NOBODY DIES IN
HOLLYWOOD

"'Nobody Dies In Hollywood' is a deliciously enjoyable thriller, beautifully written, beautifully constructed and suspenseful through the last page. A powerfully compelling hero, private detective Michael Drayton, walks the fabled 'mean streets' of Los Angeles with the courage of a Jack Reacher and the wisdom and moral compass of Raymond Chandler's legendary Philip Marlowe. Wilder's intimate knowledge of Hollywood provides for a fabulous and thoroughly modern story, filled with thrilling surprises, which nevertheless delivers the vintage depth of the great detective novel pioneers. I hope this will be the first of a long series. A very satisfying read. A true pleasure."

Anne Rice

MEGA-BEST-SELLING AUTHOR

"Great story-telling in the classic P.I. tradition. Wilder's Hollywood experience adds extra savor. Michael Drayton is a character you'll want to meet again."

John Jakes

NY TIMES BEST-SELLING AUTHOR

"With 'Nobody Dies In Hollywood,' John Wilder exploits his deep knowledge of that venerable literary form, the detective novel, and makes it new again. Through the prism of his own career as a Hollywood insider, Wilder has created a truly original hero, Mike Drayton, who walks truth to power in his pursuit for justice for a forgotten victim. Along the way, Drayton tackles challenging questions of celebrity obsession, personal identity, and race in the face of his own existential crisis. This is a stunning debut."

Howard Gordon

EMMY WINNING EXEC PRODUCER, "24";
CO-CREATOR AND EXEC PRODUCER, "HOMELAND"

"*Renowned television screenwriter John Wilder is finally publishing his first novel, and it is the real deal. 'Nobody Dies In Hollywood,' a contemporary crime book set in Los Angeles, combines the best qualities of the old masters like Chandler and Hammett, with new contemporary stars like T. Jefferson Parker and George Pelecanos. Rich characters, sparkling dialogue, a good story line, and a strong moral underpinning. Aficionados of crime writing will love this book.*"

J.F. Freedman
NY TIMES BEST-SELLING AUTHOR

"*For more than thirty years, John Wilder told the best stories on television. With 'Nobody Dies In Hollywood,' he continues that tradition on the page. Expertly paced, exquisitely observed, and compulsively readable, this novel fairly raises detective fiction up from the dead. Mike Drayton is the perfect private eye for the new millennium. Robert B. Parker would be proud.*"

Alex Gansa
EMMY WINNING CO-CREATOR, EXEC PRODUCER "HOMELAND"

"*John Wilder has written a great first novel with delicious attention to SoCal detail and a seemingly effortless literacy. 'Nobody Dies In Hollywood' is a warm-blooded tour of Hollywood's cold-blooded factories, where the star-making machines mix big money with naïve talent and loyalty is smelted into greed. This book is a page-burning pleasure and the reason for the first all-nighter I have pulled in years.*"

Patrick Hasburgh
TELEVISION PRODUCER; CO-CREATOR, 21 JUMP STREET, HARDCASTLE AND MCCORMICK; AUTHOR, ASPEN PULP

Nobody Dies In Hollywood

Dialogue quoted from *The Godfather*, motion picture, Paramount Pictures, 1972, based on the novel by Mario Puzo.

Hardcover   ISBN 978-1-939454-39-3
Softcover   ISBN 978-1-939454-40-9
Ebook   ISBN 978-1-939454-41-6
Library of Congress Control Number: 2015935838
Cataloging in Publication data pending.

Published in the United States by
Balcony 7 Media and Publishing
530 South Lake Avenue, #434
Pasadena, CA 91101
www.balcony7.com

Cover Design by Rex Perry
Interior Design by 3 Dog Design www.3dogdesign.net

Printed in the United States of America

Distributed to the trade by
Ingram Publisher Services
Mackin
Overdrive
Baker & Taylor (through IPS)
MyiLibrary

NOBODY DIES IN HOLLYWOOD

A NOVEL

JOHN WILDER

BALCONY 7
media & publishing

For Shelly,
who brightened the past.

For Tori, Christie, and Sean,
who illuminate the present.

For Vanessa, Sam, Jack, Owen, Ben,
Dillon, and Julia,
who are the future.

*"Guilt is perhaps
the most painful companion
to death."*

ELISABETH KUBLER-ROSS

PROLOGUE

Traffic swarmed the city. Endless ribbons of headlights and taillights crisscrossed vast glowing grids on either side of the shadowy mountain range snaking its way between them, people in relentless pursuit of their own potential, on the move, on the make, looking for an edge or living on it.

In a canyon carved into the gently sloping barrier between the L.A. basin and the broad valley to the north, the LED headlamps of a Porsche Cayenne swept away the darkness on a tortuous two-lane road. Coming out of a curve, the sleek SUV slowed to a stop at the unmarked entrance of a long driveway unfurling from a faint glow of light tucked into the hillside above.

"He doesn't know you're coming?"

"No."

The man behind the wheel shrugged.

"Your party," he said. "You call the shots."

The night was still. The warm, dry air bathing the grounds of the isolated estate was heavy with the scent of jasmine. Crickets called from darkness, and giant moths flitted about the floodlights shining on the flagstone path between the big house and a small cottage where a slender young man lounged barefoot and bare chested on a leather couch, studying the work of two legendary actors on a wall-mounted flat screen.

"I never wanted this for you. I worked my whole life, I don't apologize, to take care of my family."

Something more than appreciation for the subtle performances registered in the young man's light eyes as he sat up on the edge of the couch, riveted by the on-screen exchange between father and son.

"I don't know," said the father. *"There just wasn't enough time, Michael. There wasn't enough time."*

"We'll get there, Pop," said the son. *"We'll get there."*

Vito Corleone planted his hands on either side of Michael's head and kissed him.

The aspiring young actor hit the pause button on the remote resting beside him. He stared at the frozen image on the screen, a familiar knot forming in his stomach. All thoughts about learning from the veteran performers' masterful technique were gone. He was seeing himself now with his own father, feeling the pain of a wound that wouldn't heal.

The Cayenne wound its way up the grade, through overarching trees and overgrown shrubbery, toward the old Tudor-style house looming behind a stand of live oaks. The driver braked to a stop alongside a terraced tennis court and killed the engine.

In the cottage, the young man turned off the monitor and sat in darkness wrestling with his conscience, considering the consequences of actions he had taken and those he could take. He knew the only way to move on was to find forgiveness in his heart. He knew what he should do. He knew what he would do. Tomorrow.

The two uninvited visitors climbed a set of broad steps onto the wide flagstone walkway leading to the house. As they reached the intersecting path from the cottage, a lean, muscular young man in jeans and sweatshirt stepped from the house and strode down the walk to confront them.

The voices escalating outside pulled the young man in the cottage from his thoughts. He rose from the couch and looked out a window to see a friend in heated conflict with two people—and a broad-bladed weapon glinting in the bright light flooding the area from above.

He bolted out of the door—shouting a protest as his friend threw an arm up in self-defense—and finely honed steel slashed through flesh and bone.

The heavy blade sliced on through the figure slumping to his knees, swung back in a reverse arc, and slammed into the roaring skull that charged down the path from the cottage.

Wrenched from fractured cartilage and ruptured brain, the blade was drawn into a measured backswing—and a last vicious stroke hissed into the neck of the first victim just below the jaw line.

An expanding pool of blood seeped into the flags beneath the carnage as the SUV rumbled down the long drive onto the dark canyon road. And the night was still again.

CHAPTER ONE

"Drayton? My name's Chernak. Gus Chernak. I got a truckin' business. Guy I used to haul stuff for, guy worked in the movies, gave me your number. 'Call Mike Drayton,' he said. 'He's a PI, he knows people in Hollywood, knows how to get answers.' Me, I don't know anybody. I can't find out nothin'."

When I checked the voice mail on my office phone, I was standing on my deck in fading light, looking at the islands lying lavender on the far side of the channel.

"Bloody-mess pictures in the paper, all over TV. My own kid gets murdered like that, and I can't find out nothin'?"

That snapped me back from the serenity of a lazy summer evening and the delusion I'd somehow managed to become my own little island.

"Police? I ain't got a right to know what they know? What is that? It's just they don't give a damn about Kenny, that's what. Big movie star, that's all anybody cares about. My son? He's what? Nobody?"

The voice was angry, husky with booze and emotion. The level rose and fell like the arm on a Richter scale.

"'Movie hero, and friend,' they say. 'And friend?' He's got a name, goddamn it. His name's Chernak. Ken Chernak. I never seen that once. Some other name they say he called himself. And they make it sound like it was some sex thing. Like him and this hotshot were—Damn it! Talkin' to a goddamn machine. I need some help here, Drayton. I gotta find out what happened, what's true and ain't true. I don't care what it costs. You know people? You can find out what I can't? Do it. Hear me? Just do it."

End of message. No phone number, no call back. If I wanted to help someone named Gus Chernak, the first thing I'd have to do is find him.

I stepped back into the house, and punched up the message again.

Some of the words were slurred, the allusions muddled, but one thing was consistently clear. Gus Chernak's pain. I felt it to the bone.

I knew about the murder of the actor Jeremy Thomas "and friend." Every hamlet in the world with access to a satellite dish had heard all the grisly details by now. Five days earlier, the two young men were brutally killed at the film star's remote canyon home, and the media was peddling the lurid speculation surrounding the shocking crime as hard and as fast as they could. I could feel my own gut tighten at the thought of what that would do to me if the "and friend" in the story were my son. Or my daughter.

Sheridan smiled up at me from a frame on the piano. The picture was taken before her features had caught up with her front teeth, the day she won her first barrel-racing ribbon, and a grin split her freckled face from ear to ear. I thought about the tears she'd shed not long after that day. I knew she'd forgiven me for my failures with her mother, but I didn't know if I could ever forgive myself for not making her my first priority. And I wondered if a large part of Gus Chernak's agony might be some guilt that could never be absolved now that his son was dead.

My knee-jerk impulse was to respond quickly, but I set the cell down on the kitchen counter. I hadn't worked a case since a sports agent turned his Rottweiler loose on me on New Year's Eve. The dog's name was Nitro, and he'd exploded out of the night to take me through a second-story railing onto a concrete deck. It wasn't the compound fractures or the lengthy rehab that had me rethinking my future, it was more about how I was spending my holidays. And my life.

For the past ten years, I'd been chasing the truth for strangers, but the truth was I'd pretty much stopped finding personal worth in turning up larcenists and frauds, or tracking down people who didn't want to be found. I was tired of profiling killers and spending so much time with thieves and hustlers, or greedy deep-pockets convinced they can buy their way into and out of anything. The calendar said I'd hit fifty in December, and the game plan I'd been mulling didn't include getting involved in a celebrity murder case.

"I need some help here, Drayton. You know people? You can find out what I can't? Do it."

The urgency triggered the memory of another voice with a distinct West Texas drawl, one I had grown up with and would never not hear, *"Somethin' needs doin', do it."*

I went to the recycle bin, and pulled out all the articles about the murders in the last few editions of the *LA Times*. Calling Jeremy Thomas a celebrity was like calling Peyton Manning a football player. He wasn't just a flavor-of-the-month "star" on some reality show, he was a bona fide superstar. The public loved him, the press loved him, his producers and directors loved him, and the distributors loved him most of all because his last five films had grossed over two-hundred-million dollars each. In the past four years, he'd received two Academy Award nominations and won an Oscar, and he'd only turned thirty in February. But suddenly he was dead, and, like James Dean and Marilyn Monroe before him, he would be forever young to the millions who adored him in the twenty-first century and those who would see his films in the twenty-second. Meanwhile, the young man who was murdered in the same vicious attack was all but forgotten already. Except by a father reaching out to me from a world of hurt.

I turned on the *Channel Nine News at Ten*. The killing of Jeremy Thomas remained the lead story. Though nothing new had been discovered, Captain Curtis Rankin, the homicide detective ramrodding the most massive manhunt in the city's history, offered personal assurance that the killer would be brought to justice. Rankin had a face people trusted on sight, a face that inspired confidence, a face few had seen unmasked. I had. It was ugly. Curtis Rankin was a jackal masquerading as a guard dog.

I turned off the set, went back out on the deck, and sucked in a deep breath to shake off the memories of my time with Rankin. The air was warm, a mild, unseasonable Santa Ana riding across the valley, up over the mountains, and down through the canyons to the ocean in front of me. It felt clean. I couldn't.

I looked up into a field of gleaming stars, and listened to the cathartic pulse of the surf, hoping it would drown out the echo of Gus Chernak's voice. It didn't.

His grief wasn't all that haunted me, it was the anger and frustration.

"Big movie star, that's all anybody cares about. My son? He's what? Nobody?"

He was being shunted aside by a society obsessed with celebrity and short-changed by a system supposedly pledged to serve all its citizens equally.

Right. What's it ever going to take?

It was my own voice. And there was only one answer to the question.

I called the number my phone had logged. No machine was on, but the area code told me it was in Burbank. I Googled Gus Chernak and got five listings, only one in Burbank. The address was on Oak Street. It cross-checked with the trucking company he owned on Alameda Avenue. I left word there for him to call my office again and leave a number where he could be reached to set a meeting. Then I called Mari Sabusawa at home, asked her to hit the Hall of Records first thing in the morning, photograph whatever she could on the Chernak family, and email it to me by nine. That guaranteed I'd have it by eight-thirty.

CHAPTER TWO

I left Santa Barbara the next morning, and headed south on the 101 for an eleven o'clock meeting at my office in Westwood Village. Coming down the Calabasas grade into the West Valley, I could see a thin yellow haze of chemicals curling up like a giant cat against the base of the San Gabriel range on the far side of the city.

Slowing to a dead stop on the long artery clogged with cars, I thought about the pristine place where D.W. Griffith and his cronies created an industry that would eventually influence the entire world. A place that had it all, bright skies, beaches, mountains and deserts, a place where D.W. could tell any story he envisioned. Millions came later, drawn to the glitz and glamour of an industry built on an alchemic blend of illusion and reality.

Jeremy Thomas "and friend" had come to a brutal reality. The megastar got all the ink, the friend got little more than a mention, but they were both victims of the same seemingly senseless crime. Why? What was it that brought them together at that particular time in that specific place to meet such a violent end to their individual stories?

I still wasn't sure I wanted to find out. But I was certain Gus Chernak had to know.

"Took your own sweet time," he said when I opened the door into the cramped reception area at eleven-fifteen. I could smell the whiskey on his breath from across the room, which was all of six feet, but his words were crisp and the message was clear. Time is important to a guy who's punched a clock all his life.

"Traffic," I said as I closed the door and he rose from the wooden armchair alongside Mari's tidy desk. "But, I apologize, Mister Chernak. It won't happen again."

I offered my hand. Mari's bright brown eyes fixed on me. The apology seemed to catch Chernak off-guard, too.

"It's okay," he said, filing the edge off his tone. "Gave this young lady a chance to set me straight about the message I left." He took my hand. "It's me should apologize. I was pretty loaded."

"No problem," I said. "Come on in."

Mari got up as I opened the door to the inner office. Just shy of five feet, she wasn't gaining a lot of height by standing, but that wasn't why she stood. Her manners were as impeccable as her work ethic.

"More coffee, Mister Chernak?" she asked.

Her long black hair was up in a French braid. Her mint-green blouse and white skirt were as refreshing as her smile.

"No, thanks," Chernak said.

"Mister Drayton?"

"Mind making a fresh pot?," I asked.

"Already brewing," she said, as I followed Chernak through the door.

The inner office was bigger, all of ten by twelve, but seemed smaller because of the bank of filing cabinets along the length of the far wall. The other three walls were broken by the door we'd come through, another door that opened into the hallway, and two windows that looked down onto Westwood Boulevard. The space was tight, but the address had a kind of cachet that made high-end clients comfortable. The biggest plus was that my rent was less than half of any other tenant because the real estate manager knew I was aware of how he managed maintenance fees and security deposits.

"Nice kid," Chernak said as I pulled the door closed behind us and noticed a small ficus in a pot newly planted between the two windows.

"Yes, she is," I said.

"Makes a lousy cup of coffee, though."

"Yes, she does," I agreed again. I unslung my shoulder bag and set it on the desk, knowing how and why the piece of greenery had made its way into the room. The windows made it a much better place to study in my absence.

"Workin' for you while she finishes up a PhD, she says."

"The brains in the office," I said, as I slipped out of my jacket and hung it on a sturdier tree standing bleakly in the corner. "Have a seat."

He ignored the chair facing the desk, stepped to the window, and looked down at the steady flow of traffic.

"Place has really changed," he said. "T-shirt shops, fast-food joints, 7-Elevens. Used to be a real village. Hardware store, drugstore, market. College town." A trace of a smile vanished quickly. "Different times," he said. "Whole different world."

I unzipped my bag, pulled out the records Mari had dug up for me, and set them on the desk. They said Gus Chernak was born in 1933, but he looked a generation younger. And powerful. If I hadn't reviewed his service record and known he'd volunteered for the Marine Corps in 1950 and earned a chestful of medals during a twenty-four-year career that spanned Korea and Vietnam, I would have put him in his mid-sixties. He was a big man who happened to be short, five-seven to five-eight, tops, but just under two hundred pounds, and none of his weight was hanging over his belt. He wore his gray hair cropped close in military fashion, no muss, no fuss, his gray eyes framed a nose that had been hammered more than once. His wardrobe was Wal-Mart or Sears, but the tan cotton pants were creased, the scarred work boots oiled and clean. He wore a green nylon windbreaker over a navy-blue T-shirt, no logos or tags, not a shred of vanity, a pretty safe bet that what you saw was what you got.

His eyes left the street for a framed photograph on the wall. It was a picture of two men wearing the same button-front shirts, sun-bleached jeans, sweat-stained Stetsons, bandanas, gunbelts and boots. They were crouched shoulder-to-shoulder, Winchesters leveled. One of them was John Wayne. The other was younger, but physically a dead ringer for him.

"John Wayne?"

"Yeah."

"Other guy looks just like him, but younger."

"My father," I said. "He was the Duke's stunt double."

He glanced at me, back at the picture, seeming confused.

"My mother was Haitian," I explained. "Her great grandparents were from somewhere in Africa, we're not sure exactly, they left on a slave ship."

"Oh," he said, without any sign of the embarrassment I expected.

He looked back at the photograph, checking me out against my father's features. "Yeah, I can see it now. Got his size, too."

And he let it go. I liked him for that.

"You a cowboy?" he asked, noting the buckle I'd won at an RCA calf-roping contest in Bakersfield last fall.

"Not really," I said, as I sat down behind the desk.

He took the seat across from me, still sizing me up like a used car, but apparently ready for a test drive. "So where do we start?" he asked.

"Tell me about the relationship you had with your son."

"Whatta you mean?" Chernak frowned. "He was my son."

"You loved him?" I asked.

"Hell yes, I loved him."

"Did he know it?"

"Where do you come off talkin' to me like that?" he said. "What the hell do you know?"

"I know Ken was twenty-nine," I said, glancing at the papers in front of me. "I know you and his mother divorced when he was six. She moved to Oregon, raised him there, then two years ago he came to L.A. and, somehow, he found his way into the inner circle around Jeremy Thomas.

Maybe you can tell me what you know about how that happened, if you and Ken were close enough to talk about what he was doing with his life."

The gray eyes narrowed.

"And maybe you can tell me why it was he drove for a messenger service in west L.A. and waited tables at the California Pizza Kitchen in Brentwood to make his rent instead of driving for you and moving into the spare room at your place."

"What is this?"

"You said you want the truth," I said. "It starts with you."

"You messin' with me?"

"Just doing what I do, Mister Chernak. You want answers, I have to ask questions. The questions are hard because the truth is hard to find when people set out to hide it."

"You sayin' I got somethin' to hide?"

I took a stab. "You want to tell me what the problem was between you and your son?"

"Who the hell do you think you are?"

"The guy you called for help."

Mari entered with two fresh mugs of coffee, and stopped short when she saw Chernak's face. Maybe I deserved the dagger she threw at me, maybe not. Only Gus Chernak could say for sure.

CHAPTER THREE

We sat in silence staring into the coffee as it cooled. Finally, Chernak looked up across the desk and spoke in a quiet voice.

"How'd you know?"

I shrugged. "It's part of what I do."

He nodded, seeming to understand but not really care.

"Your kid?" he asked, eyeing a photograph on my desk.

"Sheridan," I said.

He nodded, sorting out the same kind of difficulty he'd had with the picture of my father. I could have explained, but I didn't, and he didn't ask. I liked him even more.

"How old?"

"That was her twelfth birthday."

"Cute," he said. "Last birthday I saw Kenny have, he was six. Took him to Knott's Berry Farm. Must've rode every ride twelve times." The memory faded. "Next day I come home from work, find a note on the kitchen table. 'Dear Gus—'" He smiled again, but this time it was pure acid.

"Did you go after them?"

"No."

"Why not?"

"I'd 've killed the sonofabitch she was with."

His eyes met mine directly. He knew himself well. I liked him a lot.
"How long before you saw Ken again?"

"Six, seven months ago. Calls out of the blue. Said he was here, said he wanted to see me."

He fell silent. I sipped my coffee and waited while he fought back a wave of emotion. It looked a lot like guilt.

"What he wanted was to let me know what a rotten bastard he thought I was for desertin' him," he said. "I heard myself tellin' my side of it and I knew he was right. I deserted him. I never thought about it that way till that very minute, but he was right."

He struggled with his emotion again, stared at the picture of Sheridan.

"I was too damn proud to care about the one thing in my life I should've cared about most."

I'd guessed right. The guilt was talking now, and I knew he had to talk to somebody. My name had come out of the hat as someone who could help him get what he wanted, but the only service I could render for the moment was to listen.

"I got no good reason for how I handled things when they took off. Excuses, alibis. That's all I got," he said. "Bullshit I fed myself so I could get on with my life. The truth was I had a son. He needed me. Now, he's gone."

He lowered his eyes, and I watched him surrender totally to the admission he had to make if he was ever going to heal.

"I wasn't there for him," he said, "He needed me, and I wasn't there."

He drew in a ragged breath, pulled a folded white handkerchief from his hip pocket and wiped his eyes, blew his nose, swallowed hard.

"I gotta be there now, Drayton. You understand?" He lifted his eyes, riveted them on mine. "There ain't nobody else who cares. He got lost before, and he's gettin' lost again."

"I hear you." And I heard my own conscience again as I glanced at the picture of Sheridan while Chernak stuffed the handkerchief back into his hip pocket, cleared his throat, worked at pulling himself together.

"Chick said you used to be a cop?"

"Ten years," I said.

It had to be a guy who owned a prop rental company named Chick Howard. A collection of antique weapons worth over six figures had been stolen from him, and the insurance company called me in. It got messy when it turned out his own sister had a big habit and hired the thieves. I wouldn't have figured him for a referral.

"He said you were a straight-shooter, and I should see you on account of you'd know people can tell you stuff about this guy Kenny was with, why somebody might want him dead. You got connections with movie people, he said. Do you?"

"Some."

"Through your father?"

"And work I used to do with him."

"Stunts?" he said. "Like jumpin' off buildings, crashin' cars, stuff like that? You did that, too?"

"For a while."

"Yeah?" he said. "A daredevil, huh?"

"That's what people think, but it's not how it works," I said. "A good stunt man doesn't take chances. He works out every detail in advance, calculates every contingency. Anybody can wreck a train, takes careful planning to jump off it at the last second and walk away in one piece."

"Sounds like a good job, how come you quit?"

"*Best laid plans of mice and men,*" I said.

"What? You had an accident?"

"My father did."

"Get hurt bad?"

"Died."

"Geezus."

He looked at the picture with John Wayne again.

"How'd it happen?"

"Battle scene. Explosion had too much powder."

"Geezus," he said. "Just like for real."

"Yeah."

Chernak looked from the picture to me, seeming satisfied.

"Okay. Whatta we talkin' here? How much?"

"Hundred-fifty an hour, plus expenses. One forty-hour week in advance, we go day to day after that. You can call it quits anytime you want."

"We sign a contract, or what?"

"We shake hands," I said.

He sized me up again, then extended his hand across the desk. I took it, and he glanced at the picture of Sheridan.

"That daughter of yours," he said. "Make sure she knows what she means to you."

His eyes bore into mine and he kept a firm grip on my hand.

"You don't do nothin' else in your life, you make damn sure of that, Drayton. You hear me? Make sure she knows."

He exited the building beneath my window, and I watched him walk briskly up the block through clusters of lanky college students in shorts and T-shirts. He looked smaller, and not very powerful at all.

"Are you okay?"

Mari stood in the open doorway. I nodded, watching Chernak cross the street and round the corner.

"Ready to come back to work?" she asked.

My eyes drifted to the picture of Sheridan.

"Yeah."

"Do you want to see the list of calls I've been keeping from people who want to meet with you?"

"No."

"But some of them keep calling back. A couple are very insistent."

I lifted my eyes to hers.

"Got it," she said. "You appreciate the interest, but you're under exclusive contract at the moment, and unable to devote your time to any other matters."

"Something like that."

She smiled.

"How about some more coffee?"

I thought about that.

"Love some."

"I've been experimenting," she said. "It's better, right?"

"Night and day."

Her smile spread, and she stepped back through the door. It was the best I'd felt about myself in six months.

CHAPTER FOUR

Southern California was built around the car, and navigating L.A.'s 468 square miles requires some 7,500 miles of streets and highways, avenues and alleys, roughly the distance from Civic Center to downtown Cairo. I'd driven most of them, sometimes feeling like I actually was passing through different countries.

Leaving Westwood, I drove east on Wilshire Boulevard, down a corridor of gleaming, multi-million dollar high-rise condominiums, straight through the heart of an international symbol of the gilded good life. The little independent city of Beverly Hills takes its name from the hills to the north, hills crammed with Spanish and Mediterranean villas, French chateaux, English country estates, and Southern mansions, creating a castles-in-the-clouds ambience that comes back to earth in short order just east of Rexford Drive. I was headed way east of Rexford. And in less than twenty minutes, I was rolling past block after block of shabby buildings, scruffy storefronts and cracked sidewalks, thinking about what a short hop it was from one kind of decadence to another.

When I pulled into the lot on the corner of Rampart and Beverly and trotted across the street to a landmark hamburger stand, Eddie Falcon was waiting for me.

"That buckle big enough?" he said.

"Working undercover," I said.

A smile flickered in his eyes and was gone in a heartbeat. In his early fifties, the DA's chief investigator looked more like a successful hedge-fund manager. His custom-tailored suit slimmed his thick frame and gave no hint of the Walther PPS strapped under his left arm.

"One with chili, one without," he said, indicating the two burgers in the box alongside two Cokes resting on the hood of his unmarked.

"Either way," I shrugged.

He picked up the burger with the chili, I took the one without. It wouldn't be any less sloppy.

The incongruity of Eddie Falcon digging into a *Tommy's* Original always amused me. Aside from this lone addiction, everything about him was precisely measured. When he took action, you knew it was the only move left on the board. I admired his approach to the work we shared, but I could never quite get there. Somewhere along the way, I'd get a hunch and have to play it, see where it led and see where the next step took me. If I wasn't dropping bread crumbs, I could get good and lost before I found my way out of the woods. Falcon never seemed lost.

"So, the NCAA ruled that tailback at SC's ineligible," he said.

"Yeah," I said, narrowly avoiding some runoff that just missed my jeans and splattered on the ground.

"No more scholarship, now, right? No more education, no chance to prove he's a first-round pick."

"All gone," I said, around a mouthful of burger.

"Because of your investigation."

"You could say that."

"What do you say?"

"He knew the rules."

I took a slug of Coke. Falcon sipped his.

"Pretty cold," he said. "Anything to do with that Rottweiler mistaking you for a bag of kibble?"

"Kid's nineteen," I said, "father's in Q, mother's on a respirator in South Central. Guy shows up in a flashy car, lets him drive it, sets him up in a Hancock Park guest house. I don't know, you tell me how that should come down."

"So, you blame the agent."

"Before I got bounced off the pavement."

"Now?"

"I wonder what I was doing in that mix in the first place."

"Job's a job."

"Not any more."

A smile kindled again in Falcon's eyes, but stopped just shy of his lips.

"Guess not," he said. "Took a 'crime of the century' to get you back on the bricks."

"I just want to get a few questions answered for a guy's getting the runaround."

I stuffed the last of the burger in my mouth, went to work on my hands with several napkins as Falcon tidily finished his meal.

"Pictures?" I asked.

"Front seat," he nodded.

I opened the driver's door of the sedan, leaned in and removed a manila envelope as Falcon carried our trash to a barrel. He returned to his drink while I opened the envelope to look at the black-and-white police photos taken at the scene where Jeremy Thomas and Gus Chernak's son had been killed.

"Thanks, Eddie. Nobody hears about these from me."

"I didn't know that, you wouldn't be looking at them."

I've been to a lot of crime scenes, studied thousands of photographs, but nothing had prepared me for the butchery. The pictures that had been released to the press showed the heavy stains that covered the walkway where the bodies had been discovered, but these were shots of the two young men lying in great pools of their own blood. Jeremy Thomas' left hand had been cut off at the forearm, his body had a deep gash that sliced through organs, and his head was severed at the neck. Ken Chernak's skull was split nearly in half.

"The press called it a stabbing," I said.

"O.J., chapter one, verse one," Falcon said. "Full disclosure before our office gets to court only helps the slicks on the other side."

CHAPTER FIVE

The autopsy pictures were equally gruesome. The blood had been washed away providing a clean view inside the gaping wounds.

"What's the coroner say about the wounds?"

"Broad blade. Like an axe."

"Whoa."

"Yeah. Up close and personal," Falcon said. "With an attitude."

I concentrated on the crime scene photos, instinctively drawing on three years of experience in homicide to turn the tableau into action and reaction.

"So, what do you figure?"

"You tell me," he said.

"Rage."

"This was a kid everybody loved."

"Kid with a great press kit, anyway."

"You're not going to disillusion me, are you?"

"*Hooray for Hollywood,*" I said.

This time the smile tugged at Falcon's mustache, but still failed to part his lips.

"Squeaky clean so far," he shrugged. "Would you believe he really was a choirboy?"

"Could be where he went wrong," I said.

The mustache twitched again.

"So, what about your client's kid?" he said. "Got anything I should know?"

"Not yet. What's it look like for him being the target instead of Thomas?"

"Could be. Moved into the guesthouse the day before," Falcon said. "But it looks more like he was just in the wrong place at the wrong time."

I looked at the pictures again.

"Floodlights on these buildings working?"

"On a timer."

"Operational?"

"Comes on at eight, goes off at six."

"Bulbs good?"

Falcon nodded. I studied the pictures.

"Rolex still on Thomas's wrist. Anything missing?"

Falcon shook his head.

"Seven hundred dollars still in his wallet, half a dozen credit cards," he said. "Another twenty-seven bucks in his friend's pocket, Visa and an ATM card in a wallet."

"Drugs?"

"Both clean. No evidence either one was using or dealing."

"Couple of stories had them sleeping together. Could have made somebody crazy, I guess."

"We're into that. Writers say they've got a credible source, but they won't give him up. We haven't turned anything says it's true."

I pored over the photographs, asking myself how the body positions and wounds conjoined to suggest a pattern, a scenario of assault and defense, a hint of motive.

"Could have been random, I guess. Just caught somebody's anger for the world in general," I said.

"Sure. But we both know that's not what happened."

"How about overly adoring fans? Any record of trouble with them?"

Falcon nodded. "Couple years ago. Guy came at Thomas with a knife, put him in emergency."

"I don't remember that."

"Never made the news. Checked into UCLA under his real name, Eugene Prentis."

I nodded, noting the name. "What about the guy who jumped him?"

"Street guy. Wacko."

"Locked up?"

"Thomas wouldn't press charges. Said the guy'd had enough hard times, didn't want to put him through any more."

"So he's still walking around?"

"Spent some time in psychiatric evaluation at the VA, supposed to continue with outpatient care, but he's been a no-show for the last six months."

"Anybody know where he is?"

"Homicide's hot for it. Won't be long."

"You don't like it?"

His eyes fell to the photographs. I followed his gaze.

"Me, either," I said. "Back to rage."

"And personal," he said. "Speaking of which," he added casually, "Rankin's in charge for Homicide."

"I saw that," I said, as I put the photographs back in the envelope.

"He knows you're into it, he'll find a way to make it hard for you."

"I'll be good."

Falcon grinned as I handed the envelope to him.

"*Buena suerte, amigo*," he said, and climbed into his unmarked.

He knew the mention of Rankin was like plucking a raw nerve, even though I had never discussed the specifics of what happened with anyone, primarily because I was still under court order not to. But friends knew about what went down, and that the charges I made about a coven of racist cops acting outside the law they were sworn to uphold had merit, even if I was the one who got the short end of the stick while Rankin didn't catch a hint of a blemish on his record.

I should have fought the countercharges he brought against me, but one of them, negligence in the line of duty, was one I wouldn't contest. The incident he was citing got my senior partner killed, and I couldn't say the blame fell anywhere else but squarely on me.

Wes Carter was straight out of Lake Wobegon, son of a Lutheran minister and an elementary school teacher, married to his high school sweetheart for thirty-five years, father of four great kids, as honest a man and dependable a partner as ever lived. And he lost his life because of a fatal mistake I made when we were on a hot pursuit.

I cornered the perp in his apartment, and his kid was crying hysterically, so I let him lift her out of the crib. My eyes were on a terrified two-year old girl, and I didn't see the piece in the blanket he picked up until it went off and slammed me to the floor. Then I saw a blurry Wes Carter come through the door and take three rounds point-blank before I passed out.

Later, I saw the face of the man who'd shot me and killed Wes lying in the morgue when I identified him the day after he'd been pulled over for a broken taillight and taken twelve rounds from a patrol team. Then I saw the faces of the cops who avenged Wes's death by gunning down his killer in the street rather than delivering him for his right to due process. They were laughing about it over beers, and being congratulated by a half-dozen other uniforms. Protocol said I had to go to Rankin with what I knew had happened.

"You expect me to file this?"

"It was murder."

"The sonofabitch killed Wes. Hell, he damn near killed you."

"So, we have the right to execute him?"

"Listen to me, Drayton, I get how you could feel. But here's how it is. They want to fight each other, kill each other, fine, but they take out one of ours, they don't just walk away. And they don't get let off by some bleeding-heart judge because of some technicality. They pay."

I lost it big time, called him out for what he was and went to Internal Affairs, naming him as a co-conspirator. I should have known my word against his wasn't going to cut it, should have been smarter than to think he was the highest ranking officer involved, but I didn't, and I wasn't.

As I watched Falcon drive off, I hoped I was smarter now—smart enough, at least, to not let the bad blood between Rankin and me blind me to the answers I'd been hired to find.

CHAPTER SIX

When I pulled out of the lot, *KNX Traffic-And-Weather-Together-On-The-Fives* said it was 92 degrees at Civic Center. The Hollywood Freeway would take me into the valley, right to the doorstep of Universal Studios, where I had a four o'clock appointment with the line producer on Jeremy Thomas's last film, and where it would be at least ten degrees hotter.

"Last gig you had was for Ed Zwick, right?"

"*Glory.*"

"Right. You were doubling Denzel. Great film. I can still see you in that TV western your dad put you in for the first time, though. You were what, ten?"

"Something like that."

"Doubling that little girl. You gave that horse one helluva ride."

"Too bad sunbonnets went out of style," I said. "Everybody said I was adorable then."

Howard Alworth laughed. It was like the rattle of a freight train in a tunnel and stirred up the tar in lungs that had been inhaling it for over half a century. He was a virile seventy-plus, a man with the broad back and strong hands of a stevedore, the smarts of a business school Dean.

"Damn, I miss your old man," he said as he took a pack of Camels from his desk top, tapped one out, and folded open a book of matches. "When he was ram-rodding the gags, my job wasn't half as hard."

My father had been the stunt coordinator on dozens of films Howard had overseen as a production manager, the man or woman directly in charge of keeping a film on budget. He was called a line producer now. Same job, better title, not that Howard cared.

"So, you still living up north?" he asked as he lit his cigarette,

"Santa Barbara."

"How's that been?"

"You mean am I the tannest guy on the beach?"

"One way to put it," he smiled, shook out the match, put it in the ashtray on his desk.

"Now, come on, Howard, don't be that way. Some of my best friends are white."

He laughed again.

"Just wondered," he said.

"I like it," I said. "Good neighbors, good restaurants, met a lot of interesting people, and nobody's ever told me to be off the streets by ten o'clock. Then again, nobody's on the streets after ten o'clock. That's part of the appeal."

"I get that," he said. "Beautiful spot. No traffic, no smog, no crime in the streets, no dog eat dog. Kind of work you do in this town, must be good to get some distance from it."

"You think?"

He laughed again, took a long drag on his cigarette, exhaled.

"So, what's going on? What do you need?"

"Jeremy Thomas," I said. "How well did you know him?"

"You working on that?" he frowned. "Jesus. You come back to work, you come back with a bang."

"Father of the kid with him wants me to fill in some blanks, that's all," I said. "Doesn't think anybody cares about his son."

"Yeah," Howard nodded. "I can see that."

"When you heard about it, what went through your mind?"

"You mean, like, did I flash on somebody who might have done it?" He shook his head. "No. Figured it was some nut. Crazy fan, maybe, something like that."

"Never heard any scuttlebutt about problems, conflicts, girls, guys, drugs?"

"Tell you the truth, Mikey, over fifty years working sets, I never saw anybody like that kid. He was something special. Never met a stranger, never made an enemy."

"No sale."

"Yeah? Why's that?"

"One or the other killed him."

The possibility that there might be a dark side to the personality of a young man he had liked and respected silenced Howard for a moment.

"Got a cast and crew sheet for that last film?"

"Yeah, sure," he said, and pulled up a file on his computer for *The Lady of the Lake*.

As he scrolled to the names and addresses of people who worked on the film, it struck me that even the title of his last film was an illustration of the unselfishness attributed to Jeremy Thomas. He certainly didn't have the title role. That had gone to a young English actress named Katherine Morris.

"How was the girl?" I asked as I glanced over the cast list.

"Kate? Scared stiff, but Jeremy was real patient with her, helped her bring her performance down for the camera."

"Peter Michaels directed. That a problem for Thomas?"

"No way. Peter's a shooter. Never says ten words to actors, doesn't speak the language," Howard said. "That's why Jeremy picked him. Wanted to work with the actors himself, and wanted to go to school on Peter's camera work for the picture after this. One he was going to direct."

"Peter still a chaser?" I asked.

"Pope still wear a tall hat?"

"Any competition between him and Thomas for the lady's special favors?"

"Nobody who got a chance to work with Jeremy Thomas was going to burn that bridge."

I nodded as I scanned the crew list.

"I thought Frankie Tate always doubled Thomas," I said. "Who's this Reggie Collingswood?"

"English. Kamala Highland brought him in."

"Thomas went along with that?"

"I don't know what happened exactly. Kamala'd done a couple of pictures with Frankie. But she said she thought they could do better. Peter liked the idea because Collingswood's so good with the period weapons."

"Kamala Highland," I said. "What's she like?"

Howard picked up a copy of *Variety*, the weekly trade paper that covers the film industry, and showed me the full-page open letter on the back. The letterhead had a logo featuring the outline of a mountain range and the words **Highland Productions.** Beneath the logo in the upper right-hand corner it said:

Kamala Highland
Chairman of The Board
Chief Executive Officer

The letter read:

*Dear **Jeremy**,*
We will never forget you. Your talent, your genius and your goodness were unparalleled in the history of our industry.
*Your final performance in **THE LADY OF THE LAKE** will live on to rival the legend of King Arthur itself.*
Farewell, dear friend. And Godspeed.

My eternal affection,
Kamala

"Touching, huh?" Howard said.

"I'm all choked up," I said.

"Ran it on her web site, too," he said as he tossed the paper back on the desk. "You see stuff like that all the time. Letters to people that read like they're personal and private and sincere. But to a dead man? Come on."

"You don't think that's personal and private and sincere?" I said.

"What I think, they couldn't print."

"What did Thomas think of her?"

"Had to know she's a snake," he said. "If he could read that piece of garbage, he'd laugh his ass off."

"So there was somebody who might have been an enemy."

"Enemy? No. She didn't threaten him."

"Maybe he threatened her."

"How?"

"I don't know. Just a possibility," I said. "That's all I have to work with so far. Possibilities."

Another name jumped off the crew sheet.

"Leah Sanders held book?" I asked.

"First person I ever go to," he said. "You know that."

"I just didn't know she was working again."

"Thing she had going with that DP blew up."

"She was pregnant."

"Lost it," he said.

"She okay?"

"Still too good for you, Mikey."

"No argument here," I said. "Tell her hello for me."

"Tell her yourself," he said. "She's on stage 12."

Chapter Seven

A naked young goddess lay on a bed bathed in soft light streaming through lace curtains. A naked young Adonis lowered himself onto her while a camera focused on the couple like a voyeuristic Cyclops. I watched from the shadows beside a stand with a naked red light.

A dozen crew members clustered around a video monitor several feet behind the camera. No one moved, no one spoke, until a buzzer sounded. Then the red light went off, the lights on the catwalk fifty feet overhead came on, and an air-conditioning unit groaned to life. What had been a frozen tableau broke into kaleidoscopic disarray with twenty people talking at once. My eyes remained focused on a shapely woman seated near the camera in a folding chair. The word *Script* was stenciled in white on the black-canvas back.

"Leah?" a long-haired young man in jeans, denim shirt and aviator-style glasses stepping away from the monitor called for her attention. "Print three, six, and nine."

"What about the hold you had on seven?"

"Yeah," the man mused. "Yeah, I liked what she did when he first slid in there. Let's look at that, too."

He turned back to the actors on the bed, their nudity now covered by large terrycloth robes, as Leah circled the numbers of the designated takes at the top of the nine lines she had drawn along a ruler's edge down through the scene. Her detailed record of the shoot would become the bible for postproduction, and her concentration was complete as I stepped up behind her.

"I missed one through eight," I said. "But nine had me blushing."

I couldn't see her smile, but I could feel it as she closed the leather binder, then stood up to face me.

"My God, did you get taller?"

"I think it's the human growth hormones," I said.

"Just what you never needed," she grinned. It was a top-ten grin. Snow-white teeth trapped between two giant dimples. No lipstick, no eye shadow, no mascara. A natural beauty flowing across the centuries from a cool spring somewhere deep in the barren hills of Israel.

"Buy you a cup of coffee?" I asked.

"It's been a long time between cups," she said.

The craft services table near the stage entrance was well stocked with energy sources for quick consumption and three large stainless-steel urns with hot water, ice water, and coffee. I filled two Styrofoam cups, added milk and two sugars for Leah.

"You remember," she said.

"All the important stuff," I said.

Her smile softened as we drifted away from the table to isolate ourselves from the snackers that came and went.

"Howard told me you were here."

"Told me you were coming down," she said.

"Still playing matchmaker," I grinned.

Leah held script on the first film Howard Alworth hired me on as stunt coordinator. He had suggested then that I should get to know her, but told me flat out what he would do to me if I played fast and loose with her emotions.

It wasn't any fear of Howard that set the guidelines for the relationship that blossomed, it was the lady herself. She was young then, just twenty-two, but definitely a lady, with an innate sense of propriety and decorum that demanded respect and was balanced by a spontaneous sense of fun that provided plenty of "sugar and spice." I fell hard, and tried hard to be the mature man I wasn't. We were together for two years before she left. I hurt for two more, but understood why she wasn't going to wait around for me to grow up. She seemed to understand my need for going it alone more than any woman I'd met since. Time had eventually healed mutually inflicted wounds and, in the converse of the old song, made two friends of lovers.

"He said you might want to ask me some questions about Jeremy Thomas."

"Yeah."

We stopped near another naked red light on a stand and a large sign posted on the stage door that said QUIET! NO MOVEMENT WHILE RED LIGHT IS ON!

"So, you're working for Chad Kennedy's father?"

"Ken Chernak's father. Chad Kennedy was a name Gus Chernak never heard before homicide paid him a visit to say the friend of the movie star who got butchered was his son."

"God," she said.

"Yeah," I agreed.

"What can you do that the police aren't doing?"

"Maybe just give him the feeling somebody cares about his son more than the movie star."

She nodded thoughtfully, sipped her coffee.

"So, he was number sixty-five on the cast list," I said. "He was on the shoot, what, couple days?"

"Five weeks," she said. "Part of the corps of young men surrounding Arthur."

"Courtesy of Thomas?"

"Yes."

"Any idea what it was Thomas saw in him?"

"I've thought about that," she said, "He had talent, I think. Hard to tell how much from what I saw him do, but it was there. Very poised. And he had a lot of drive. I think maybe Jeremy saw somebody a lot like himself and wanted to reward that."

"Couple papers said the two of them were gay. Anything to that?"

"Not Jeremy," she said. "Not the last time he had me run lines with him in his trailer, anyway."

"So? Did he live up to the legend?"

"Thanks, Michael."

"Hey, hottest thing on the planet? Who's going to throw stones?"

"I wasn't about to make that mistake. Not just coming back from where I'd been. I needed the work, not the complication."

"Anybody else you know he hit on?"

"I don't like to talk about that stuff, Mike."

"I know. But somebody gets chopped up like he did, my antenna says sex and all its crazy complications is a definite front-runner for motive."

She dropped her eyes into her cup, chewed on her bottom lip. I knew that expression. It meant there was more. It did not necessarily mean she would tell me what it was.

"He get it on with Katherine Morris?"

She glanced around, then nodded. "Yes. I think so."

"Anybody else?"

"I—" She stopped herself. "I really don't like this, Michael."

"Me, either," I said. "But I already care more about Ken Chernak than Jeremy Thomas."

CHAPTER EIGHT

She was biting down lightly on her bottom lip, balancing ingrained mores and virgin insight, when the big door to the soundproof entrance chamber behind us opened. It sucked the air around us toward it and pulled Leah's attention to the woman who entered like a commanding officer arriving to review the troops. Two minions followed in her wake as the heavy door pushed the air back into place and resealed the stage.

Instant recognition flashed across Leah's face. She tensed slightly as the woman approached, wearing a couple thousand dollars in summer-weight clothing and an all-weather, perma-press smile. She was shadowed by a thin-lipped, thin-hipped, young blonde dressed in thrift-shop chic and two-hundred dollar combat boots, and a skinny, shaggy-haired kid in jeans, Doc Martens, rumpled shirt, and small wire-rimmed glasses.

"Leah," the woman said. "Are we on schedule?"

"Close," Leah said. "We should wrap this set today."

"Bobby's doing a fabulous job, isn't he?" the woman gushed. "Dailies are great," she added without waiting for Leah's reply. "He keeps that long lens working, gets us right inside the characters. I love it."

Leah nodded a smile that I knew was as synthetic as the woman's.

"You picked the right guy," she said. But the woman's eyes had already left her to size me up.

"Kamala Highland," she said, offering her hand.

"Mike Drayton," I said, taking it.

A tall woman in her late-forties, her grip was firm for effect. Everything about her was for effect, starting with the top two buttons of her silk blouse which were undone to draw attention to major cleavage. Her pampered skin had a dusky hue, and her nose was perfectly sculpted, no doubt by a very expensive sculptor who may have also provided the cleavage. She was a natural brunette, but blonde by choice, the green eyes and full lips were God-given and remained her most attractive features.

"Are you working with us, Mike?" she asked. "I thought I knew everyone."

Her voice was husky, with a trace of Dixie she didn't want you to miss.

"Just stopped by to see an old friend," I said.

She broadened the smile. "I love it," she said. "We need more of that. Kind of set I like to run." And she winked at me as she patted Leah on the arm.

"Excuse me," she said. "I need to talk to Bobby."

"Sure," Leah said.

Having already dismissed us, Kamala Highland moved off. Thin Lips and Baggy Pants tossed condescending smiles Leah's way as they followed their mentor toward where more important people awaited anointing.

"So that's her." I said.

"What?" Leah said.

"The other woman Thomas hit on."

"Why did you say that?"

"You lost your tan when she walked in."

Leah glanced anxiously toward the set and then at the few crew members helping themselves to the free snacks.

"Not now, Mike," she said. "Not here."

CHAPTER NINE

It was a record day for heat in North Hollywood and a record day for phone calls in Westwood. Mari was giddy. Seven calls were more than she had fielded all week. Two from potential clients got her rehearsed speech, one from Pidge Connors was reminding me to get my entry fee in for the rodeo coming up at the Earl Warren Showgrounds, one was Frankie Tate returning my call with a cell phone number, two were from Gus Chernak, and one from Leah Sanders.

"Leah?" I just left her a few minutes ago.

"She said. And then the director told her he wanted to get a couple of insert shots, and she wants to know if you can make dinner at eight o'clock instead of seven."

"Fine."

"Who is she?"

"An old friend."

"Her name isn't in your address book."

"We haven't seen each other in a while." I wiped the sweat from my cell and switched ears as I walked through a corridor of sound stages toward the parking lot.

"Chernak called twice? What did he want?"

"He was going to be out all day and he didn't have a cell phone, so he thought he should check in to see if you had anything for him."

"It's only been what, three hours?"

"The second time he said he'd just bought a cell phone, and he wanted us to have the number so you could call him anytime, night or day. I told him we appreciated that, and you'd call if you needed to talk."

"Masterful."

"*Arigatou*, Drayton-*san*," Mari said. "Your date tonight, is that Miss Sanders, or Mrs.?"

"Does it matter?"

"Just looking out for your reputation."

"Where were you when I needed you?"

"Kindergarten."

"Ouch."

I wiped the sweat away again and shifted the cell back to the other ear.

"Listen, Lotus Blossom, I've got another half mile hike to my car, but since you're feeling so chatty, I've got a couple other calls you can make after you call *Miss* Sanders back and tell her—"

"Whatever time is best for her works for you."

"Couldn't have said it better myself."

"That's what you have me for."

"I thought it was to maintain humility and practice patience."

"That, too," she said. "You want me to make a reser?"

"*Musso's.*"

"A booth on the bar side at Danny's station and the *Frog's Leap Rutherford?*"

"Got all my moves down pat, huh?"

"Wait till they read my dissertation. The Psych department will never be the same."

"You little snitch. There's a law about full disclosure when you fill out a job application, you know. I do have some recourse here."

"If the other call is to the W hotel, they know you're coming and your bag will be in your room."

"I'd like to know what you've been doing all day."

"Studying."

"Might be good for the tree if you open the windows."

"Not today. I've got the air on. You want Mr. Tate's cell number?"

"Shoot."

She read the number twice and I repeated it aloud twice to program it securely into a brain that was beginning to feel like a baked apple.

"Pretty warm over here," Mari said. "How's the heat in the valley?"

I ended the call and punched in the number for Frankie Tate.

CHAPTER TEN

Refrigerated air blew from ceiling vents, chilling the long narrow room of a windowless bar in Toluca Lake called *Out Takes*. I entered through the rear door from the sun-broiled parking lot, pocketed my shades, and stood for a moment, letting my eyes adjust to the dark interior.

A former director of photography named Henry Figueroa owned the place. The theme of its decor featured everyday objects from sound stages, camera trucks, and editing rooms. But the uniqueness of its appeal came from a DP's understanding of how to use light and shadow for dramatic effect. Shafts of light raked across the stools at the long teak bar, rim light found each table, and the booths were all backlit. Once the alcohol kicked in, everything in the room glowed like a Rembrandt.

Frankie Tate saw me before I spotted him, waved me to a booth where he was sitting close to a copper-skinned woman with a coal-black ponytail. He was wearing a white T-shirt with a logo, a small blue circle around a small blue image of a thirty-five millimeter camera sitting on a tripod. The circle was formed from the words Stuntmen's Association. I'd worn the same badge with pride in another life.

"Hey, hoss," he said, putting out his hand. "Good to see you."

Like all the best stunt men, Frankie had the cool confidence of those blessed with superior athleticism. If he had a shortcoming as a professional it was overconfidence, the conviction that he could pull off any stunt that could be imagined on land, sea, or in the air. It was a kind of wild streak that you knew he had when he first climbed out of the crib. He had a mean streak, too, which I had seen unleashed on back lots and in bar rooms, but it was always masked behind a lazy smile that reeled in most of the women on any set he worked. He might have made the transition from stunts to stardom for himself if he had a voice to match his looks, but when Frankie spoke, his Oklahoma twang sounded more like Mickey Mouse than Mickey Rourke.

"This is Twila," he said. "From Tulsa. Full-blooded Cherokee. Ain't she somethin'?"

Twila from Tulsa smiled with her black eyes. The corners of her mouth arced up shyly toward the classic high cheekbones of the first Americans.

"This is Mike Drayton, honey. Real-life private eye I told you 'bout."

"Twila," I nodded as I slid into the booth alongside her. "Nice to meet you."

Twila smiled again. I still couldn't tell if she had any teeth, but she had an undeniable exotic beauty and a full figure tantalizingly displayed in a white tank top.

"What's on your mind, *Miguel?*" Frankie asked.

"Anything cold," I said.

Frankie grinned and signaled a waitress to the table.

"*Pacifico.*" I said.

"And *dos mas margaritas,*" Frankie said.

Twila from Tulsa caught his glance and smiled again. Still no hint of teeth.

"So?" Frankie said as the waitress moved off.

"Jeremy Thomas," I said. "What happened?"

Frankie's smile faded. "How do you mean?"

"His last picture, he went with somebody else. English guy. Collingswood?"

"Yeah."

"Why?"

Frankie found his smile again, but he had to dig for it, and his high, nasal voice remained disinterested.

"Who knows?" he shrugged.

"I was hoping you did," I said. "I'm working for the father of the kid who got killed with him. Looking for things that don't square with the squeaky-clean image."

"What's that got to do with me?" There was a defensiveness in his tone. I tried to defuse it with a fraternal smile.

"Loyalty," I said. "You made him look good every time out. What kind of guy cuts you loose after a run like you had together?"

"Happens," Frankie shrugged, and drained the last of his drink.

"You two get into it over something?"

"Guy's dead, Mike. Okay?"

"So's my client's son. He's trying to find out why."

"Maybe JT'd still be alive if he didn't have that little faggot around."

"The kid was gay?"

"I don't know what the fuck he was, okay? Just leave me out of it."

"What about Thomas? Switch hitter?"

"He's dead. I got nothin' to say 'bout a dead man."

"Nothing good, you mean?"

"Don't press it, man."

"Sorry, Frankie. I have to. Everybody talks about the guy like he was a saint. A right guy doesn't just dump a buddy for no reason. Especially not a buddy who's helped him scale Everest."

"I'll give you a reason, okay? The assholes he was runnin' with. That whole artsy-fartsy crowd."

"Like?"

"You know Reggie Collingswood?"

"No."

"You're lookin' under rocks? Start with him."

CHAPTER ELEVEN

.

When the waitress arrived with the drinks, I pulled a twenty and a ten from my pocket as she set the margaritas in front of Frankie and his Cherokee maiden, the brown longneck in front of me.

"You don't have to do that," Frankie said.

"Done," I said, dropping the bills on the tray. Frankie lowered his eyes to his drink.

"Sorry I lost it, *hermano*," he said.

"No harm, no foul." I took a pull on the bottle, focusing on the icy flow of the Pacifico.

"It hurt," he said. Then he smiled ironically. "Hurt the ol' bank book, too."

"You think somebody else talked him into it?"

"He changed, man. That's all I know. Just wasn't JT any more. Hit him like it hits all of 'em sooner or later."

"The big head?"

"Hard not to get that way, I guess. People blowin' smoke up your ass eight days a week. I just didn't ever think it'd happen to JT. Hell, I'd known him since the first part he ever got. We started ridin' bikes together, chasin' *Señoritas*, got Laker seats with Billy Barton and Big Don Harris. Kings games, Dodgers. We were like brothers. Way you showed me the ropes when I was first out here? I did the same for him. Really threw me, man, I'll tell you. Guess you don't ever know anybody good as you think."

"Probably not," I said. "Could have been drugs."

"Nah. Just all that smoke, man. I've seen it over and over, so 've you," he said. "After a while, they want to b'lieve all that shit people they pay to write about 'em say. They ain't hearin' it all the time from folks they hang with, they start hangin' with folks who won't say nothin' else. But they don't ever see that. Funny, ain't it?"

"Not this time," I said.

He nodded. "No." He took a long pull on his margarita. "Sorry I said what I did 'bout the kid with him, too," he said. "Wasn't right."

"You know how they hooked up?"

"Some chick, I think."

"Know her name?"

He shook his head. "Never met her. Never met half the women JT knew." A grudging smile perched on the salted rim of his glass. "That ol' boy was one busy bird dog, I'll tell you."

He smiled at the young woman beside him.

"Young lady like this? Hell, I'd hold it all night 'fore I'd hit the head and leave her alone with JT."

"Competitive?"

"You had somethin', he had to prove he could have it, too."

"So much for loyalty," I said. "I guess the handwriting was on the wall."

"Somehow with JT, that never mattered. Had a way of makin' everythin' feel like a fun game. I never could get mad at him, don't know anybody who did."

"Not even when he hurt you?"

He shook his head. "Nah. It just hurt." He smiled again slowly. "Hell, when my agent told me they were makin' a change, I was hotter 'n hell. Got a call from JT ten minutes later, wound up thankin' him for all the good times. Meant it, too," he said. "Like thankin' the cop for the ticket he hands you 'fore he climbs back on his bike. He's gone, you look at the dang ticket, you say what the hell was I thankin' him for? But you know you owe him. Man coulda just saved your life."

"Yeah," I said. "Maybe Jeremy Thomas saved yours."

"Crossed m' mind more 'n once," he said. "That an' how I owed him, too. It was a helluva ride."

He nodded to my near-empty bottle.

"'Nother *cervesa?*"

"Better push off," I said. "Think of anything else, let me know."

I pulled a card from my pocket, handed it to him. He stared at it.

"I can think of one thing right now," he said.

"What's that?"

"I miss him."

I nodded, then looked to the young woman beside him.

"Twila. He's all yours."

She smiled again shyly without parting her lips. I offered my hand to Frankie.

"Thanks," I said.

"Any time, *hermano*," he said, as he gripped my hand firmly.

I left the two of them sitting in silence, a striking couple in chiaroscuro. Made for each other, maybe. One with a voice that didn't fit his physique and one who might not have any voice at all. Or any teeth.

CHAPTER TWELVE

I headed directly into blinding sunlight when I left Toluca Lake on Riverside Drive. As I angled northwest toward the hills on Moorpark avenue, a black-and-white cruiser pulled out of a parking lot at a Pizza Hut and swung in behind me. I checked the speedometer and eased off to a steady thirty-five.

As I crossed Fulton, the black-and-white turned right and headed north. LAPD is divided into eighteen regional areas, and Fulton is the western boundary for the boys from north Hollywood's area fifteen. But, as luck would have it, a Van Nuys unit heading south turned right onto Moorpark two cars behind me. I was glad I wasn't in a hurry.

A couple of miles later, I caught a green light at Ventura and started up Beverly Glen. The cruiser took a left at the signal and headed east again on Ventura, paralleling the hills. When a motorcycle cop heading east on Valley Vista fell in behind me as I crossed it, I started thinking it might not be my five-year-old Volvo Cross Country drawing all the attention. It might be me.

The temperature dropped ten degrees as I climbed the long two-lane grade at the base of Beverly Glen Canyon. Flat-roofed houses built on stilts lined the hillside to the left. I'd lived in a house like that years ago, on the Hollywood side of the hills. Seeing them brought back memories of warm summer nights and the faces of girls who shared them with me, girls who waited tables or worked in shops and took voice lessons and dance lessons and acting lessons, girls with stardust in their eyes, girls who saw me as an entree into a world they were determined to be a part of, probably the same way Twila from Tulsa saw Frankie Tate. Where were they now, I wondered, those beautiful, starry-eyed girls who never saw their names in lights? Did they have daughters themselves? Or sons like Ken Chernak who wanted to be like Jeremy Thomas? What would they say to them, if they did? What would it matter if the bug had already bitten?

I stopped in the left lane for another light at Mulholland Drive. The bike cop braked and sat idling behind me, his face in the mirror a Ray-Banned mask of nonchalance. It was the end of the line for him now, the north-south boundary between LAPD's Van Nuys area and the West L.A. area. It was also the crest of the range that divides desert heat from ocean breezes, a level spot that affords a breathtaking view. To one side you can see the San Fernando valley sprawling out to the northeast where it eventually blends into the great Mojave. To the other, the city of Los Angeles spills southwestward to the sparkling Pacific. It is an awesome sight by day or night. But the day or night has to be clear. Those unparalleled vistas come with the strong winds of March, and again in October and November, never in July. All I could see was a wall of smog that smothered the entire panorama. And a cop I thought could be following orders passed down from a mortal enemy.

The light changed and I crossed the threshold un-ticketed as the bike turned left, rumbling off to the east on Mulholland, and I began a descent down the southern slope into the deep shadows that come early to the canyon dwellers, thinking I didn't have any reason to be so paranoid.

CHAPTER THIRTEEN

Doing business in a city as spread out as L.A. means you spend plenty of time isolated in your own mobile cocoon. Short-distance commuters tend to keep their minds engaged by tuning in a favorite station for music or talk radio, long-haulers lean more to music or audiobooks, the fast-trackers keep the cellular circuits busy and don't miss a beat. The ninety miles from Santa Barbara to my Westwood office gave me quiet time to go over whatever puzzle I was working on. There weren't many pieces to this one yet, and none of them seemed to fit together to form any kind of recognizable pattern, but they were all I had.

Two young men had been hacked to death. One was world famous and would be eulogized at his funeral the next day as a saint in an industry of sinners, the other seemed to have found his "fifteen minutes of fame" in a rumor intended to incite lurid speculation. One had a position of tremendous power, the other appeared to have been a willing lackey. One was envied for his success, the other may have been envied for his admittance into an inner circle of companions. A former friend categorized those current companions of Jeremy Thomas as "artsy-fartsy" and seemed bitterly disappointed at being replaced by them. Resentment is a powerful emotion, how strong was Frankie Tate's? He claimed he held no hard feelings, but it didn't sound that way when I first mentioned the name Jeremy Thomas. Put Tate to one side.

Falcon had said it didn't figure that Ken Chernak was the primary target. Probably right. But don't close the door on the possibility.

Falcon had also said there was no indication of anything drug related, there was no burglary involved, and the rumor of homosexuality was unconfirmed. Scratch burglary, put a pin in drugs and sex.

The most likely suspect for the police was an unstable man who had assaulted Thomas before. Could be. But it didn't jibe with the crime scene photos.

On the face of it, then, the killer was either a homicidal maniac or a person enraged by some action committed by Jeremy Thomas. Howard Alworth said he knew of no one Jeremy Thomas had ever alienated, knew of no indiscretions the star had ever committed. That squared with the general public's impression as well as what the police and the DA's investigators had turned up so far. And it argued strongly for the Jack-the-Ripper theory the press was pushing on a public anxiously hanging on every word being printed or broadcast. Falcon wasn't buying into the Mister-Clean-Jeans publicity any more than I was, though. And Leah Sanders had restored my faith in the consistency of human nature. She said Thomas hit on her, bedded his co-star, and she didn't deny he had been sexually involved with his producer.

So, what did I know for sure? Not much. But it looked like the saintly super star was a mere mortal. His Achilles heel seemed to have been the fairer sex. Frankie Tate called Thomas a bird dog who was 'compulsive' about outscoring his pals. He also said he thought Thomas had met Ken Chernak through a young woman.

A couplet kept running through my mind. Kipling, I think. *If you love me as I love you, what knife can cut our love in two?* Or what broader blade?

The photographs of what an axe can do to a human body gave me the most to work with.

The tale the pictures told the trained eye was as enlightening as it was grim. Jeremy Thomas's home was on a secluded hillside in Benedict

Canyon, but the area where the bodies were found was a well-lighted open space between the main house and the guest cottage where Ken Chernak was staying. The coroner had placed the time of death at somewhere between midnight and six a.m. The floodlights were on. The two victims would have seen their assassin before they were attacked, seen a madman with an axe. And yet the mortal wounds to both men had been delivered from the front, meaning the victims had either come toward the killer or been with him when he struck. Ken Chernak's body was between Jeremy Thomas's and the guesthouse, indicating he had been the second victim. Clearly he had not tried to run away. If he had run at all, it was to charge Thomas's attacker. Both young men were six-feet tall, fit and athletic. They could have defended themselves given the opportunity. It followed as night after day that Thomas, at least, had known the killer and had been taken totally by surprise.

If you love me as I love you...

CHAPTER FOURTEEN

I came out of the canyon at Sunset Boulevard, and hung a right toward Westwood. When I drove past the gates leading into Bel-Air, another black-and-white pulled out and followed me up a slight grade bordered by expensive homes and manicured yards. It wasn't paranoia. It was Rankin.

I made a left on a green arrow at Hilgard Avenue. The cruiser followed suit, switching on its reds while we paralleled the northeast perimeter of the UCLA campus. I turned into an entrance leading to an information booth, stopped at the curb, and turned off the engine as the patrol car stopped behind me. I took off my sunglasses, put them on the dashboard, and planted my hands on the wheel at ten and two, watching in the rearview mirror as two officers got out of the car. The driver was dark-haired, broad-shouldered, flat-bellied, in his early thirties. His partner was younger, taller, broader, with close-cropped red hair. They each wore military creases and green-tinted Ray-Bans, each unsnapped the straps on their sidearms as they approached. The tall one positioned himself casually on the curb by my rear bumper, the driver came up alongside me and leaned down to the open window.

"Is there a problem, officer?" I asked.

"May I see your driver's license, please?" he said.

"It's in my coat pocket."

"Would you remove it, please?"

"I'm armed," I said. "A forty-caliber automatic in a shoulder harness."

"Would you get out of the car, please?" he said.

"Sure thing."

He took a step away from the door and let his right hand hang near the butt of his sidearm. I didn't look to see what his partner was doing, I already knew his hand was resting on the grip of his gun and his adrenaline was flowing. I climbed out from behind the wheel, closed the door, faced the officer with me and carefully pulled the left side of my blazer jacket away from my body to reveal the weapon.

"You have a permit for that?" he said.

"With the driver's license and my private license," I said. "Should I take the wallet out now?"

"Go ahead," he said.

A helmeted kid on a Vespa slowed as he approached from campus. He saw the gun and the two cops and sped out onto Hilgard. The student working the information booth stepped out to see what was going on, then ducked quickly back inside. The cop with me studied my licenses and my permit.

"This your current address, Mister Drayton?"

"Yes."

"Santa Barbara?"

"Yes."

"This address on the permit. What's that?"

"My office."

"Westwood?"

"Yes."

"Long drive."

"Worth every mile."

He waited for me to confess it was all a lie. I waited for him to get to whatever it was he stopped me for.

"May I see the registration on the vehicle, please?"

"Sure thing," I said. "It's in the glove box."

He nodded permission to reach back into the car. I removed the registration and handed it to him.

"May I ask what it was you stopped me for, officer?"

"You made a lane change and a left turn without signaling."

"I signaled twice," I said. "Once for the change, once for the turn."

"Maybe your blinker's not working," he said.

"Maybe." I reached inside the window to the steering column to depress the turn indicator. The blinker flashed rhythmically. We both looked at it. The cop on the curb looked at me.

"It's fine," I said.

"That's too bad," the cop beside me said. "Equipment failure wouldn't affect your insurance."

"You're going to write me up?"

"Illegal lane change, illegal turn."

"I signaled."

"We didn't see it."

"You were right behind me." I nodded at the blinker. "Hard to believe you didn't see that."

"You can turn it off now," he said.

I did. He watched me closely.

"Have you been drinking, Mr. Drayton?"

"One beer. Thirty minutes ago."

"Would you step around to the front of the car, please?"

It made sense. All the cops in my wake from the valley on up over the hill couldn't have been so interested for any other reason.

"You know a homicide captain named Rankin?"

"Front of the car, please."

"Sure you do," I said and stepped to the front of the car.

I could feel the cop behind me come up alongside the car, staying just outside the periphery of my vision as my inquisitor moved with me.

"I'm going to remove your weapon," he said.

"You're the man," I said. And I took hold of the bottom of my blazer with my left hand again, pulled it away from my body. The cop still held his citation book, my IDs and the registration in his left hand, his right still hung near his weapon. The younger cop behind me stepped off the curb and removed my automatic. I kept my eyes welded to the Ray-Bans in front of me, couldn't suppress a smile.

"You find this funny, Mr. Drayton?"

"Not yet," I said. "Maybe when we're in a courtroom with a transcript of the radio logs for your unit, the area fifteen boys, and the area nine tag team that took me to the top of the Glen."

"I want you to touch your right hand to the tip of your nose," he said.

"Yeah, this could get real funny," I said as I complied. "Maybe Rankin should be there, too. He can tell the judge about the drive-on passes at Universal being screened for any names that jumped out at him, who the driver visited, the alert he put out for the plates on this car."

The cop kept a stony face, but he handed back the registration and the IDs.

"Okay, Mister Drayton," he said. "I'm not going to write you up this time."

"Good move," I said.

"Consider it a warning."

"For what? Making lane changes in front of blind cops or investigating a case headed up by Curtis Rankin?"

He stiffened.

"You don't have to answer that," I said. "On the grounds it would definitely incriminate you."

I turned to the young giant behind me and held out my hand. His veiled eyes checked his partner's, then he reluctantly gave back the gun. He grew taller as I slid the automatic back into the holster.

"I don't know who you are, mister," he said. "But if I were you, I'd watch my mouth."

"If you were me, we wouldn't be standing here putting your job on the line as a favor to a total dirtbag ," I said. "And you can quote me on that, if your partner wants to change his mind again and start writing your way into a courtroom and an Internal Affairs hearing."

I turned away from the giant to look back at his partner. His black book remained clenched tightly in his hand. I moved past him, climbed into the car, and started the engine.

"Quote me anyway," I said. And drove off.

As I rolled past the information booth and on down the campus road toward the next exit, I watched the two cops in the rearview mirror again. They were engaged in an animated exchange. As they got back into the cruiser, I could see the giant's door slam. And I could see Curtis Rankin's face.

CHAPTER FIFTEEN

The head of security at the W hotel in Westwood was a guy named Bert Quint. He'd been an instructor at the Police Academy when I was in training and we'd stayed in touch after I graduated. I'd gone undercover for him a year ago and collared a couple working a sting on a string of guests. When he found out I'd moved to Santa Barbara, he said there'd always be a room for me at the hotel if I needed it. There always was. And there was never a bill to go with it.

My room, the night I started work for Gus Chernak, was a suite. It was, in fact, the Governor's suite, and took up the whole top floor. I'd have felt pretty important if I didn't know the hotel was overbooked and there weren't any takers for that high-priced a ticket, or any Governors in town to pay for it with tax money.

My gym bag looked anemic sitting on the King-size bed in the largest of the three bedrooms. I carried it to the smallest room. It didn't look any bigger there.

I took out the shaving kit, clean clothes, and dress loafers Mari had pulled from a filing cabinet, found an iron and ironing board in a closet, set them up to press the shirt, and stripped down for a quick shave and shower. As I headed for the bathroom, I saw the red light on the phone blinking. I punched a button and picked up two voice-mail messages.

One was Mari saying Gus Chernak had called three times and wanted me to call him. The other one was Gus Chernak. There wasn't any anger in his voice this time, just the pain, and the alcohol.

I called the number he left. He answered on the first ring.

"Chernak."

"Gus, it's Mike Drayton."

"What room you in?"

"What?"

"I'm downstairs. What's your number?"

"I don't think you can get up here, Gus."

"What, I can't punch a button? Just gimme the number."

"You have to have a card key to get to this floor."

"A what?"

I tried to explain, decided it was easier to call the front desk and have someone bring him up. When I opened the door in a plush monogrammed robe and he stepped into the lavishly appointed suite, his hackles went up.

"This what you call expenses?" he said.

I told him about Quint. He went straight for the mini-bar.

"Got the key to this thing?"

"It stays locked."

"What?"

"You want me to work for you, I want something from you besides my fee."

"What's that?"

"Lay off the booze, get eight hours, three squares, exercise. You don't help Ken any by losing your health, your business, control of your own life. And you're no help to me if you're in this kind of condition all the time."

"What do you know?" he erupted.

"I know it's hard," I said. "But you can't change that. And if you want to be there for Ken now, like you said, that's what you have to do. Be there."

His eyes locked on mine. The whites were red, but the gaze was rock solid. After a moment, he nodded. "Yeah, okay," he said quietly. "You got it."

"Good," I said, and checked my watch. "Listen, I have to keep moving here." I headed for the bedroom and the ironing board. He followed on my heels.

"So, anything yet?"

I couldn't tell him about the pictures Falcon had shared with me. But he had to hear something. "Friend of mine with the DA's plugging me into what they have," I said as I unfolded the dress shirt, laid it out on the board. "Met the producer on the movie Ken was working on, couple of people who knew Thomas pretty well. Seeing one of them again in a half hour to go over some things, and I have to shave and shower, so—"

"Somebody's got an idea what happened?" Gus interrupted.

"No. Just pick and shovel work."

"You turn up anythin', I wanna hear about it. I don't care what time it is."

"Sure."

I started pressing the shirt. He watched for as long as he could stand it.

"Here. Lemme do that. You're gonna be late." He took the iron from my hand. "Go. Do what you gotta do."

"Thanks," I said, and stepped into the bathroom.

"That a habit of yours?" he called after me. "Bein' late?"

I turned on the tap and took out my razor, ignoring the question.

"'Punctuality is the courtesy of kings,'" I heard him call from the other room. "You ever hear that?"

Only every day of my life till I was seventeen, I thought. But I pretended not to hear as I lathered my face and started to scrape off the shadow. It was quiet until I saw Gus over my shoulder in the mirror.

"I appreciate what you're doin'," he said. "Shirt's in the closet. I'm gonna go grab a steak."

"I'll keep you posted. But it'll take some time, Gus."

"One-fifty an hour, right?"

I could see him converting hours into days into weeks into months, into whatever retirement he had planned on.

"Right," I said.

His hesitation was slight. "It don't matter," he said. "Do what you gotta do. I gotta sell my trucks, I will. House, too. Just find out what the hell happened, tell me who the sonofabitch was who killed Kenny."

He remained in the doorway. "One other thing," he said.

"Yeah?"

"Kenny's funeral. It's tomorrow. I'd like you to come."

It wasn't an order. If anything, there was a fragility in his tone that made me feel his pain again. "Sure," I said.

"I'll write the time and the address down, leave it on the desk," he said.

"I'll be there."

He nodded and was gone. I stood alone at the sink, and my eyes found the phone on the wall. As I thought about calling Sheridan, it wasn't Gus Chernak's pain I was feeling. It was my own.

CHAPTER SIXTEEN

"So, how's camp?"

"Fine."

"You're a junior lifeguard now?"

"Yeah."

"You made it out to the buoy and back all by yourself?"

"Yeah."

I was seeing her smile, but the voice on the end of the line wasn't smiling.

"That's pretty darn good."

Silence.

"I wish I'd seen it."

Painful silence.

"I'm proud of you."

Really painful silence.

"Showground rodeo's coming up. You ready?"

"Yeah."

"What about Shadow? How's she doing?"

"Fine."

Three yeah's, two fine's, and five major stomach churns. I was shooting double bogeys on what had become a very hard course.

"She going to be ready to win?"

"Yeah."

Six. It hadn't been easy to talk since the day I'd tried to explain why she couldn't live with me after her mother died.

"You guys are on a streak now. Four in a row?"

"Three."

"I'm already counting this next one."

"My friend's here. I have to go now."

Two whole sentences. But just to get rid of me.

"Who's that, Cindy?"

"Mel."

"Mel?"

I hadn't thought about her friend being a boy. She caught the concern in my voice.

"Melanie," she said.

"Oh," I said, trying for nonchalance, but not getting there. "Have I met her?"

"No. Her dad's waiting for me."

Bull's-eye. And didn't she know it.

"You're going to her place?"

"Yeah."

"Well, have a great time. I'll be up as soon as I can, okay?"

"Okay."

"Bye, pal."

"Bye."

The disconnect was loud. The dial tone louder. The long silence deafening.

I stood under a stream of hot water, feeling the sting of it as I replayed the awkward, self-consciously boring conversation with a twelve-year-old girl who was never long out of my thoughts. I wished I could have that moment and too many like it back to live over again. I should have told her I missed her. I should have told her I'd drop everything and come up on the weekend, so we could talk. But knowing what I should've done after it was too late was a failing I seemed to have perfected, even after years of warning.

"*Prime Minister of Shoulda, that what you are, son? Shoulda done this, shoulda done that?*"

The drawl cut through the rush of water pounding on my head and shoulders. It was the voice I always heard when I was thinking about things he'd tried to teach me. I could see that half-smile everyone else thought was so charismatic. The one I knew meant you were three-feet shy of whatever mark he thought you should be hitting.

"*Shoulda, coulda, woulda, them's words say you didn't get the job done, boy. Words I don't wanta hear. Supper'll be waitin' when you finish up.*"

He thought if he put the spurs to me enough, I'd finally start doing things the way he wanted them done. But it didn't always work. Doing the right thing at the right time was still a problem for me.

As I dressed, I focused on the present, knowing that the choice I had made to help Gus Chernak was already taking me back into the past.

CHAPTER SEVENTEEN

Danny watched scornfully as I swirled the contents of a long-stemmed, wide-brimmed glass.

"Volatilizing the esters," I said.

"I only knew one Esther." He spoke in a flat New York accent. "She came volatilized."

Leah cracked a smile behind the daily menu that proclaimed *The Musso & Frank Grill to be The Oldest Restaurant in Hollywood, Providing Fine Cuisine Since 1919.* I inhaled and tasted. Danny was already filling Leah's glass.

"It's fine," I said. "You may pour."

He connected the two glasses with a trail of ruby-red dots dripping from the bottle.

"Know what you want yet?"

"How are the cherrystone clams?" Leah asked.

"Okay, you like clams."

He set the bottle down to make a ruby ring on the white tablecloth.

"I do," Leah said, and looked at me. "Split a Caesar?"

"Read my mind," I said.

"And?"

Danny's eyes were back on me, demanding.

"Anything in the kitchen's not on the menu?" I asked.

"You'll love it," he said, and moved off.

"To mystery," I said as I lifted my glass.

"And attitude," Leah grinned as she touched her glass to mine.

We sipped, savored the subtle aroma of chocolate and cherries, and shared a smile. It was a room we both liked. A big high-ceilinged room with dark-wood paneling topped by pastel murals of eighteenth-century pastoral scenes, peaceful settings incongruent with the hard sounds that caromed off the walls from all points of the compass. Bright light and the constant din prevented intimacy, but provided a curtain of privacy for conversation. There was a lot I wanted to hear from Leah, but first I just wanted to look at a face I hadn't seen for too long.

She had come straight from the studio, but there was a pale gloss on her lips now, a touch of color over the eyes that made them even darker, and complemented the Hunter green of her sweater. I could smell the clean scent of freesia in what I remembered was called *Antonia's Flowers* cutting through the aroma of garlic and *bouillabaisse* coming from the next booth.

She lowered her eyes self-consciously. "I guess Howard told you about Rob and me."

"Hey, I'm a licensed Shamus, sweetheart," I said with a Bogart lisp that brought her eyes back to mine. "Dragging what I need to know out of people's not a problem."

She shook her head, smiled, then asked, "So, what about you? Anybody in your life I should know about?"

"Nobody," I said.

"I didn't hear how sick Julie was till it was too late to see her," she said.

"Not much time left when they found it."

I offered the breadbasket. She declined, and I took a piece of sourdough.

"Did you talk before she died?" she asked.

"I tried."

I sampled the sourdough, sipped some wine.

"How did Sheridan handle it?"

"Not real well."

It wasn't a topic I wanted to go any further with, and Danny's green jacket returned mercifully with a tray. He slid our salads in front of us and moved off as quickly as he had materialized.

I took another sip of wine. "You were going to tell me about Kamala Highland and Thomas," I said.

"Wow," she said.

"What?"

"That look."

"What look?"

"I used to call it your game face."

"What are you talking about?"

"The way you get so nonchalant when something's really important to you," she said. "I could always tell. When you look like you're about to yawn? Inside you're like a dog with a bone."

She was right. I was in a lot deeper than I wanted to be. I set my glass down, swirled the wine, and a plaid jacket on a stool at the end of the long bar caught my eye. I'd seen it before less than two hours ago in the lounge just off the main entrance to the W. The guy wearing it shifted his eyes from the mirror. He was several shades darker than me, had a thick neck and a neatly trimmed mustache. Definitely a cop. Definitely on duty. The bad hairpiece didn't mean he was working undercover, it just went with the plaid polyester jacket.

Chapter Eighteen

I dropped my eyes to my glass, then looked back up at Leah.

"You see any pictures of the place they found the bodies?" I asked.

She nodded, picked up her salad fork, and took a bite.

"Pictures I saw had the bodies," I said.

She looked in my eyes, glimpsing what I didn't describe.

"If one of them was my kid, I'd hope to hell anybody who knew anything that might lead me to the killer wouldn't hold back."

She hesitated, but didn't flinch.

"I can't tell you it has anything to do with them being killed."

"What can you tell me?"

She bit her lip. I took a bite of salad and waited, resisting the urge to check back on the cop at the bar.

"Couple of things, I guess," she said. "First was when I walked in on Jeremy and Kamala. In his bungalow."

"Doing the deed?"

She nodded, took small bites of the crisp Romaine as she continued.

"Jeremy always wanted to see my notes first thing in the morning, so I swung by to drop them off. It was after midnight. We'd gone into golden time doing some second-unit shots, coverage on a big battle sequence we shot in Ireland. I didn't think he'd still be there. The key he kept under a brick outside wasn't there, so I tried the door and it was open. I was just going to leave the notes on his desk like I always did, then lock the door I thought he forgot to lock. It was dark inside, so I turned on the light in the entry. They were on the couch. I don't think Jeremy even saw me, but Kamala sure did."

"Either one of them ever say anything to you about it?"

"No. It was like it never happened," she said. "Of course, all three of us knew it did."

"You said 'a couple of things.'"

"I saw them alone together one other time," she said. "But they weren't having sex. They were at each other hammer and tongs."

"You remember anything they said?"

"More than I wanted to," she said. "It was in Kamala's bungalow. She'd asked me to bring her some timings. When I got there, Billie, her assistant, was on the phone with a day-care center. Her boy friend was supposed to pick up her daughter, but he hadn't done it yet and they said she had to come get her little girl right then. She didn't know what to do, so I told her I'd take her desk. She said Kamala was in a meeting and didn't want to be interrupted. I said she should just go, I could handle the phones. So, I'm sitting there taking a few calls and Jeremy opened the door of Kamala's office. She shouted at him. 'It was a mistake,' she said. He turned back into the room and blew off at her."

"What'd he say?"

"He said she sure as hell made the most of it. He said she was a user, but she wouldn't be using him any more."

"You sure about that?"

"Come on, Mike. I'm sitting where I shouldn't be sitting, hearing what I shouldn't be hearing, you think I'm going to forget what it was?"

"Go on."

"She really went off then, said they had an agreement and she expected him to honor it. He said, 'What the hell do you know about honor?' She said something like, 'Do you really want to start that? What's the public going to think about the All-American boy fucking his leading

lady? What's her husband going to think about it?' He said, 'You want
to play that game? Let's go. Let's see what the press does with your little
mistake. Let's see what the studio thinks about you balling the stunt man
scoring your coke.' Then it got really rank. She called him something
I'd just as soon not say, and he called her a phony bitch. He started to
leave and she grabbed him from behind, spun him around hard. I think
it surprised him, but she's a pretty big girl."

"I noticed. What'd he do?"

"She said she needed one more picture with him. He said, 'Not in
this lifetime, lady.' He shoved her away and slammed the door to the
bungalow on his way out."

"He never saw you?"

"No. Billie's desk is set back in an alcove."

"What about her?"

"She went back into her office and slammed that door."

"So she didn't see you, either?"

"I don't think so. I knew I didn't want to be there when she came
out, but I didn't want to get Billie fired, either, so I wrote a quick note
about Billie having to leave, put it on the desk with the timings and left."

"And she never mentioned anything about it?"

"No."

"You remember the date?"

"The date? No. Last week in May, I think."

"What about the time they were having sex?"

"A couple weeks before, ten days, maybe. Why?"

"Just keeping a timeline. If it comes to you, let me know."

Danny returned with an aromatic tray, set a beautiful arrangement
of cherrystone clams on the half shell in front of Leah and slid a plate of
dark meat and garden vegetables across to me.

"Roast duckling," I inhaled. "In sherry sauce?"

"Already volatilized," Danny snarled as he moved off to cross paths
with other green-jacketed waiters reminding customers that they were as
busy as anybody else in a very busy town.

CHAPTER NINETEEN

The plaid jacket was still nursing a drink and watching us in the mirror when Danny showed up with a slice of chocolate rum cake for Leah, and two cups of fresh-ground Mocha Java.

"I almost called you," Leah said, touching on a personal topic for the first time.

"You should have."

She lowered her eyes. "No. I had to work it out myself." A wry smile spilled into her cup. "You wouldn't understand about that."

"Are you insinuating I'm not good at sharing?"

The smile became a laugh as she lifted her eyes again, the dimples imploding.

"It's great to see you," she said.

I put my hand over hers, felt what she was feeling squared.

"Funny how it never worked out for us," she said. "Hard as we tried."

"Too hard, maybe."

Her eyes softened, the dimples deflated. "Let's go," she said quietly.

"Leah," I said, "I don't think—"

"I want you to hold me," she said. "That's all. Just hold me. Very close for a very long time."

For a brief moment, I felt almost whole. I felt safe, like I was home, wherever that was. But the guy at the bar wouldn't let me relax, and I knew I had to get Leah out of there.

"I could use some of that myself," I said.

The dimples indented again. Slowly.

When we moved past the bar into the adjoining room on the way to the parking lot, the plaid jacket slid off the stool to pay his tab. And I felt my collar tightening, my body hardening like a bike tire being inflated.

I let Leah's taillights disappear before I pulled out, but I didn't follow them. My whole shirt was feeling two sizes too small as I headed north up the backstreets to Franklin Avenue and swung east. A gray Taurus followed about as discreetly as the plaid polyester clung to the cop driving it.

I turned left off Franklin, followed one of the quiet, narrow streets up the hill. When I had two curves between me and the Taurus, I punched it up a block where little houses sat high above the street, and pulled to the curb just past a van parked on the other side in the shadows of a big jacaranda. I got out of the car, crossed the street and crouched behind the van, swelling with the lethal energy I knew I had to control unless it was needed. When the Taurus rounded the corner and braked to a stop just short of the Volvo, I stepped away from the van. The driver was peering through the windshield to see if I was still behind the wheel when I opened his door.

"We should talk," I said.

He went for the gun in his shoulder holster, and I grabbed a handful of shirt. As I pulled him out of the car, he dug a wild right into my body and I hit him hard with a left that exploded from the ball of my left foot. Whoever he was, he wouldn't be waking up quickly.

I dragged him onto the curb, and pulled his car in behind the Volvo. When his glassy eyes started trying to focus, his cerebellum was still reconnecting dots and his cerebrum scanning for data to place him in time and space.

"Gerald Mohr. Private License in the employ of Frontline Security and Investigation, Inc. Born May 2, 1974, New Orleans, Louisiana," I said from where I squatted on the curb beside him with his ID in hand. "African American, six-two, one-hundred ninety-seven pounds, brown hair, brown eyes. That help?"

He tried to sit, instinctively reaching for his gun again. I dangled the .38 snub-nose off my right index finger. He glared, then groaned as the knot forming where the back of his head hit the asphalt made its presence known, and grimaced as he became aware of the source of the blood splattered on his coat and shirt.

"Too bad about the coat," I said. "One of a kind, right?"

He struggled to sit, pressing his thumb against the side of his nose to stanch the bleeding.

"Look, man, I was just doing my job, you know?"

"Who for?"

"I don't know."

"Well, when you do, we'll swap."

I slid the .38 into my blazer pocket as I stood up. He winced as he tried to get up with me and thought better of it.

"I just take assignments, man. Strictly 'need to know.'"

"I need to know."

"All anybody said to me was to tail you and keep a log."

"But being in the same business, both of us know somebody's paying for it, don't we?"

"I don't have access to that."

"Or this."

I slipped his ID into a breast pocket and started for the Volvo.

"Those records are secure," he said as he labored to his feet.

"Good. You know right where to find them."

"Are you crazy? I can't do that..."

"'Can't' isn't an option for you, Gerry. Breakfast at *Mojo*. Eight o'clock. Bring a copy of the report,"

"There's no way I can bust into those files."

"There's always a way, Gerry," I said as I opened the car door. "Eight sharp. You don't show, what's in my pockets gets hand-delivered to Frontline with a detailed explanation of how I got them."

I climbed in behind the wheel, keyed the ignition, and Gerald Mohr's consternation shone in the afterglow of my taillights as I drove away.

Chapter Twenty

"He followed you from the hotel?"

I sat at Leah's kitchen table resting my left hand in a bowl of ice water while she gave me the third degree.

"And you knew he was at the bar? How could you do something like that without even letting me know? What if he'd surprised you instead?"

"Then I'd be wearing plaid polyester coats," I said. "Not my style."

"You know damn well what I mean. You should have told me, so if anything happened, I'd be able to tell the police."

"I thought he was the police."

"What do you mean, you thought he was the police? Why would the police be following you? Why would you attack them if they were?"

"In that exact order?" I asked. "I thought he was a cop because he looked like a cop. He could have been following me for the same reason I was followed by cops this afternoon, I hit him because he went for his weapon, and when I stopped him he hit me, which is not a complete answer to your question, I know, but I can't give you that because I don't know for sure yet. I think it's because Curtis Rankin knows I'm asking questions about the case he's running."

"Curtis Rankin?"

"You remember the name."

"I remember what he did to you."

"Allegedly."

"Why would he care what you're doing?"

"I don't know. And I don't know why somebody hired a big PI firm like Frontline to shadow me," I said. "But I'll know who that was by eight o'clock in the morning. Then maybe some pieces will fall into place. You wouldn't have any Paddy's, would you?"

"What?"

"Irish whiskey?"

Leah turned to a cupboard, pulled out a fifth of Cutty Sark and put it on the table.

"Remind me to talk to you sometime about the subtleties of distilled beverages."

"Just tell me why you think people are watching you," she said as she turned for two glasses and shoved one under the ice dispenser on the refrigerator door.

"Besides my animal magnetism?"

"Damn it, Michael—" She set the glass with the ice down hard on the counter. "You always do that. So damn cool."

She was right, "cool" was my reflexive defense mechanism, the heat shield that guarded against congenital self-destructive impulses. But her anger came from someplace else. I didn't know where exactly.

"Sorry," I said.

She bit her lip, dropped her head, and set the other glass down. I stood and wrapped my arms around her. I felt the short, choppy intake of breath that begins a sob.

"I keep losing things."

The words coming out on the reverse chop of air were muffled in my chest. But I heard them. I knew what she'd recently lost, what having a child would have meant to her, and I understood where that someplace was.

"I'm here," I said.

They come sometimes in summer. Unexpected, unheralded and unsettling. An awesome force unsheathed with a sudden ferocity as seductive as it is terrifying.

It was almost two in the morning when I heard the first faint tapping on the window. The door from the bedroom to the redwood deck overlooking the canyon was open, and the breeze that swept in over us had a sense of urgency.

Leah had finally drifted off to sleep a little after midnight. I had held her close for a long time, and she was still nestled into my side when I slid my arm out from under her and got up. She didn't move when I slipped a pillow under her head or her shoes off her feet. I envied her that kind of sleep.

A blanket of clouds was unfurling across the moon outside, drawing a shadow up over her, and I drew the comforter up behind it. The tapping grew louder and came faster. I walked to the door and stepped out under the wide eave as the giant drops of rain splattered the deck with magnum force. The breeze was still warm, but stronger. Thunder rumbled in the distance. It segued into the faint, far-off sound of a siren coming or going to an attack or an assault, a violent collision or a violent crime, to where a building was ablaze or a pursuit in progress. Even in the dead of night, even in the recesses of a city renowned for its promise, its big dreams and bright lights, something was being lost or violated, stolen or broken, something good was most likely gone forever.

I don't remember much about my mother, don't think of her often, but as I stood staring up into the storm, I heard her soft voice, with its island accent, whispering to me a long time ago, "*When it rains, Michael, God is crying.*"

Lightning flashed somewhere over the hills above me. A clap of thunder boomed off the canyon walls. And as I thought about Gus Chernak and his son's brutal death, I felt for a moment like my mother was right. God had to be crying.

Chapter Twenty-One

When I stepped into the chic, Latin-influenced restaurant, I saw a somewhat battered, and noticeably balding Gerald Mohr sitting at a corner table. He was wearing a dark jacket, yellow shirt, and an angry welt left by the imprint of my knuckles.

"'Mornin', Ger. Hardly recognized you."

"Sonofabitch," Mohr growled.

"Don't tell me," I said as I slid into a chair across from him. "You didn't get any sleep last night."

The welt purpled beneath his dark skin as he pulled a folded computer printout from an inside pocket and handed it to me.

"I got what you wanted, asshole," he grumbled. "You don't have any idea what I had to do to get it, either."

"Nothing immoral, I hope."

"Damn near got caught."

"But you didn't," I said as I opened the report. "Take some pride in that."

"Gimme my stuff."

"Did you read this?" I asked as I stared at the name of the person who hired the investigation.

"Kamala Highland," he said. "Somebody you know?"

A white-jacketed waiter stepped to the table with a pot of coffee, refilled Mohr's cup and poured for me.

"*Buenos dias, Señor* Drayton. Your usual?"

"Thanks, Eligio."

"And for you, *Señor*?"

"He'll have the *huevos rancheros*."

"*Bueno*," the waiter smiled at Mohr. "Best in town."

He moved off to the kitchen. I unfolded my napkin, put it on my lap, and looked into two smoldering slits.

"Come on, Ger. You look like a heuvos rancheros kind of guy."

"I got work to do."

"Gerry, I am your work, remember? And I'm buying. How bad is that?"

"I don't like you."

"Give it some time," I smiled demurely. "I'll grow on you."

"Just gimme back my stuff."

"'Stuff?' Is that how you refer to the tools of your trade, Ger? 'Stuff?' Your license to practice your profession? The weapon you depend on to keep you alive? 'Stuff?'"

The welt grew darker.

"Hey, man, give a brother a break, okay?"

"The old race card. Very disappointing, Gerry."

"I worked hard to get this job."

"I'm sure you did. But this isn't about race. It's about people. Good people and bad people. They come in all colors."

"I got a family, man."

"So, let's think this through."

"Whatta you mean?"

"Look, we're two pro's, right? There's nothing personal between us, it's pure business."

"So?"

"So, your business in this case is prying into my business, and I can't have that. Any idea how we get around that little problem?"

I waited for a response. It wasn't going to come swiftly.

"Let me make a suggestion," I said. "I give you my itinerary every day. My secretary will have it for you at nine o'clock sharp. Dates, times, places, people, everything you need to file a detailed report."

"Why would you do that?"

"To save your job."

"You mean, you tell me where you go so I don't have to be there?"

"You spend the day doing anything you want, and so do I. And the two of us are the only ones who know you weren't glued to me the whole time."

"How do I know you're going where you say you are?"

"You have to trust me."

While he considered the prospect, I spelled out his option.

"Your choice, Gerry. Best huevos rancheros in town, or pick up your 'stuff' in the shoebox at the front desk right now, go your merry way, and know the next time I see you you'll wind up in a wheelchair sucking meals through a straw."

"You think I'm scared of you?"

"I think you should consider your options very carefully."

The waiter returned with breakfast. Gerald Mohr studied me long and hard, then folded his hand.

We ate in silence. The huevos rancheros looked delicious. But it figured I'd soon be dealing with somebody a lot brighter than Gerald Mohr, and I couldn't afford to be feeling content. The slice of melon was a slice of melon, the oatmeal was oatmeal. It was fuel for the day.

CHAPTER TWENTY-TWO

It drizzled all morning. The storm's energy was spent, but the front had stalled and low clouds eclipsed the ridgeline behind Forest Lawn Memorial Park. Leah's Saab inched forward in a long line of cars crawling toward the double-gated entrance on Forest Lawn Drive just across the river from The Burbank Studios. The wipers were on intermittent, only an occasional swipe of the blades interrupting the long silence between us. It wasn't just the solemn occasion that kept us quiet, it was the puzzle we were working on.

"It doesn't make sense."

"Not yet," I agreed.

"I mean, she'd never seen you before yesterday."

"Far as we know."

"She thinks you're just a friend of mine."

"Assumption," I said.

She fell silent again, nodding in accord. She hadn't planned on attending the service for Jeremy Thomas, but agreed to let me escort her. I hadn't planned on attending, either, but it gave me a chance to eyeball all the players who showed up, and I knew Kamala Highland would be there front and center. I thought it might be a good idea to let her see me there. I didn't know why exactly, but I didn't know much of anything yet and she was apparently concerned enough about what I was doing to pay somebody to find out what it was.

"This used to be our race track," I said.

"What?"

"High school. Summer nights, kids from all over the valley, San Fernando, Van Nuys, Burbank, Glendale. We rallied over here at midnight, paired off, and let it rip. Lost a good friend on this curve," I pointed. "Right over there. Donnie Jensen. Good guy, hell of a linebacker. SC wanted him, Cal, Washington. Rolled three times. First dead body I ever saw. We were seventeen."

She looked at me along her eyes.

"How many since, Mike?" she asked quietly. "How many killings? How many rolls of crime-scene tape, body bags, forensic reports? How do you live with that?"

"You been reading my mail?"

I was sorry the minute I said it. It wasn't anything I wanted to be chewing on while I was working. It could make me careless, and careless could get me hurt, maybe permanently.

"Meaning?"

"Nothing."

"Thanks," she said, fixing her eyes on the car in front of us again. "God, Michael, there're so many other things you could be doing. Move up by Pidge and Liz, raise horses, grow grapes. Or go find a beach and tend bar where nobody can tell you how things have to be done." She caught herself. "I guess that wouldn't work for Sheridan, though, would it?"

It was hard to pick up the pieces with someone when there were so many pieces you hadn't shared.

"I never was much good with mixed drinks, anyway."

"Yawn," she said.

"Okay, I'm ducking the question," I said. "How about a rain check?"

Silence set in again, the wipers slapping it away every few seconds to clear the mist from the windshield.

Chapter Twenty-three

A city cop stood beside his bike in the middle of the street, funneling cars arriving from both directions through the stone-pillared wrought-iron gate. We fell in between a black Jaguar and a silver Mercedes, drove a quarter mile up the carefully tended hillside where hundreds of headstones lay flat in the grass. We parked and walked past more graves covered by manicured lawn and dotted with pools of shade from leafy trees to where a crowd ringed a white chapel with a tall spire that looked like a transplant from a village in Vermont.

Strobes flickered against the gray sky and battery packs glared atop handheld cameras as TV crews and members of the press covered the entrance like it was an awards night or an old-fashioned world premiere. Two dozen rent-a-cops and security people in tan uniforms kept hundreds of stargazers and autograph hounds at bay, while four young men in dark suits admitted faces and names they recognized to the roped-off chapel, or directed them to the tarp-covered overflow areas where folding chairs were filling with lower profile mourners.

One of the young men screening arrivals knew Leah and nodded us into the building past a young fan he was fending off who was pleading for admission with a baby in her arms.

In the foyer of the chapel, a woman handed us a five-by-seven program with a picture of Jeremy Thomas on the front. It was SRO inside the chapel itself, but we nestled in beside a column against a sidewall that gave us a view of the flower-draped casket, the lectern, and the people sitting in the roped-off rows down front. I only noticed a dozen people with skin anywhere close to my color who had made the A-list. But that was pretty good for Hollywood.

I thought about what had to be inside the casket and the arrangements that had been made to keep the people crowding the service from knowing what I knew. I looked inside the program. There would be three speakers in addition to a Minister, nobody with the surname Prentis, none of them designated as family. One of them, however, was the newly self-appointed president of my fan club, Kamala Highland.

An organ began to play. At that precise moment, one of the young men from outside ushered a tall woman in black suit and veil to a front-row seat.

"Timing is everything," I said to Leah.

Her eyes, and all others, focused on Kamala Highland.

"Who's in the house seats?"

She craned her neck to sweep her eyes over the pew down front where Kamala Highland was being seated.

"Studio execs, agents, his business manager."

"Is that the leading lady?" I nodded.

"Katherine Morris."

"The gray-haired guy beside her?"

"Her husband, Nigel Crane."

"What would you say, thirty-five year spread? Forty?"

"She's twenty-six, he's sixty-four."

"The plot thickens."

"Is everyone a suspect?"

"Guilty until proven innocent," I said. "Is that Peter Michaels?"

She followed my look.

"Sir Peter," she corrected.

"Ah, yes. *Knight of the Realm*. For directing damsels in distress, was it? Or distressing damsels he directed into his motor home?"

"For 'reflecting glory on the Crown.'"

"Oh, like Shakespeare, you mean. No, wait a minute. He never got dubbed Sir William, did he? You have to be really good for that, I guess."

"Stop it," she said, dimples twitching.

"How about the guy beside Sir Peter, gotta be the double for Thomas, right?"

"Reggie Collingswood," she said. "Strong resemblance."

I looked around the chapel and found Frankie Tate about eight rows back. A little older, but another ringer for the guy in the casket. *Only in Hollywood,* I thought.

"I don't know the man next to him," Leah said.

I looked back to the first Jeremy Thomas look-alike, and the man seated beside him. "Marty Mishkin," I said. "Think Robert DuVal in *The Godfather.*"

"Mafia?"

"Is Phil Adams mafioso? Nobody's ever proved it. Lot of people say that's because of Mishkin."

She looked back at the slender man in the dark-blue, eight-thousand-dollar Attolini suit and silver tie. He was in his early forties, had a full head of black hair combed straight back like a GQ model approaching middle age.

"He represents Phil Adams?"

"His one and only client," I said, nodding to the man next to Mishkin. "On his right."

Leah stared at the tan, white-haired man in the black, ten-thousand-dollar Kiton suit.

"Phil Adams?" she said.

It was a name everybody in L.A. knew. He kept a very high profile, chaired fund-raisers for worthy causes and candidates from both major political parties, owned a downtown office building that towered above the city, but nobody knew exactly where his wealth came from. Rumors were rampant and reporters had dug into his background for years, but they seemed to have a way of never finishing their stories. Some left for better jobs that suddenly materialized, some took early retirement, and a couple had fatal accidents. The only guy who knew for sure just how Phil Adams made his millions and whether or not he was mob-connected was Marty Mishkin. And maybe the FBI.

"What's he doing here?" Leah wondered out loud.

"Maybe he was a fan," I said, and stuck my tongue into my cheek as the unseen organist stopped playing and the Minister stepped to the lectern.

The man in the royal blue robe was another face everyone knew, a silver-haired evangelist with a national television congregation. He was a tall, commanding figure who delivered a dramatic account of the character and qualities of a young man he'd never met.

A young actor named Mark Ford followed the good Reverend and read from Scripture. I knew Mark Ford by reputation. He was a heller. He was also quite good at cold readings, because the words of *Revelations* seemed as comfortable in his mouth as the profanities I'd heard him hurl at a parking lot attendant last fall outside a little club on the Sunset Strip.

The next speaker was Grant Collier, an executive vice president of worldwide distribution at Universal. As he delivered some remarks about "a young man beloved the world over," his voice thickened, suggesting that he was fully aware of what the popular young star's absence from his lineup would mean to profits from foreign markets. An agent named Freddie Getz followed Collier. He was, like a lot of agents, not very tall, barely visible, in fact, behind the lectern. He had represented the young man in the casket ever since he became an established international star worthy of the time and attention of a power player like Getz, and he spoke reverently about the "spiritual adventure" the two of them had shared on a white-water rafting trip through the Grand Canyon with a group of fifty close friends from different areas of the industry.

"Like the run through the rapids," Getz declared, "Jeremy Thomas's life was a great ride."

I had the feeling I was living Holden Caulfield's worst nightmare. And when Kamala Highland rose to give the eulogy for her "trusted partner and dearest friend in all the world," I was sure of it.

Her performance was masterful. She only faltered once. That was when her eyes brushed over the wall where Leah and I were standing and bounced back to focus briefly on me.

Leah's hand tightened on mine.

"In the immortal words of Vernon Jordan," I whispered, "'mission accomplished.'"

When the panegyric concluded, there wasn't a dry eye in the house. Except for mine and Leah's. That's what I thought, anyway, until I saw Howard Alworth standing against the wall on the other side of the chapel smiling at me.

CHAPTER TWENTY-FOUR

As we filed out with the crowd, Howard fell in with us.

"So, who came with who?" he said, keeping his nicotine-stained voice geared to a confidential level.

"I'm his cover," Leah said.

"Yeah?" Howard said. "You're actually working a funeral?"

"Reason I got the job," I said. "Rubbing elbows with the Bigs."

"So you fit right in with some of the other phonies who showed up."

"My kind of town," I said.

Howard glanced around, steered us out of the mainstream as we cleared the crowd of fans, reporters and cameras still engulfing the chapel and reached the street.

"Hey, you know a cop named Rankin?" he asked as he pulled a pack of Camels and a book of matches from his raincoat pocket.

"Yeah. Homicide."

"You tell him we talked?"

"No. Why?"

"He called to ask me what it was we talked about."

He tapped the last cigarette from the pack, crumpled the empty wrapper and jammed it back into his pocket.

"What'd you say?"

Howard gave the cigarette three sharp raps on the back of his left hand and put it between his lips.

"I didn't know what I should say."

"So, you told the truth?"

"Yeah. That okay?" he asked as he ripped a match from the book and lit the cigarette.

"It isn't, I'm in the wrong racket."

"He said he's in charge of the investigation?"

"Right."

"But you didn't tell him you were coming to see me," he said as he exhaled a stream of smoke.

"No."

"Then how the hell did he know?"

"Case like this can make his career. Won't be much gets past him."

"So you guys are pals?"

"He say that?"

"Not exactly. Said you used to work together downtown."

"I worked for him, actually."

Howard stopped in mid drag.

"Jesus," he said. "Is he the one?"

"I'm still under court order not to name names."

"Jesus." He removed a fleck of tobacco from his tongue. "He's the sonofabitch went after your hide?"

"Don't worry about it," I said. "We understand each other. There won't be any problem."

Howard studied me skeptically through the smoke he exhaled. Leah bit her lower lip.

"Going to the burial?" Howard asked.

"Not this one," I said. "You?"

"Like I said, far as I know he was a good kid. I want to pay my respects without all the bullshit."

"See you at the open house Kamala Highland's having this afternoon?"

"Sure," he said. "Right after I take out an open letter in the trades."

The committal was on a hillside above the chapel. We could hear the nasal skirl of bagpipes as we got back in the car and saw a hearse approaching an array of lights and cameras amidst a forest of black umbrellas clustered around the graveside.

Off to one side, Howard Alworth stood alone, bareheaded beneath the sullen sky.

CHAPTER TWENTY-FIVE

"She saw you," Leah said.

"Tough not to stand out in a room that white."

"You knew that when you asked me to take you."

"I did."

"And you were right about Rankin."

I nodded. We were driving east along the south bank of the Los Angeles River. The broad thirty-foot high concrete channel still had runoff from the storm flowing through the trench at its center. Three kids were floating along the rusty brown water in a yellow-rubber raft. Three new-millennium pirates in baggy pants and ball caps, spiritual descendants of Tom Sawyer, Huck Finn, and Joe Harper on the Mississippi. But there was no forested island in sight, only massive gray walls tagged with graffiti. I wondered what this young trio had stolen for their adventure, and mourned what had been stolen from them. It was the first time I'd felt sad all morning.

"This is creepy, Michael. These are funerals we're going to. Young men who were murdered. And now?"

Concern and confusion collided, silencing her. She looked at me.

"Is this something you really have to do?" She bit her lower lip, shook her head in surrender.

I remembered all the opportunities she'd given me to explain myself a lifetime ago, none of the reasons I hadn't. But I knew they probably all came down to the same one.

"Okay," I said. "Rain check time."

"No. It's all right," she said. "I don't have to understand. But now I can't help worrying."

"I don't want that."

"Tough."

She wasn't smiling. I saw her in her twenties. I saw her tears, and anger, and pride. I saw the note I found in our bedroom.

"You were right on target," I said.

Her eyes shifted from the road, questioning.

"About your mail?"

"Yeah. Gets old," I said. "Sort of like proctology must. Always looking up the ass end of the world."

"You really feel that way? Then you get yourself into something like this?"

"Hang a left here," I said, indicating the bridge at Riverside Drive. She made the turn and we started across the channel. I could see the raft way down the river.

"I don't get it," she said. "I'll never get it."

"I'm pretty much my father's son, I guess." I could hear his voice in mine. I could hear him saying for the hundredth time, *'You see somethin' needs doin', do it.'*

"His dream for you was college. That's what you always said, a formal education, a profession."

"It was," I said, thinking about the kind of student I'd been, or hadn't been, how formally educated people had intimidated me the same way they intimidated my father.

"Far as I could see, there wasn't much wrong working with him, making good money taking chances that gave you a rush. How do you beat that when you're twenty years old?"

"But you did what he told you to do. You went back to school."

"He never told me what to do. He showed me why one choice might be better than another," I said, and pointed to the intersection ahead of us. "To the right."

As we left the bridge, I caught one last glimpse of the yellow raft floating around a bend and out of sight. Leah turned onto Alameda Avenue, crossed Victory Boulevard and headed into Glendale.

"He dumped some books on me, whole world of ideas, talked about doing something with my life, different kinds of service, different kinds of challenges. Medicine, law, teaching. Things he said mattered, things he never tackled, wished he had. He said I had my mother's intelligence, I should put it to good use."

I remembered the look in his eyes that day, a look that was always a challenge in itself, always a yardstick for what you were made of. I remembered the first time I had to stare straight back into that look or catch another rap under my chin that rattled my teeth. I remembered a day so hot and dry I could hardly draw a breath, and wondering how my eyes could puddle up when there wasn't enough spit in my mouth to swallow. *"Fear's a thing you got to conquer, son,"* he said. *"The one thing you can't let whip you."*

We were walking to the corral. Pidge Connors stood with the colt tied off to the snubbing post, a little buckskin, twelve hands high, no more, but he looked like a Clydesdale to a six-year old. *"There's a taste comes to your mouth like suckin' on a copper penny,"* he said. *"You just swallow that down, an' hold 'er down. After a few times, you find out it ain't all that big a deal. But knowin' you can take whatever comes at you, now there's the whole world in a nutshell."*

I smiled at the thought of all the copper pennies I'd sucked on since that day.

"I think the biggest draw for me," I said to Leah, "was finally doing something he hadn't done better."

"But then you quit. Why?"

Quit. The word cracked like a rifle shot. It always had since I was just shy of twelve years old. His image came back across the years again, his voice as steady and clear as his eyes. *"That what you are, son? A quitter? One o' them fellas folks count on ain't around when you need 'em? One o'them kind says this is too tough for me, I want out?"*

The words stung then, and they had never stopped stinging. *"What happened to that goal you set? That buckle you was after? That dream of provin' to the world you could hang an' rattle with the best of 'em? You just givin' up on that 'cause you got hurt? You got scared? Hell, you ain't a man if you never been hurt. An' you'll never be a man, you back away from whatever it is got you cowed. You ain't learned it yet, I guess, but you better start lookin' around, see how many boys you're ridin' against look like you. You get older, get out in the world, you're gonna hit some things head on you can't back down from. Lot of them things'll come from men look like them other boys. Like me. But they won't be me. Nor Pidge, neither. Things they do or say won't be fair, they won't be right, but you're gonna have to stand tall and face 'em down. You better not ever quit."*

He turned and walked away. I hated him. That part of him anyway, that part that demanded the best effort anytime I tackled anything, the guts and the will to see whatever it was through to the end without showing any fear, without leaning on others, or blaming others, or caring about what others thought. The emotion I felt that day didn't really die until he did, and I finally began to understand him. To understand what he'd given me. What he knew he had to give me in a world that kept talking about being color-blind but never quite seemed to make it over the hump.

Leah's voice pierced the memory.

"I never understood that. You got into UCLA, got into your last year. Why just drop out like that?"

"He died," I said.

"You just said you weren't doing it for him."

"He died, and nobody cared."

"What do you mean?" she said. "An army of people mourned him."

"Yeah," I said. "And believed what they read in the papers. *'Legendary Hollywood stunt man dies in miscalculation of explosives.'*"

"You don't think that's what happened?"

"Miscalculation? Never."

"His doctor did say he had cancer."

"I know what he said, and I know what people thought. But quit? On his own life? That wasn't consistent with anything in it."

She looked back at the road. "I wish we'd been together then."

"No, you don't."

She glanced at me again. "You never got any closure, did you?"

"I just knew nobody cared enough to find out for sure what really happened. Made me want to do that kind of work, be somebody who tried to sort things out and set them straight."

"Okay. I get that. Police work. But you quit that, too," she reminded without casting judgment.

"Yeah," I said. "When I saw victims wearing body bags and killers wearing badges. I couldn't stop it, but I didn't have to be part of it. I thought if I could work alone, help level the field, maybe, for people on the outside looking in, I'd feel like I was doing something worthwhile."

"And now?"

"Now I'm talking too much."

Her right hand left the wheel for my left. She squeezed it firmly.

"Thank you," she said.

What I hadn't said was that the truth I'd learned about human nature in the years since my father died had dulled my convictions about taking on corrupt self-interest, about trying to be some kind of equalizing force. I wasn't sure any more if the time I'd spent looking for justice was justified, if it wouldn't have been better spent with a daughter I loved.

"Helping a father," Leah said. "That's the reason you took this case, isn't it?"

"Part of it."

"What's the other part?"

"Being a father."

CHAPTER TWENTY-SIX

There were no cars waiting to get into the little cemetery just east of the railroad tracks on Glenoaks Boulevard, no ornate gate, nobody in the information booth to direct us. We took the only route available, a narrow two-way street lined by Acacia trees sadly in need of pruning. On either side, there was a broad expanse of water-shy Saint Augustine grass bordered by chain-link fencing. We drove past the few isolated dots of color from small bouquets scattered among the headstones to where a half-dozen cars were parked near a mound of earth covered with a piece of vivid-green indoor-outdoor carpeting.

I saw Gus Chernak standing on the far side of a mahogany casket that rested on a hydraulic lift over the grave. He looked ten years older than when I had first seen him the day before. Grief, guilt, and pent-up rage were ravaging the inner core of a very strong man.

Whoever prepared the remains for burial would have been instructed by the coroner and the PD to protect family members from the gruesome details, but enough details had been released by the media to make it impossible for a combat veteran like Gus Chernak not to know what lay in the wooden box in front of him. Burying it would not be this father's final act of duty. Until he found out who had savaged his son, and why, there would be no rest, no way that any amount of time could ever heal his own gaping wound.

He stood bareheaded in a tan raincoat over a dark blue suit. A minister stood beside him in a black raincoat, Bible in hand. Four other people, three men and a woman, stood beneath a brace of umbrellas a few feet from the curb with their backs to us.

We sat for a moment in the car, moved by the stark contrast to the mob scene we had left less than twenty minutes ago.

"'*Full many a flower,*'" I said.

Leah spoke more softly, more eloquently. "Dear God," she said. "How hard."

Gus Chernak looked up at the sound of the doors closing on the Saab, saw me open the pop-up umbrella, get Leah under it. As we approached the grave, his eyes latched onto mine like a lifeline. His face was a grim mask holding raw emotion in check as only very brave men can do.

"Ready, Reverend," Gus said as he spread his legs and settled into a Marine Corps at-ease. He held fast to a lifetime of discipline as the Minister offered a prayer, read from Scripture, and remarked on the suffering of family and friends when a soul is summoned early to the life that follows this temporal existence.

Unlike the clergyman who'd officiated at the service for Jeremy Thomas, the only identification this unassuming pastor made with the young man whose life he had come to consecrate was that of a fellow sojourner. The only portrait he attempted to paint was not of a Ken Chernak he hadn't known, but of a benevolent Creator who regards all life as precious, as having equal value. The words were simple, sincere, designed to bring solace and ease grief. When he finished, he asked if anyone had any memories they wanted to share.

A young man as brown as me responded from beneath a black umbrella with an L.A. Raiders' logo held by a stocky Latino in his early twenties. Both men wore rain jackets from Eddie Bauer or Big Five. The Latino's was dark green, the thin black man's a Tyrian purple.

"My name is Rowland." The young man spoke with a pronounced feminine manner. "Rowland Martin. Chad, that's the name I knew him by, Chad was my friend. He was a beautiful person. He helped me be a better person, I think, and a better actor."

Gus Chernak's face reflected a mounting discomfort as Rowland Martin's voice thickened with emotion.

"I loved him," the young man said. "And I'll miss him."

He ducked out from under the umbrella, blinking back tears as he pulled a long-stemmed red rose from beneath his purple jacket. He planted a kiss on the rose, placed it with precision atop the casket, and turned back to the shelter of the umbrella.

Gus worked hard to veil his reaction to the young man's testimonial. The man beneath the other umbrella cleared his throat to speak. He was ninety-plus or -minus, and gravity was hard at work on his slender frame. As he shifted his weight to face Gus more directly, I could see that the young woman beside him was holding a baby.

Clearing his throat again more forcefully, the old man's words found passage on a raspy voice that was incongruent with a soft drawl that sounded vaguely Virginian.

"I'm Leon DuMont. I was Chad's—" He stopped and fixed a dull gaze on Gus. "I was Ken's agent."

Gus acknowledged the old man's considerate correction with a nod.

"We shared a belief. A belief in his talent. And we shared a dream, a dream of his future," he grated on. "It's hard to believe we won't ever see that dream come true. We were so close. Right on the verge, working with one of the greatest stars in the history of film."

I felt Leah's hand squeezing mine.

"Jeremy Thomas. A giant like that. He saw what I saw in Chad."

Leah's nails were creasing my skin. But the pain was in my ears as the old Virginian cleared his throat again, unearthing genuine emotion.

"That was validation of the highest order. I'm proud to have put Chad in his very first film. A Jeremy Thomas film. It's just such a—such a shame that—"

Tears mercifully silenced the old man. His arm sagged, and the young woman grabbed the umbrella. It struck me slowly, but I was certain. It was the same young woman who was begging to get into the chapel at the memorial service for Jeremy Thomas.

"My name is Ernie Rubalcava? I worked with Ch...with Ken, at First-Run Messenger Service?"

The stocky Latino beside Rowland Martin glanced at Gus, then included the rest of us fleetingly as he shifted his weight from one foot to another.

"He was a good guy, man, you know? Good worker? Like, you gave him something to do, man, you could count on him, you know? Like, he'd get it done, man, whatever it was. On time, no problems, you know? You wouldn't ever look bad because of him, man. He was a good guy. I liked him, you know? I think God will too, man."

He crossed himself quickly and shifted his weight again. The hand Leah was squeezing was numb, but I knew she needed it to keep from screaming.

The Minister's eyes focused on the young woman holding the baby. She shook her head, swallowed hard, silent tears drowning any words she might have wanted to say.

The Minister looked to me.

"Michael Drayton," I said. "Friend of Ken's father. Witness to his love for his son."

Gus kept his chin high and his gut tight.

"Leah Sanders." Her voice came softly from beside me. "I worked with Ken, too. On the film he was featured in at Universal Studios, *Lady Of The Lake.*"

She let go of my hand as Gus fixed his eyes on her. I worked my fingers to draw back the circulation. She spoke directly to Gus.

Chapter Twenty-seven

"Ken Chernak was talented, dedicated, and always conducted himself as a professional," Leah said, lending her own quiet dignity to the image she offered. "I remember one scene, a long scene with hundreds of extras and five cameras rolling," she continued, letting her gaze drift over everyone but me, letting each individual know that what she had to say was for all of them.

"It was the most important moment in the film, the action climax. It was the last shot of our last scheduled day on location in Ireland. If we didn't get it before we lost the light, we'd have to bring everybody back the next day and hold the company over in their hotels or pay a huge penalty enforced by the unions to travel them on a weekend. Either way it was an enormous expense to the studio and we were already thirty million dollars over budget, so nobody wanted the responsibility for that."

All eyes were fixed on Leah. Mine, too, since it was a story she hadn't shared with me.

"About two minutes into the shot," she went on with a smile that bordered on a laugh, "the star, Jeremy Thomas, forgot his lines. But Ken knew them. And he delivered them as if they belonged to his character speaking for Arthur, the young King of England."

Her radiance was putting smiles on all the faces around the grave. Mine, too, since I was pretty sure I knew why she hadn't told me the story.

"It saved the scene. It saved the day for the company," Leah continued, dimples expanding. "And Ken just shrugged it off, like it was something anyone could have done. But we all knew no one else did it. It was him. His ability to stay cool under pressure."

Gus inhaled deeply, seemed to stand taller.

"It took amazing creative reflexes," Leah said. "Something actors with years more experience couldn't have pulled off."

Her smile was full-blown now, and everyone basked in it. The young woman with the baby hugged it as if she wanted it to remember every word of what they were hearing.

"It was a proud moment for Ken, and a rare experience for all of us who witnessed it," Leah said. "It wasn't just a movie any more, it was life. It was one quick-thinking, totally committed individual stepping up to a challenge no one else was prepared to meet. It was heroic," she concluded. "And that's how I'll always remember Ken Chernak."

It was like Lincoln at Gettysburg. No one spoke, no one moved, each person savoring her words, matching them with their own memory of the young man to whom they had come to pay homage. Finally, the Minister looked to Gus whose iron-willed stoicism was all but destroyed.

"Thank you," Gus said to those of us assembled across from him. "For coming. For being his friends."

Another thought formed on his face, but it would remain unspoken. The Minister bowed his head.

"Let us pray," he began, and led us in the twenty-third Psalm. When he finished, the little crowd dispersed, and I made a mental note of the license plate on the '97 Honda the young woman with the baby got into as she drove away. When Leon DuMont folded himself in behind the wheel of a vintage Rolls Royce and lurched away from the curb after the Honda, I thought about taking his license, too, and alerting the local PD to a potential disaster, but Gus joined Leah and me, his eyes brimming.

"Thank you, young lady," he said.

"Leah," I said. "Leah Sanders. Gus Chernak."

"Mister Chernak," she said, taking his hand. "You're welcome."

"What you said, Leah. That meant a lot."

He was about to lose it. I brought him back to me, and the reason I was there.

"How'd you contact the people who were here?" I asked.

"Called the places Kenny worked. Restaurant, Messenger Service. Screen Actor's Guild gave me the agent."

"What about the girl with the baby?"

"I think she was with one of the guys," he said. "How you comin'?"

"I'll call you tonight, walk you through everything I know so far."

"Yeah. Good," he said, and settled his gray eyes back on Leah.

"I won't ever forget you."

Leah smiled softly. He turned to rejoin the Minister, and Leah turned back toward the street without looking at me. I moved beside her, keeping the little umbrella over her head.

"You mind driving?" she asked as we reached the Saab.

"Sure."

I opened the curbside door, collapsed the umbrella and handed it to her as she got in. I circled the car, slid the seat all the way back and climbed in behind the wheel. Leah handed me the keys, and opened the glove compartment to get a tissue.

"How much of it was true?" I asked.

She ignored me, blotting her eyes, wiping her nose.

"What I thought," I said.

She balled up the tissue, stuffed it in a small litterbag clipped to the pocket on the door panel.

"Pretty damned impressive, lady," I said.

"Does that mean I scored some points with you?" she asked.

"Heavy duty."

"Oh, good."

I leaned to kiss her on the cheek, and she turned to meet my lips with hers. It was very gentle, but very deep.

"Wow," I said.

"Yeah," she said.

I held onto that look for a moment longer, then put the key in the ignition and started the engine.

CHAPTER TWENTY-EIGHT

The foyer of Kamala Highland's Holmby Hills mansion was three stories high and domed with a beveled skylight. Sweeping staircases on either side of the terrazzo floor rose to a second-floor landing, each one wide enough for a Busby Berkeley grand finale.

"Good Lord. Look at what's inside," Leah said, straining for a better view into the grand salon as I helped her out of her coat.

"The jousting arena, mayhap?"

I handed our coats to a liveried servant and pocketed the number I got in return. We moved slowly with the people entering the large room, where the babble of several hundred voices battled the baroque music of a string quartet, and I was very aware that—save for some young people carrying trays—I was one of very few chocolate chips in a swirl of vanilla. The eyes that darted toward me, however, weren't disapproving, just feverishly checking to see if I was anyone important enough to acknowledge. It wasn't the first time I'd disappointed a Hollywood crowd.

We continued with the flow into an area the size of centre court at Wimbledon. An interior veranda with a verdigris wrought-iron railing bordered the entire room and provided a broad platform for the formally attired musicians. Beneath it, vaulted windows looked onto flowered gardens and courtyard fountains on both sides. A stone fireplace wide enough for a banquet table and tall enough for me to stand in was the focal point of the back wall. Antiqued mirrors flanked the fireplace, and matching mirrors on the walls inside the giant doors to the foyer behind us created the illusion of standing in the middle of infinity.

Large floral arrangements exploded with violent bursts of color atop antique tables and chests that also displayed framed photographs of Kamala Highland at work and at play with the great or near-great. Seating areas were grouped at intervals throughout the room, oversized pillow-back couches and chairs facing oversized coffee tables holding crystal bowls filled with candies and nuts.

The art on the walls was an eclectic mix from the past four centuries, save for the centerpiece over the mantel, a regally posed portrait of the mistress of the manor in one of her gardens surrounded by seven small, white dogs, bounding around her like soap bubbles on a stretch of emerald-green grass. In the background was the travertine facade of the mansion rising three stories to the mansard roof beneath a blue sky and billowing white clouds that would have been scudding if oil on canvas could scud.

We were staring at the portrait when I felt something hit my left leg just below the knee. I looked down into soft brown eyes looking up at me through wisps of snow-white hair.

"*Bichon Frise,*" Leah said.

"*Gezundheit,*" I responded.

"The seven little dogs in the painting," she said as she kneeled to pet one of the trio at our feet.

"So who's this, Dopey or Doc?" I said.

"It isn't Bashful," Leah said.

"That's Boomer," a rich voice with a soft Southern inflection said. It was the grand duchess from the painting, and Leah rose to greet her. I hesitated, trying to remember if I was supposed to kiss her ring or the hem of her dress.

"And that's Maggie, and Katie. I thought they'd bring out some smiles," she said.

"They're adorable," Leah said. "You remember my friend, Michael Drayton."

"Michael," came softly across a smile that projected genuine warmth and appropriate sadness as her hand was offered and the three little snowballs trotted off to make new friends.

"Kamala," I nodded, admiring her considerable acting skills as I took her hand. "This is very good of you."

"He was an incredibly gifted human being," Kamala said. "Thank you for being here," she said to Leah as she kissed the air beside her cheek. "You, too, Michael," she added as she smiled gravely again at me. "Enjoy yourselves. That's what he'd have wanted."

"Yes," Leah said. "We will."

I nodded as she moved away to join three men seated around one of the coffee tables. They stood to greet her. One of them was blocked from view, but I could see that the other two were Marty Mishkin and Phil Adams.

"Caviar croutons?"

A uniformed young Latina offered a selection of hot hors d'oeuvres on a large silver platter, "Smoked-salmon quiches, barbecued *Csabai?*"

"How spicy?" Leah asked while I watched the men with Kamala Highland, wondering what their connection was to Jeremy Thomas.

"Mild. Really tender," the young woman said. "These are my favorites. Lamb triangles, garlic, gingerroot, mixed with egg and a hint of mint."

"Gotta go with the lamb," I said as I lifted a flaky golden triangle and a cocktail napkin from the tray, still angling for a glimpse of the third man talking with Kamala Highland.

Leah went for the caviar and the Csabai, and pointed over my shoulder.

"Don't let that man get away," she commanded.

I popped the Lamb triangle into my mouth and moved to a jacketed man carrying a tray of flutes filled with pale sparkling wine. As I lifted a glass, I saw our hostess with her hand on the arm of the man I hadn't been able to see before.

"Who is that?" Leah asked as she joined me.

"Guy I knew at the department," I said.

He had me in his sights and headed toward me as Kamala Highland left him to greet some other guests. I handed the glass to Leah.

"I'll find you," I said, and moved across the room toward Curtis Rankin.

CHAPTER TWENTY-NINE

He pulled the heavy door closed behind us as we stepped into a big room with red velvet loveseats sitting abreast of one another on three separate tiers covered in a plush black-pile carpet. A thick glass window at the rear housed digital and film projectora, and a beaded screen filled the opposite high-ceilinged wall.

"Time for dailies?" I asked, reaching deep to keep a hair trigger from the slightest pressure.

"Save it, Drayton," Rankin said.

He was in his late fifties, a wiry six-two. He wore his silver hair short, the deep tan born on the private courts of public people he cultivated with the patience of Albert Pujols sitting on fastballs. He knew they'd be there for him someday. And here he was inside the palace, sipping champagne and nibbling dainty tidbits with Hollywood royalty. But so was I, and his pale eyes couldn't conceal how he felt about that unhappy circumstance.

"What are you doing here?" he asked.

"You first."

"I don't answer to you."

"Let me guess. You were another one of the superstar's closest friends."

"I knew him. You?"

"I'm escorting a friend who wanted to pay her respects."

"Bullshit. Who are you working for?"

"A father who couldn't get the time of day from you about his son."

"The faggot?"

"The young man who caught an axe blade in the skull for trying to help a buddy."

"Who told you that?"

"Who told you Ken Chernak was gay?"

"Don't get in my way, Drayton. You hear me?"

"Or what? You'll get me busted for an illegal lane change?"

A thin smile settled on his lips. Nothing rattled the man, you had to give him that.

"I don't need a pissant private cop poking around in this."

He deftly avoided identifying my heritage, but I knew what the full sentence was that had formed in his mind.

"*This* being a case that can make you a household name ready for the State ballot?"

"A crime that's strictly police business. I can't have a clown like you stirring things up and spilling information that spooks the sick sonofabitch who did it."

"We're on the same side this time, Captain. Since nobody involved other than me is black, I wouldn't think you'd have a problem treating any of them right."

The eyes remained remote, but we were finally engaged.

"If you wanted to make that charge stick, you should've had the balls to press it instead of tucking your tail between your legs and turning in your shield."

"Maybe if I had it to do over again, I would."

"No. You never would've fit, Drayton. How many partners you get shot up?"

"One was enough."

"Wes Carter was ten times the cop you ever were."

"*Nolle prosequi.*"

"No. You won't pursue that. You won't touch it with a ten-foot pole. Fucking asshole."

"So. Sounds like I shouldn't look to the department for any help?"

His eyes froze me in the crosshairs.

"Stay out of it, Drayton," he said. "You don't, your license gets yanked. That's a promise."

He opened the heavy door effortlessly, and went back into the palace to work the well-heeled crowd for future favors. I exhaled a blast of air from a furnace deep inside my core.

CHAPTER THIRTY

"You're awfully quiet," Leah said when we turned off Sunset onto Coldwater Canyon and started up into the hills.

"Sorry," I said. "Thinking."

Thoughts I'd never not have. Images of what happened to Wes Carter. Of the shooter dumping the kid back in the crib and taking off. Of an ambulance and an ER and not knowing if I'd live or die. Of seeing what other cops did to avenge my mistake. Of knowing what I had done was not the same as what they had done. Of knowing, but still feeling the guilt for all of it.

"Me, too," Leah said, pulling me back to the moment.

"What about?"

"If Curtis Rankin knew you were on the lot like Howard said, and he told Kamala about it, maybe that's why she hired the PI firm to follow you."

"Great minds think alike."

"Because she saw us together, and she knows I saw her and Jeremy together."

"Be my guess."

"Then she's worried about me telling you what I saw?"

"Fits."

"And I did tell you."

"Which worries me."

"But that would mean—" she paused, glancing at me. "You don't think Kamala had anything to do with the murders."

"No?"

"You mean, like why else would she care about what you're doing?"

"You're not bad at this," I said.

"You said you were worried."

"Uh-huh."

"About me?"

"How would you like to hang out in Santa Barbara for a while?"

"What?"

"Not suggesting anything, not assuming anything," I said. "Hanky-panky might be desired, but not required, just a good no-cost-to-you vacation. White sand, blue water. That's the front yard. Back faces the mountains. Sun paints them a different color every hour."

"Why?"

"Darned if I know, but it sure is pretty."

"Okay, you won't be serious, so you really are serious," she said.

"I have to keep digging," I said. "And it looks like Kamala Highland is the place to start. She's not going to like that."

"So?"

"So, come to Santa Barbara."

"Michael, that's crazy. The way they were killed? Kamala? Me? No. No, that doesn't make any sense," she said. "Besides, I have to work."

"You wrap Saturday?"

"Should."

"So, figure out what you're going to pack."

"But you'll be down here. How do I not worry about you?" she said.

"Remember the last time we lived under the same roof?"

"Oh."

I cut a glance at her. The dimples framed a mellow smile.

The smell of moist eucalyptus, cedar, and damp earth drying in the sun permeated the canyon and wafted through the open windows of Leah's little hillside cottage. The pungent earthiness of *eau de* canyon mingling with the delicate fragrance of *Antonia's Flowers* gave a tug like Charybdis.

"Don't go," she said.

"Don't want to," I said.

"The other night," she said, "I wasn't ready."

"Me, either."

"Now?"

I could feel myself drifting into a perfumed pool of ecstasy. It would have been easy to build a fire, send out for a pizza, pull a couple of cold Pale Ales from the fridge, and snuggle in for a long, cozy midsummer afternoon and evening. But not on Gus Chernak's money. And not with his short fuse burning.

"Santa Barbara," I said.

"Maybe."

CHAPTER THIRTY-ONE

Before I dug into Kamala Highland, I wanted to clear up the matter of Ken Chernak's sexuality. Contact would have been minimal at the Messenger Service, but the personal interaction with management, staff and customers at a high-volume restaurant might give me something, so I headed for the California Pizza Kitchen in Brentwood.

Coming around the first curve on Coldwater, I passed a Ducati 916 parked on the side of the road in the shade of two large pine trees. The man sitting astride it eating an apple wore jeans, boots, and a black-leather jacket.

A half mile down the canyon, I could hear the distinctive two-cylinder engine running at high RPMs before he showed up in my rear-view mirror, visored helmet low over the handlebars, left knee inches off the pavement, running on the inside of his tires. He gained ground as the road bent back to the right and his right knee skimmed over it, then he rocketed past me as we hit the next straightaway.

As he went into the next curve, I slowed down, half expecting to come around a corner and find bike and rider wrapped around a tree. Instead, the guy was poking along in the middle of the lane and I had to brake to keep from climbing up his tailpipe.

He slowed more as I heard another twin-cylinder blasting in, and saw a second Ducati in the mirror. It fell in behind me, and the rider in front picked up speed. I anticipated the guy in the mirror shooting past after what was probably his buddy, but he stayed in the middle of the road, and I found myself sandwiched between the two 916s.

The rider in front started weaving back and forth, making it clear there would never be an opportunity to pass. The rider behind me came up alongside on the left, then dropped back and cut behind me to shoot past on the right and take the lead while his playmate dropped back behind me. They didn't seem to want me to stop, but they weren't about to let me carry on unescorted, either.

Darting around like dragonflies on a pond, they stayed with me all the way down the canyon. When we reached Sunset and stopped for the light in front of the Beverly Hills Hotel, they pulled up together in the right lane as I braked in the left. They sat there grinning at me beneath the tinted visors of their helmets. Then the light changed and they blasted off. Two testosterone-driven idiots whose idea of fun would probably kill somebody some day. I was glad it hadn't been me.

When I slowed to turn into the underground parking of a two-story, nouveau-Mediterranean mini-mall on San Vicente, I saw the Ducatis again. This time the object of their fun and games was a little silver Mercedes convertible with two blonde ponytails blowing in the breeze.

I drove by valet parking and wound my way down past a million dollars worth of shiny high-end brand names to where older models that were lower on style and higher on gas mileage were parked and locked by people of more modest means. I rode the escalator to the second courtyard level and the brightly lit indoor-outdoor pizza-plus eatery.

Business was slow in the late afternoon. The leggy blonde at the reception counter just inside the glass door brightened when she saw me enter from the patio. "Inside or outside?" she asked.

"Right here's fine," I said, and gave her a look at my license.

"So, what are you investigating, Mister Drayton?"

"Did you know Chad Kennedy?"

"Oh, my God," she said with an inflection that placed her roots deep in the San Fernando Valley.

"What can you tell me about him?"

"Not much," she said. "I mean, he was an okay guy, I guess. Worked hard, hauled in big tips."

"From the boys or the girls?"

"What do you mean?"

"Word is he was gay. Know anything about that?"

She frowned. "No way. He had fan clubs that wouldn't sit anyplace but his station. Girls from Uni High, Crossroads, the Brentwood School, UCLA. Didn't surprise me when he quit to go work on a movie."

"With Jeremy Thomas."

"Yes," she said. "God, that was awful. I couldn't believe it. None of us could."

"Any idea how he got hooked up with Thomas?"

"No. We didn't talk that much. He just flirted with me like he did all the girls."

"Anybody here who was close to him?"

"Yes. A girl who used to work here, Karen Miller. I think they knew each other for a pretty long time. Up in Seattle, or Portland, maybe, I don't remember. She went to work doing nails somewhere. After that, I guess, maybe Rowland."

"Rowland Martin?"

"Yes. You know him?"

"I've seen him. He still work here?"

"Comes on at six."

"And the girl, Karen Miller, you said?"

"Yes."

"Any chance you could find a number for her in a file? An address, maybe?"

"What do you want it for?"

"Chad's father hired me to find out what I can about his son, why he died the way he did. I'm just looking for answers anyplace I can think of."

She studied me in a different light for a moment, then nodded. "Okay," she said. "I'll look."

CHAPTER THIRTY-TWO

I was working on a Heineken when Rowland Martin came up two flights of steps from the sidewalk and through the glass door at the front of the restaurant. I watched him from beneath a yellow market umbrella at a table overlooking the street. He was wearing the same purple rain jacket, but there wasn't any need for it now. The tires still hissed on the wet pavement below, but the rain had stopped and we might not see any more for six months.

The blonde at the reservation counter inside spoke with Rowland for a moment, and pointed toward me. He came back outside more slowly. I ducked out from under the umbrella, and offered my hand.

"Rowland. Mike Drayton."

"You were at the funeral," he said, eying me skeptically.

"Right."

"And you're a detective?"

"Private."

He didn't seem to want to shake my hand, so I gestured with it to a chair.

"Have a seat."

"I have to work."

"I just need a couple minutes."

I sat back down. He reluctantly took the chair across from me.

"You an actor, too?"

"I'm studying."

"That how you and Ken hooked up? Acting class?"

"He hated that name," Rowland said. "It was weird to have people calling him Ken all the time at the funeral."

"His father paid for the funeral."

"Funky place."

"He did what he could," I said. "I didn't see anyone else doing any better. I didn't see hardly anyone, period."

"That's because of what happened, the pictures, the stories in the papers. People didn't know what to think."

"What people? From your class? This place? Why would what happened scare them?"

"What's going down here, man?" he said. "You got something to ask me straight out, let's hear it."

"Okay," I said. "Was Ken gay?"

He smiled scornfully. "I knew it," he said. "What's it matter if he was gay or not?"

"Maybe it doesn't."

"So why ask?"

"Because it might lead to something that could help me find out why he died."

"Whoever killed him like that was sick? And you think homosexuality is sick?"

"What I think is any sexuality can be passionate. The crime against Ken may have been a crime of passion," I said. "What I know is only eight people showed up for his funeral, nine, if you count the baby. The minister was working, so was I, and my friend just happened to know him. That means you, the guy from the messenger service, his agent, a young mother, and his own father were the only people who came to pay their respects. He must've had more friends than that."

"I gotta go inside now."

"Sure. You've done all you can do."

His emotions rushed to the surface.

"Look, man, don't dis me," he said. "I don't know why people he knew didn't come today. Maybe it's because he changed when he got in with Jeremy Thomas. Maybe some people got bent a little because he didn't have time for them anymore, I don't know. Maybe what happened scared them because they didn't feel like they knew who he really was, what he might be into. I really don't know. I just know it didn't change how I felt about him, okay? I said how I felt, and maybe that *is* all I can do."

"Did he ever talk to you about Jeremy Thomas?"

"So what?"

"How did it sound when he talked about him?"

"You mean do I know if they were lovers?"

"Do you?"

"He had a big capacity for love. That was part of his gift, part of why everybody loved him."

"All five of them."

"You're making fun of me."

"Just stating a fact. Facts are what I work with. I'm only pressing you because I believed what you said today."

"And because I'm gay."

"And because somebody put out the word that Ken was gay."

"You think I did?"

"Did you?"

"Why the hell would I do that?"

"I don't know. Maybe it's true. If it is, maybe it's something people should know, maybe it isn't. But somebody said it and the papers printed it and it's something his father has a right to know, don't you think?"

"Chad hated his father."

"He knows that."

"Good."

"Why do you say that?"

"Because he hurt Chad, hurt him bad."

"So he should be made to suffer?"

"He shouldn't ever forget how much he hurt him."

"I don't think he ever will."

Chapter Thirty-three

I took the escalator back down to the underground parking lot, where I'd backed into a corner stall. The Volvo was now flanked by a gleaming, black Bentley sedan nosed in parallel to it one stall away and looking very out of place in the low-rent district. A slender dark-haired man in a black blazer got out from behind the wheel and opened the rear door as I approached. I could see another dark-haired man in a white-linen suit sitting in the back seat. A tall black man got out of the right front seat. He had a black T-shirt stretched tight over a fifty-plus chest, a heavy gold-rope chain draped around his thick neck, and biceps that looked like granite Gorgonzolas.

My antennae shot up instinctively, but while I was taking careful note of the trio, they weren't paying any attention at all to a guy unlocking an old, gray Volvo.

The full-throated roar of a big twin-cylinder igniting and revving nearby caught my attention, and I looked down the long concrete corridor to see a second bike fire up beside the first one. As the Ducatis leaped forward, the sound that filled the structure was deafening.

Every muscle in my body tightened as I realized the two riders could have been posted to either side of Leah's house earlier, covering the only two routes I could take. They could have made radio contact when either one saw me. I also realized I could be getting paranoid again.

They braked to a stop, and grinned at me. Their visors were up this time, and I could see their eyes clearly. Adrenalin rushed to every nerve ending as they revved the powerful engines, making any attempt to speak senseless as we looked at each other. Then they shifted into low and gunned off.

I watched them shoot around the corner and up the ramp leading to an alley behind the building. As the sound of their engines faded, I was aware that I had been joined by two of the men from the Bentley. The hand protruding from the black blazer held a Beretta 92 automatic with a silencer screwed into the barrel. The jolly black giant towered over me on the left.

"I hear you're a smart guy," the man in the car said in a non-threatening tone.

"Obviously not smart enough," I said.

"That remains to be seen."

He nodded to the hulk, who patted me down, removed my automatic, and stuck it in his waistband as the other man kept the Beretta leveled on my chest. This was a whole different league from the agency Kamala Highland had hired to follow me. And they wouldn't be working for Rankin, but that didn't mean they weren't working with him.

"Is there something I can do for you?" I asked.

"You can make my job easy," he said. "Get in."

He was in his late fifties, a thickset man with a set of teeth that would be the envy of any operatic baritone. His suit set off the deep tan.

"And what line of work is it you're engaged in, Mister—" I paused for effect. And to figure out my next move.

"Get in the fucking car," he said without a ripple of emotion.

I looked to the shooter. He just smiled. The shot that hit me was a short right to my rib cage delivered by a man who had pulverized many a heavy bag. It was followed in rapid succession by two more body shots that spun me around and left me draped over the hood of the Volvo.

Neon pain jangled to all four extremities as my sparring partner peeled me off the car and poured me through the open door of the Bentley where the man in white waited patiently.

The man with the Beretta smiled again as he laid the extended barrel on the door frame of the open window and kept it trained on me while the muscle outside leaned casually against my car, ejected the clip from my automatic, and checked the chamber to satisfy himself it was unloaded.

"I hope the rest of this conversation is a little easier," said my host.

"I'm all ears," I managed.

"Smarter than all mouth, *amicone*," the man said. "I understand you're working for the father of the young man who was with the movie star."

"May I ask who told you that?"

"Suffice it to say that certain individuals do not want the official investigation complicated by any outside interference. *Capisce?*"

"Suffice it to say," I said as my head began to clear.

"You want to go another round with Karim?" he asked with the bored indifference of a man who knew he was in yet one more encounter with an inconvenience he could snuff out in the blink of an eye.

I was thinking straight enough to start narrowing things down, and to know not to be afraid. Whoever he worked for, if they wanted me dead, we wouldn't be talking.

"These 'certain individuals'," I said. "Do they have names?"

"They prefer to remain anonymous."

"Then your name would be Duke Catalano?"

His expression didn't change, his voice remained emotionless.

"I would not repeat that," he said.

If he was who I thought he was, he was a hit man's hit man, an enforcer who worked exclusively in "security" for Phil Adams. He withdrew an envelope from his inside coat pocket and put it on the seat between us.

"I would put that in my pocket, consider myself a very lucky man, and take some erotic broad to some exotic place a long way from here."

"If I'm supposed to send you a postcard, I'll need an address."

"You are going to make this difficult, aren't you?"

"Believe it or not, I have friends, too," I said. "And my dead body, even my disappearance, would start them asking questions your friends won't like half as much as the ones I've been asking."

"Take the money," he said, seemingly unimpressed with my logic.

I got the drift of his. I picked up the envelope, hefted it.

"Heavy," I said.

"Twenty large. Tax free."

"For work I don't have to do."

"You got it."

"How long do I have to think about this?"

"Let's say I count to ten. Then my nephew gets his rocks off with one twitch of his finger."

I looked at the man with the gun. He smiled again. It was not an endearing smile.

"I'd really like to know if you can count to ten, Duke. But I'm sure your friends would rather stick to Plan A, and I'd hate to have them upset with you."

Even that didn't get a rise out of him. He was every bit as cool as I'd heard. I didn't doubt for a second that he would not hesitate to go to Plan B if I didn't pocket the money like the two-bit hustler he was sure I was. So I did.

"Get the fuck out of my face," he said without a trace of emotion.

I managed to get out of the car unassisted, and the black giant handed me my empty gun, looped back around the car to the passenger's side. The man with the Beretta smiled as he closed the back door, opened the driver's door and climbed in behind the wheel.

"Nice meeting all of you," I said.

Duke Catalano fixed his passionless expression on me through the open window.

"I ever see you again, you'll be wearing your smartass tongue for a necktie."

"Not if I see you first," I said.

But not until after the Bentley had backed out and pulled away.

Chapter Thirty-Four

I definitely had a problem. It was a lot bigger than finding out if my client's son was gay, a lot bigger even than trying to find out who killed him. I had to take the money to stay alive, but I couldn't keep the money and live with myself.

I sat behind the wheel in the parking lot of a Rite Aid drug store on Wilshire with an Ace cold-wrap around my rib cage. I slugged down four Advil with a bottle of water, and reflected on my dilemma.

I knew the money in my pocket was a kind of contract. I also knew there would be another kind of contract if I caused any trouble for Phil Adams. I didn't know what to do. And I didn't know enough to figure out what to do. If inaction was the only course of action I could come up with, I might as well have given Catalano's nephew his jollies and let him put a bullet in my heart.

"Knowledge is power," somebody said. I needed some power to stand up to a guy like Phil Adams. That meant I had to know why a controversial businessman and philanthropist was bothered by my trying to find out what I could about the private life of a bit player in a movie.

It was the same question I'd been asking about Kamala Highland and Curtis Rankin. On the surface, they were three distinctly different individuals with three distinctly different agendas. How could what I might find out about Ken Chernak threaten any one of them, let alone all three of them? What was their game? What tied them together, and what made them all so concerned about not being able to control a wild card like me turning up in that game?

Rankin was ambitious. He wanted political power and needed ties to people who would ultimately fill the coffers for him. Kamala Highland wanted prestige in a celebrity-studded industry. She needed big paydays to maintain the lifestyle that helped her impress and intimidate most of the people in it. Phil Adams was always about greed and the appearance of respectability. Money seemed to be the common link. It usually is. And yet the crime itself appeared to be a crime of passion. It still felt like square pegs and round holes.

Kamala Highland had needed to know where I was going and whom I was talking to, Curtis Rankin had warned me to stay out of his way, but Phil Adams' play was the most intriguing. A preemptive bid to make me back off that carried an implicit threat of death. Heavy. Why?

What was clear was that the three of them were in communication about my activities, and those activities were a major concern for all of them. Being top dog in that trio, Adams would have said he'd handle it. So he made me the proverbial offer I couldn't refuse.

I don't like being threatened. I don't like being worked over. I really don't like being called a whore. And I hate being a guy who doesn't know what's what. I couldn't leave it at that.

Chapter Thirty-Five

When I got back to the hotel, I put the envelope in the room safe. The mini-bar and the blackout drapes did their job, and I didn't roll out till well past noon the next day to search for Karen Miller. The hostess at CPK, had come through with her last-known address, but was pretty sure she'd moved. She was right. The Santa Monica phone directory gave me Karen Miller's current address. Sometimes it's that simple.

The Honda at the cemetery was parked in front of a duplex on Eleventh Street, just south of Montana. I parked directly across the street and congratulated myself for being such a tenacious tracker.

I crossed the street and walked up a narrow brick walk to the duplex. It had a small front yard and a small lattice-covered front porch framed by hibiscus plants with big showy yellow flowers. There was trumpet vine on the latticework and cobwebs along the lintel over the door. There were more cobwebs in the open-bottomed porch light that hung from a link chain mounted to the beam over the center of the porch. Small moths and winged bugs were trapped inside the light waiting to be devoured. One of them was still wriggling.

Norah Jones filtered through an open window, a lighter, untrained voice sang along. I rang the doorbell and glanced up at the moth again. The more it wriggled, the more ensnared it became. I reached up inside the light and ran two fingers around the bulb, pulled out the web and shook the moth free. It flew off into the trumpet vine to wait for the light to come on again.

I wiped the web off my hand, and a copper-haired girl in an orange University of Tennessee T-shirt and tan shorts opened the door. She was freckled from her hairline to the toes of her bare feet. She was not Karen Miller.

"Hi," she said. "Whatever it is, I don't need it."

I pulled my ID from my inner coat pocket and flipped it open.

"Private investigator. Are you Karen Miller?" I asked, knowing it would bring a quick denial and we could get on with things.

"No."

"Is she here?"

Decisions, decisions.

"She's not in any trouble," I said. "I just need to talk to her about a friend of hers."

The girl turned and called over Norah's *Seven Years*. "Karen... Somebody for you!" She turned back to me. "Just moving in," she said, indicating the cardboard boxes strewn around the living room behind her.

"And you never knew you had so much stuff."

"Totally."

I gave her a smile to relax to. "Good song."

"Yeah, I love her."

"Who is it?" another voice carried over the music.

"Somebody wants to talk to you about a friend of yours," the barefoot girl said. She nodded a smile at me, turning away from the door as a tall, slender, dark-complected young woman in jeans, tennies, and a faded-red halter top took her place. And placed me on sight.

"Hi," I said.

"Hi," she replied tentatively.

I showed her the ID. "Michael Drayton," I said. "I'm doing some work for Ken Chernak's dad."

"What kind of work?"

"Finding out what I can about Ken's life, how he got hooked up with Jeremy Thomas."

"Who told you to talk to me?"

"A little voice inside. After I saw you at two funerals yesterday."

She held my eyes in hers for a moment, then turned into the house again, called to the red-haired roommate.

"Sharon?"

"Yeah?"

"I just put Eugene down. You mind looking after him for a little bit?"

"No problem."

"Thanks," said the young mother. Then she looked back at me.

"There's a place up the block we can talk."

We walked toward Montana along the needle-strewn sidewalk beneath tall pines that line the street. My ribs were still aching, but I didn't figure Karen Miller would be delivering any sneak punches.

"Eugene?"

"Yes." The answer came with a smile.

"How old?"

"Six months."

"And you're on your own?"

"Since I was fourteen." The smile faded.

"I mean, no father in the picture?"

The smile vanished. And I backed off.

"That storm was really something, huh?" I said.

"Not if you're from Portland," she said, clutching at another small smile.

"That's where you and Ken met?"

"Yeah."

"How long ago?"

"Fifth grade."

"Long time. Were you here when he came to L.A.?"

"We came together."

She stopped, waved her hand, eyed the sidewalk as she tried to find her voice.

"I don't know if I can do this," she said softly.

"It's important," I said.

"I just don't know."

"I'll shut up for a while," I said. "We'll get some coffee."

She nodded, and we walked on in silence.

CHAPTER THIRTY-SIX

We sipped fresh-ground French Roast under a faded-green umbrella outside the restaurant. A steady stream of traffic rolled east and west. It was still light, but the shadows were lengthening and some of the cars had their headlights on.

"Feel better?"

She nodded. "Sorry."

"Me, too," I said. "But there's a lot about what happened to your friend that doesn't make sense. I need to shine as much light on it as I can find."

A ruddy-faced, white-haired man and his blue-haired wife seemed to have focused on us. The expression they shared wasn't one I saw often in L.A., but me sitting with a beautiful young white woman was clearly not high on their approval rating.

"He didn't seem like such a bad guy," Karen said softly.

"Gus Chernak?"

She nodded. "Ken hated him."

"He knows that. And he knows why," I said. "That's why it means so much to him to know he's doing what he can for Ken now."

"What can he do? Nothing's going to bring Ken back."

"No. But some of the things people have said about Ken have been pretty rough. Sex, drugs. Things that make it look like he might have been responsible for what happened. Or like his life didn't count for much when you stack it up against Jeremy Thomas's. That's not right."

She nodded, stared into her cup.

Before I left Rowland Martin, I'd asked if he knew Karen Miller. *"Tight-assed bitch,"* he said. I asked if he thought she might be able to fill in some blanks for me. He said he wouldn't trust anything she told anybody about anything. I reminded him that she was one of only four friends to go to his buddy Chad's funeral. *"Don't mean she ain't a tight-assed bitch,"* he said.

At first I couldn't figure what his assessment of Karen Miller was based on. She seemed genuine and so did her emotion. Given his sexuality, I thought maybe she just wasn't a woman's kind of woman. But as we sat across from one another longer, I began to realize it might have been a prejudice born more of ethnicity. In the thinning light, her skin had the color of heavily creamed coffee. Her features were finely formed, Mediterranean, her eyes a sea green, but the pigmentation and the hair were African at their roots. She had the look of the young women who drove white Creole planters wild with desire at the *Salle D'Orleans* in the eighteenth and nineteenth centuries, the legendary octoroons of New Orleans' French Quarter.

"Gus knows he wasn't there for Ken when he should have been," I said. "He can't just stand on the sidelines now."

She lifted her eyes to mine.

"What can you do for him?"

"Look for the truth. Help him clear Ken's reputation, if some of what's been said wasn't true."

"How will you know what's true and what isn't?"

"Let's find out."

"What do you mean?"

"Your new roommate. You just left your baby with her. That's a lot of trust."

"She helped raise five brothers and sisters."

"Was she at the apartment yesterday morning?"

"Yes."

"So, you could have left him with her then. But you didn't. You took him out in the rain instead. To two funerals."

She was silent. She was smart. She saw where I was going.

"I thought you were just another groupie when I saw you trying to get into the chapel at Forest Lawn," I said. "I thought it was weird, taking a baby who wouldn't have any idea what was going on to a movie star's funeral. But Ken Chernak wasn't a star. And there you were again. With your baby."

Her eyes glazed. She lowered them.

"You obviously knew Ken. So well you were too emotional to say anything about him when you were asked. You knew Jeremy, too, didn't you?"

Tears slid silently down her cheeks.

I saw the older couple exchange comments, the first words they'd spoken since we sat down. Their expressions said they didn't see what I did in the young woman seated across from me.

"The baby's name is Eugene," I said, and took a shot. "For Eugene Prentis?"

She was taken aback, looked up at me through her tears.

"Was he the father?"

She remained silent.

"We're looking for the truth," I said. "What is it?"

She shook her head, her voice thickening as she answered. "No."

"Then Ken was."

She began sobbing quietly, the tightly contained sobs of a person who was no stranger to tears.

The woman with the blue hair glared at me. Her husband put his hand on her arm, said something I couldn't hear but had probably heard before.

"Did he know that?" I asked Karen.

Indignation flashed in her eyes. "Of course," she said.

"Did Jeremy?"

"Yes."

"Anyone else?"

"My mother," she said. "But she didn't even want to see—"

She broke off bitterly, and shook her head. Her throat clamped shut again.

"And now me," I said. "But it won't go anywhere else unless you tell me you want it to."

She searched my eyes, wanting to trust me, needing to trust me, needing someone to confide in.

"Truth," I said.

Chapter Thirty-seven

We moved inside to a quiet corner table away from prying eyes and prejudice, ordered the special pasta and a half bottle of the house Chianti. The waitress brought a basket of small, freshly baked garlic rolls with the wine.

"Your friend was wonderful," Karen Miller said, finding her voice after a sip of Chianti.

"Leah? Yeah, she has a habit of being that way."

I took a bite of garlic roll. It was rich with flavor and aroma. I finished it off, washed it down with a swallow of Chianti and took another one out of the basket between us. I'd done my thing. Whatever came out now, Karen Miller would have to volunteer.

"He was helping out," she said. "Taking care of us."

"Ken?"

She nodded. "But he couldn't be married, couldn't be tied down to a family. Not and do what he wanted to do."

"Be a star?"

"More. Like a really good actor."

"Like Jeremy Thomas."

"I think he could have been," she said. "I think Jeremy thought so, too. That's part of what made them friends."

"Somebody told me they met through a 'chick,' I believe was the term he used. In it's most complimentary definition, I'd say you could be described as a 'chick,'" I said. "But if that's too politically incorrect for you, don't haul off and throw the wine at me, okay?"

She actually tossed me a small smile.

"Chick's okay," she said, and sipped her Chianti. "Yeah. I do manicures at a hair stylist's in Beverly Hills. Jeremy started coming in, and he was always like real nice to me when I worked on him."

"Holding hands with you? I'd say that was a pleasant way to spend an hour."

"He said that." She smiled. "But I told him I lived with someone I loved."

"He respected that?"

"Totally."

I was comparing what I was learning with what I had learned from Frankie Tate. It didn't quite square, but then Frankie's liaisons didn't tend to be monogamous and maybe that factored into Jeremy Thomas's code of conduct if the lady said no. Like Leah, Karen Miller had said no. Apparently Katherine Morris had not.

I offered the basket of rolls to her. She shook her head. I took another.

"So, you had Ken drop by one day when Jeremy was coming in?"

"No. I told Jeremy that Ken and I were both in the same acting class. He said he didn't know I wanted to be an actress. I told him I didn't, I wanted to be a writer, but I was studying acting to understand what actors look for, like what they need in character and dialogue. He thought that was pretty cool, and he wanted to know about Ken."

She sipped her wine again, and I refilled the glass when she set it down, emptied the rest of the bottle into my glass.

"You talk a lot with the people you work on when you do what I do," she said. "It's like, if you get along, you get to be friends. Anyway, I told him about Ken, and he told me to bring in a picture the next time he came in. I gave him Ken's composite. That's like an eight-by-ten print with, like, four pictures on it?"

I nodded. "Four different looks," I said.

"Right. And Jeremy really looked at it. I mean, like, he studied each shot, and he said he wanted to meet him."

She sipped some more Chianti. I eyed the basket. Willpower finally overcame gluttony.

"They really hit it off," she said, shrugging a lovely bare shoulder, "and Ken went to work on *Lady Of The Lake*."

Her eyes dropped to the table as an unexpected wave of emotion flooded over her.

"Now I feel like, if I hadn't talked to Jeremy, or given him the picture—"

"You wouldn't be the kind of person you are," I said, "the kind of friend. You helped Ken get the break he wanted. What happened later had nothing to do with you."

She was mining my eyes, desperately needing to believe that what I said was true. I hoped it was.

CHAPTER THIRTY-EIGHT

The Village looked different from my window at night. The streets weren't quiet, but they were less crowded, the traffic moved slower, people walked slower. I'd always found it a better time to think. But sitting alone with the lights off wasn't giving birth to any brainstorms. I couldn't tell my client about the payoff I'd had forced on me, and I couldn't tell him he had a grandson unless Karen Miller said it was what she wanted. That client still needed what he came to me for, and I had to find a way to get it for him without exposing him to the same degree of risk I knew I'd be facing.

Before I called it a day, I called Leah. She was on the back lot at Universal getting ready to shoot a night sequence and couldn't talk long, but I didn't have much to say.

I walked to the hotel, went to my room, turned on the TV and watched the Dodger game. They lost to the Giants seven to one. I went to sleep grumpy and woke up grumpy, grabbed breakfast and headed for Glendale.

"You got any leads?"

"Some questions," I said. "No answers."

"Like what?"

"Sorry, Gus," I said. "I don't work that way. I can prove something, you'll hear it. Right now, I just want to talk."

The disappointment on his face was heavier than the grease on his hands. He stepped out from under the transmission of a five-ton truck sitting on a hydraulic lube rack above him and hit the switch that lowered the truck to the ground.

"Yeah, okay. I understand," he said, keeping his eyes on the descending truck. Just before it settled onto the spotless concrete floor, he leaned against the front bumper with one hand to line it up perfectly with the workbench that ran the length of the garage. I had the feeling there was only one untidy corner in Gus Chernak's life and he was nearly resolved to accepting the fact that there was nothing he could ever do about it.

"I can tell you he didn't use drugs."

He nodded and stepped to the workbench.

"That's good," he said. "Good to know."

He took the top off a can, and the pungency of ammonia knifed through the smell of gasoline and oil hanging in the air. The whirr of a pneumatic drill came from the far end of the garage where another uniformed man spun the lug nuts off an oversized wheel.

"What about the other stuff?" He rubbed the white gel in his hands to liquid. "You know, that story. About them bein' more than just good buddies. I mean, the black kid at the funeral, he seemed pretty—" He searched for a word. I gave him one.

"Theatrical?"

"Geezus."

He shook his head, put the lid back on the can, pulled a faded red rag from his hip pocket. "And the stuff he said. You know, about lovin' Ken."

"Just a friend."

"Yeah?" He searched my eyes as he wiped his hands with the rag.

"I had a long talk with him."

"You did?"

"And a couple young women who knew Ken. There wasn't anything physical between Ken and the kid you saw. Nothing between him and Jeremy Thomas, either. Just mutual respect and a solid friendship."

"Yeah? You sure?"

"Positive."

"Then where'd all that shit in the papers come from?"

"Somebody made it up. That's what tabloids do, how they make money."

He tossed the rag onto the workbench and started for the door to the offices.

"I oughtta sue their ass."

"You don't want to do that," I said, moving with him.

"Why not? It ain't right what they do."

"No, it isn't. But what's important is that you know what's true and what isn't. That's why you called me, remember?"

"Yeah, but those bastards—"

"You said you could live with whatever I found out." I stopped him just short of the door. "I found out Ken was a man who didn't look down on people because they weren't just like him, a man who didn't pick his friends by the color of their skin or their sexuality. He liked somebody, felt he could trust them, that was all he needed. And he stood by his friends. He gave up his life to try and save one of them. That's what's important to know about your son, Gus. Just hang onto that."

He heard me, but he was all bulldog, didn't like the idea of backing down at all.

"Somebody should teach 'em a lesson," he said as he opened the door and led me into a wide hallway.

"You don't want to go to court, Gus. Not against the kind of legal team you'll run into. You'll be duking it out for months, maybe years."

"I told you before, I don't care what it costs," he said as we passed a small office where a heavy-set young woman was hunched over a steel desk talking on a telephone.

"You don't know what it costs," I said. "I don't mean dollars. You start rolling around in the gutter with the people who print that kind of trash, that's all you'll be thinking about. It's poison. Let it die. It'll go away and you won't even notice."

"I gotta look out for him," he said. "I don't, who will?"

He opened a door to a small interior office. I followed him inside, closing the door behind me.

"When the police and the DA know everything there is to know about how Ken and his buddy got killed, it'll be on the front page of every legit paper in the country. People are going to know he was the kind of friend everybody wants and hardly anybody ever finds, a guy with more loyalty and more guts than most ten guys have."

He rolled a chair back from a battle-scarred desk, sat down, still looking for a way to land a counterpunch.

"Whaddif you just dug into whoever wrote the stories?"

"Dig for some dirt, you mean?"

"We all got wash we don't want hangin' on the line, don't we? So, you find somethin' on them. Get 'em to print a whatchamacallit."

"Retraction?"

"Yeah. You could do that right? "

"No."

"Why not?"

"That's not my line of work."

"Whatta you mean?"

"I guess I mean we are what we do, Gus," I said. "I don't do that."

There was a long silence as he thought about it. I sat down in the wooden chair across the desk from him. "Just give it time. Ken's buddy was a hero to a lot of people. They're always going to remember how their movie hero died, and they're going to remember how a real hero gave up his life trying to save him."

He thought about that, too.

"Listen," I said. "I don't think I need to be on your payroll any more."

"Because of what I just asked you to do?"

"Because I don't know what else I can do right now." And because I still didn't know what to do about Phil Adams. Whatever I did, I wanted Gus safely on the sidelines before the game got any rougher.

"You said you had questions about who the killer was."

"And no answers. I'm not even sure the questions are valid. I could just be barking at shadows."

"I don't want you to quit."

"The police are all over this. The DA's all over them. I'm like a fifth wheel out there," I said.

"Tell me about the shadows."

"I can't fit the pieces together, they probably come from some other puzzle," I said. "You don't need me, Gus."

"Let me call that shot," he said. "Tell me about your kid. What's her name? Sheridan?"

"Yeah."

"You take time off. Go see her, that's okay by me."

He stood up, signaling the end of discussion. "I ain't lettin' you quit," he snapped, his gray eyes glinting like my father's when he was through listening, beyond hearing or weighing the worth of whatever words might follow.

"One thing I hate it's a quitter," he said.

It was simultaneously an angry declaration of impatience and a personal challenge. He couldn't know how familiar it was to me, how many times I'd stared in the mirror and seen my father staring back, testing my will, digging, daring, demanding.

"You just keep doin' whatever the hell it is you're doin'," he said. "I know you ain't rippin' me off."

He lowered his eyes, fished for a smile he couldn't hook.

"Nothin' else, I don't feel so damned alone."

It was a quieter, less desperate call for help. But it was still a call for help.

CHAPTER THIRTY-NINE

"Eugene?" Falcon said. "Jeremy Thomas's real name."

"Right."

"She tell you how that happened?"

We were standing by our cars outside a Starbuck's in Hancock Park. Falcon sucked on an iced coffee as he digested what I told him.

"They all three had rough backgrounds," I said. "She was adopted at birth, raised in Portland. She met Ken in fifth grade, they started having sex in junior high. Same year, a logging truck ran away on a downgrade, killed both parents, put her in a series of foster homes. Ken stuck by her, kept her head together. She was doing the same for him, really."

"How's that?"

"No contact with his father, alcoholic mother brought home a series of live-in losers took out their own problems on him. Pretty much all they had was each other."

I drank my coffee, Falcon filed the information.

"What brought them here?

"His dreams mostly. And she thought maybe she could find her birth mother."

"In L.A.?"

"She was born here. The Millers interviewed the mother before she gave birth, kept tabs on her afterwards. Felt Karen should be able to look her up, if she ever wanted to. She'd hung onto that information."

"Find her?"

"Yeah. Didn't go that well, I guess. She didn't want to say much about it."

"What'd she say about Thomas?"

"Same kind of background. Mother ran a boarding house in Seattle, father was a sailor never came back. She shipped the boy off to her parents in South Dakota. Had some juvie problems, bit of a hood. A coach straightened him out, hooked him up with a football scholarship at Boise State."

"How'd he get into acting?"

"Some girl he had the hots for. Took a class to get close to her, wound up with a lead role, liked it, and took off for Hollywood to be a star.

"Easy as that."

"Right up to the end."

I finished my coffee, dropped the cup in a trash bin. Falcon was still fleshing out the images on his mental sketch pad.

"This young mother know why Thomas and your client's kid got so close so fast?"

"She thinks it's because Ken stuck with her and the baby."

Falcon finished his drink, mused. "So Jeremy Thomas helping out Chad Kennedy was probably more about Eugene Prentis helping Ken Chernak because he was committed to little Eugene."

"And little Eugene losing his father was about Chad trying to help Jeremy when somebody came at him with an axe."

Silence fell over us, the grizzly crime photos still vivid in our minds. Falcon dropped his plastic cup and straw in the bin.

"Doesn't get us any closer," he said.

"But it tells us how they wound up together that night."

"Two pretty tough kids, really," Falcon said.

"Karen said she only saw Ken cry once. Right after he ripped into Gus. Said he didn't want it to be like that, but he couldn't help it."

"Might have been different next time."

"Yeah," I said. "But there wasn't any next time."

Chapter Forty

My view was from the second floor on the east side of the Village's first building. It was built in 1927, and I was beginning to feel like I'd been standing there from day one.

The people passing below my office were all going somewhere. I had few roads to travel. Trying to smoke out Curtis Rankin was a dead end. Messing with Phil Adams was a way to end up dead. Kamala Highland was my best shot at getting to the truth. Maybe my only shot at staying alive.

I heard the outer office door open, turned from the window as Mari stepped into the doorway between the two rooms with a file folder in her hand.

"What'd you do?" I said.

"Got everything you wanted."

"To your hair."

"Cut it."

She pirouetted, tossing her head like a girl in a shampoo commercial.

"What do you think?"

"It's the real you," I said.

"It doesn't make me look too tall?"

"Well, now that you mention it."

She grinned, and spun around one more time.

"I feel so light," she said.

"Well, tie yourself down and show me what's in there."

She put the folder on my desk, opened it.

"That's an email from Mr. Alworth at Universal. He sent us Miss Highland's studio biography, I printed it out. She really shattered the glass ceiling, didn't she?"

I scanned the pages, looked at the next document.

"Background check," Mari said. "County clerk's office, credit bureau, newspaper, morgue. She's single, owns her home. Oh, yeah, what was that like?"

"Understated," I said.

"Fifty thousand square feet for a single woman?"

"And a staff of twenty."

"How do people ever get that kind of money?"

"Probably not working for private investigators," I said. "What's all this?"

"You said everything," Mari said. "Pays her bills on time. Supports those charities. Spoke at all those events. Registered Independent, doesn't gamble, conservative investor."

"How'd you get all that?"

"Online. Scary, isn't it?"

"How's she get paid? Corporation?"

"Right here." She pulled another sheet, put it on top. "Highland Productions, incorporated in Delaware, 2001. And HighNote Productions, Delaware, July, 2012."

"We need a look at the Domestic Stock Statements."

"What's that?"

"Tells you who's in the corporation," I said. "Officers and directors. You can request a certified copy from the Secretary of State's Office. Should be here in a couple days."

"Might even get more online."

"How's that?"

"If we run a search by name and address of the corporation, we should get the registration number and get into anything we need."

"Yeah?"

"Simple."

"You think my not being a techie gives you job security?"

"I think my salary's job security," she said.

"How much am I paying you?" I said.

"Given inflation, probably less than my great-great grandfather got paid for picking sugar beets in Colorado in 1875."

"But look at your benefits."

"What benefits?"

"Working with a world-class detective."

"Who's being dragged into the twenty-first century kicking and screaming."

"And who knows a great haircut when he sees one."

She grinned again. And lit up the room.

CHAPTER FORTY-ONE

"Kamala Highland?"

She smiled sweetly as she said the name with a trace of Texas in her voice.

"Want to tell me why you're interested?"

"Not if I don't have to," I said.

"You just want to dish?"

"Whatever you've got."

Flora Richards was an ash-blonde in her late sixties who could still claim fifties in a community where at least five years were eventually shaved off everyone's resume. She flashed a more insidious smile as she leaned toward me across the table.

"Baby, you have struck the mother lode."

We were seated under an old Brazilian pepper tree on the patio outside the Polo Lounge at the Beverly Hills Hotel. A dappled light softened Flora's features.

"Kamala Highland," she said as she set her glass squarely in front of her, turned it slowly on the pale pink tablecloth, staring into it like a soothsayer with a crystal ball. "First of all, where did she get that name?"

"Stage name?" I said.

"I don't know. But it's beautiful, isn't it? Kamala. Floats right off your tongue. Kamala."

She took another sip of her martini, smiled again. It was becoming a full two-martini smile, promising a well-oiled tongue that loved talking trash.

"I mean, that is a truly beautiful name. And unique. Nobody's ever going to ask, 'Kamala who?' are they? Took some thought. East Indian, right? *Kama*, the Hindu god of love. *La*, feminine diminutive. Literally? Little goddess of love." She smiled. "But trust me, baby, that name and that woman together? That's a real, live, walkin', talkin' oxymoron."

I had known Flora since I was a boy. I didn't know how she and my father had met, but I knew it had been a torrid affair. And I knew she had encyclopedic recall of every peccadillo anybody who was ever anybody committed in a town where the peccadillo population outnumbered all the armadillos from Texas to Argentina.

"I was her idol once, you know," she said. "Oh, yeah. Her idol. That's what she told me when I was running drama development at the network and she was an assistant to the kid who worked for me."

She took a long sip, as if to wash the taste from her mouth.

"We got close when he left and she took his place, and we were best buds when I took over programming. Then when I got canned, she moved into my office. You didn't know that?"

"I wasn't paying a lot of attention to show biz when I was with the department."

"Gospel," she said. "Took my job, then never returned my calls."

She drained her glass, signaled a waiter for two more. I waved one off.

"Oh, pooh," she said. "You sure you're Jack Drayton's son?"

"Did he drink?"

She laughed. It was a deep, throaty laugh.

"Oh, honey," she said. "You want stories?"

"Let's stick to Kamala Highland today. How'd she do when she got behind your desk?"

"Couldn't cut it, I'm happy to say. Put the hits I had in the wrong spots, put some junk on the air nobody can remember and went down in flames. But, she had the proverbial golden parachute. Set up Barry Lowenstein with a raft of on-air commitments, then went partners with him when she was 'allowed to resign to pursue her first love and become an independent producer.'"

"Pretty smooth."

"Crafty, too. Dumped Barry somehow, but hung onto the commitments. Made a fortune with shows that put nurses in nightgowns between the sheets, lady doctors in silk teddies between the sheets, and lady cops in the raw between the sheets. Stories were crap, but the babes were hot. So were the hunks, and bare butts were *de rigueur*, wall-to-wall music took your mind off the bad dialogue," she said.

"Soft porn?"

"More like eye candy."

"Made some serious money off it," I said.

"Serious and then some," Flora said. "Knows how to flaunt it, too."

"What do you know about her before she got to the network?"

"Came from Mississippi, I think. Said she was a cheerleader at Ole Miss."

"So, she came to ABC right out of college?"

"No. A lot more colorful than that."

She took the olive from her glass, put it in her mouth and chewed it slowly, knowing she had me hanging.

"Her first job was as a receptionist with a small talent agency. Lou Dodds. Little office on Holloway Plaza just off Sunset. He had mostly good character actors who worked all the time, kept him in Rolls Royces and racehorses. Then one of the real tough-guy types broke through and won an Oscar, became a big star," she said. "The story I heard was the star got her pregnant, but couldn't let his wife and five kids in on the secret, so he bought her off."

"When was this?"

"Early eighties."

I started flipping through an *Academy Players Directory* in my mind, scanning actor's faces and names.

"Lee Marvin?"

"Eighties," she repeated as the waiter stepped to the table, picked up her empty glass and set another martini in front of her.

"Yummy," she said, eyeing the young man, not the drink. He returned her smile as he moved off.

"Cochran," I said. "James Cochran."

"Bull's-eye." She lifted her glass, sipped from it. "Anyway," she said, smiling across the martini, "he had a brother who was an executive at the network, and Kamala got a job in daytime programming in New York."

"Did you know the brother?"

"I did."

"And you think he got her into the network?"

"I do."

"In daytime?"

"But she wanted film," Flora said. "And she got film. Then she got my job." She took another drink, but it didn't wash away the memory.

"She partnered up with Jeremy Thomas," I said. "You know how that came about?"

"Not really." She set her glass down squarely in front of her again, a wicked smile forming. "But I know the story."

CHAPTER FORTY-TWO

"I'll have him call you," Mari said as I opened the door. "Wait a moment. He just walked in, Mister Falcon."

Her Spanish pronunciation was meticulous, soft "a," long "o." She had just scored points with Eddie Falcon as she hit the hold button.

"It's the Falcon," she said melodramatically, pronouncing the name like an Anglo talking about a bird. "I want to meet him some day."

"He's not in the movies," I said as I stepped to my office.

"I know," she said. "But it's a cool name. I picture this really cool-looking old guy. Like Antonio Banderas."

"Antonio Banderas is an old guy?"

"Way old."

I winced as I reached my desk and picked up the phone.

"Eddie?"

"Thought I'd give you a heads-up," he said. "Rankin got his guy."

"The guy from the VA?"

"He's going live with it on the four o'clock news."

"Does it fit?"

"It does for Rankin."

"I'm asking you."

There was a long silence.

"Am I reading between the lines?" I asked.

"They found the guy in the hills up in Bel Air," Falcon said. "He came at the arresting officer with a machete."

"I thought the ME said it was a bigger blade."

"He did. Could be a different weapon, but it's the same MO."

"The cop okay?"

"Lucky guy," he said. "Got off five rounds point-blank."

I felt the chill that comes when you get the answer you knew you would to a question you knew you didn't have to ask.

"Is that why you're calling me?"

There was another extended silence, then he said, "I just thought you should know they'll be shutting down the investigation."

"So, I'm on my own?"

"I'm always available for a *Tommy's* Original."

"I hear you, Eddie. Thanks."

"Take care of yourself, Cowboy."

Twenty minutes later, Mari and I were perched on stools at the bar in the restaurant downstairs. She was on her second Coke and I was still nursing a Corona when the news story broke at the top of the hour on the TV set behind the bar.

A local anchor began the coverage with an unofficial report that said the killer of film star Jeremy Thomas was believed to have been found and was believed to be dead. An on-scene reporter outside the Parker Center added more unofficial information from "reliable sources" within the police department, and then Captain Curtis Rankin stepped in front of a camera in the briefing room jammed with journalists.

Sounding like a modern-day George Patton and looking like a yester-year Wyatt Earp, he was at his Rock of Gibraltar camouflage best for the cameras that surrounded him as he read an official statement verifying that a savage killer had been caught and would not strike again. He gave the date, time, and place that the primary suspect in the brutal slaying of film star, Jeremy Thomas, and his friend, Chad Kennedy, had been confronted and told how that confrontation had erupted into an assault on the arresting officers by an enraged man wielding the two-and-a-half-foot-long machete he held up in a clear-plastic evidence bag.

In defense of their own lives, Rankin said, one of the officers had managed to shoot the suspect. Unfortunately, or, perhaps, mercifully, he said, the suspect, who had attacked Thomas in the past, died immediately. Then he passed out kudos to all the regional areas of the LAPD, the DA's investigators, the men and women of the County Sheriff's department and the officers of the Beverly Hills PD for the coordinated effort that brought such swift results.

He deflected questions, saying there would be a more detailed briefing to follow, but that residents in the Westside hills and throughout the entire city could feel certain that the deranged man was no longer a threat to anyone's safety.

Then something interesting happened. The news anchor put up a police booking photo of a slender, wide-eyed black man in jheri curls. My blood ran cold.

The young woman standing behind the bar reacted to the picture, too. "That's Willie," she said.

Mari and I looked at her. "That's Willie," she repeated as though to convince herself.

"You know him, Diane?" I said.

"Yeah."

Diane Tuiasosopo was a big girl, five-eleven to six feet, a good two-hundred-twenty pounds and more African-American than Samoan. She'd been pouring the best drinks in Westwood for the past six months. But I loved her more for her laugh than her undeniable skills with jiggers and shakers and blenders. It rolled out readily and resonated above the other sounds in the room. Diane wasn't laughing as she looked at the TV set I'd asked her to turn on.

"Before I came here, I worked for six years at *Ben Gunn's* in Santa Monica," she said. "Scared the hell out of me first time I saw him. I was going to my car about two-thirty in the morning and he comes at me shouting at the top of his lungs. Saying all kinds of shit. Every damn cuss word you can think of and some you ain't even heard."

"What'd he do?" Mari said, anticipating an account of a gory encounter.

"Just stood there and shouted at me."

"Did you run?"

"I make damn near three of you, honey. More 'n two of him. Soon as I saw how scrawny he was, I just told him to chill."

"What'd he do then?" said Mari, taking the words out of my mouth.

"Stopped shouting and started grumbling. Same foul-mouthed stuff as before, just not so loud. And I realized what he wanted was money."

"Money?" Mari said. "Did you give it to him?"

"Hell, no," Diane said. "I went back inside and took him with me."

"Into the bar?"

"No, girl. Kitchen. Sat his boney ass down and filled his belly. Man, that little sucker could eat. Sat there for an hour, scarfed down everything I put in his way. Took me the rest of the night to air the place out. He was ripe."

"He didn't try to hurt you?" Another key question I didn't have to ask.

"Ain't a whole helluva lot of hurt he could put on me, honey. He's all skin and bone."

"And mouth," Mari said.

"Yeah. And all twitchy, too," Diane said. "Damndest thing was when he settled down and stopped cussin', he got into repeating whatever I'd say to him."

"Repeating?" There was no hint of surprise. Mari was onto something. I sat back and let her run with it.

"I'd say, 'How's that going down?' He'd say, 'How's that going down?' I'd say, 'What's your name?' He'd say, 'What's your name?' Like talking to a damn parrot."

"Echolalia," Mari said.

"Say what?" Diane said.

"Repetition of what other people say. It's called echolalia. I did a paper on variable verbal utterances displayed in the syndromes manifested by massive disruption of thinking."

"I got no idea what you just said, girl, but you know what I'm saying, then, right? He's got that thing. Whatta they call it? Some kind of nutso thing makes him act that way."

"Schizophrenia."

"That's it. Guy from the VA hospital came around looking for him once, told me. 'Schizophrenia.' That's exactly what he said."

"But he's not necessarily dangerous," I finally chimed in. It wasn't a question. I knew.

Mari shook her head "His appearance, behavior, the verbal tics, it's definitely a psychotic disorder. But from what Diane described, and the fact he hadn't been committed, it doesn't sound like he was physically violent. Something must have pushed him over the edge."

Chapter Forty-three

Mari told Diane and me about her paper and everything she'd learned about schizophrenic disorders. As I digested what she was telling us, I kept seeing Curtis Rankin's face when I told him what was going on with a small band of racist cops under his command ten years ago. Alongside it, I saw the face I'd seen for less than ten seconds on the television set. The black face of Willie Gates.

A mental patient who'd "attacked" one of the victims years before was a sitting duck for a sharpshooter like Rankin. A homeless person with no resources, no one to protest the end he came to without benefit of due process. What kind of defense could he mount if he was brought to trial? Would he even know what was happening to him when Rankin put him in the crosshairs?

There was no chance that a man like Willie Gates would slip out of the net once it was cast over him. No chance anyone would ever hear any other side of the story. Because Rankin operated on the principle that dead men tell no tales.

When Mari and I got back upstairs to the office, there were three messages from Gus Chernak, each urging more forcefully than the previous one that I get back to him as soon as possible.

The girl in his front office answered on the first ring and put me through to him without hesitation.

"You heard the news? They got the sonofabitch," he said. "They got him."

"Seems like it."

"Tried to cut up the other guy once before," Gus said. "How come they let people like that loose? Why the hell didn't they put him away for good the first time?"

"Thomas didn't press charges the first time," I said.

"A guy jumps him with a knife and he doesn't press charges? What the hell was he thinkin'? He does what he shoulda done, Kenny ain't dead now."

"I guess he felt the man had suffered enough. He's a 'Nam vet, been a patient at the Veterans Hospital."

"Prob'ly fried his brain on all that hash those dumb-ass kids got into over there. One of those punks made us all look bad."

"I thought maybe I'd hit the hospital, get a look at his file, if I can."

"Stow it," Gus said. "He killed Kenny. He deserved to die."

"I'd just like a look at his records, maybe talk to whoever's worked with him."

"Whose side are you on here all of a sudden? You lookin' for some kinda excuse for what he did?"

"If he did it, no, I don't want anybody giving him an excuse. But if he didn't—"

"What the hell are you talkin' about? Didn't you hear that cop? Didn't you see that machete?"

"I just think, maybe—"

"Hey, tell you what, Drayton—" he cut me off in mid-sentence. "I don't like what I'm hearin' outta you right now, okay? You want to go diggin' up alibis for the crazy bastard who hacked my son to death, you sure as hell ain't doin' it outta my wallet, you know what I mean?"

"I guess you mean stop."

"I guess you got it."

There was a silence, then he spoke again.

"I didn't mean to jump on you like that," he said. "I appreciate everything you did. But like you said before, there's nothin' needs to be done anymore."

"That's your call," I said.

"So, that's it then, I guess, huh? Like the rest of life, no rhyme, no reason. Some wacko gets it in his head to chop somebody up, my kid just happens to be there so he gets chopped, too."

He inhaled heavily, and I heard the pain I'd heard when I first listened to his voice.

"I gotta ask myself, though, ask myself forever, if my kid woulda even been where he was if I'd been there for him when he needed me."

It was the same deep, unbearable guilt I'd detected in that first message. And I felt the same chill.

"So, listen," he said. "I want to thank you for what you did, okay?"

"I didn't do much of anything."

"You did what I asked you to do. That's good enough for me. You keep the dough I gave you. Expenses run more, send me a bill."

"Everything's covered," I said.

"If there's anything you forgot, you know where I am."

"Yeah."

"They got the sonofabitch," he said, his voice thickening again. "They blew him away."

Yeah, I thought. *That's exactly what they did.*

"Anything else I can do for you, Gus, you know where I am, too."

"One thing," he said.

"What's that?"

"Be there for that kid of yours. Be there every goddamn day."

It wasn't intended as a point of discussion. He was giving me a piece of hard-learned wisdom intended to spare me any measure of the grief he would never stop feeling. It was a gift straight from the heart.

"Thanks, Gus," I said.

"Hey, Drayton?"

"Yeah?"

"Maybe we could have a beer sometime."

"I'd like that."

"Me, too," he said. "See ya then."

"So long, Gus."

CHAPTER FORTY-FOUR

I should have felt a burden lifted from my shoulders, but I didn't. It was more like being buried beneath an avalanche of responsibility I had no way of sharing with anyone.

"Is he all right?" Mari asked with genuine concern.

"I think he's relieved."

"You're not."

"Relieved of duty."

"But you don't think Willie Gates is the killer, do you?"

"What do I know? On the job four days, no leads that take me any place solid, no other real suspects with real motives."

"Are you going to go to the hospital?"

"And say what? I'm a concerned citizen who wants to know whether or not a man who just tried to kill two cops with a machete was capable of murdering two other people? They'd probably want to run a psychiatric evaluation on me."

"So, that's it? I just close the file?"

"Did you order those stock certificates?"

"Yes."

"Let me know when they show up. And see if you can find a number in Century City for an attorney named Martin Mishkin. Century Park East, I think."

I stepped into my office, and stood staring at the picture of Sheridan on my desk. This case was never just about getting information for Gus Chernak, it was always about knowing the only way I could make any sense of my own existence was to do a job that had to be done.

I turned to the window, looked out at the passing parade on the boulevard below and considered the obvious. If Willie Gates was the killer, what did anybody else have to hide? Specifically, what did Kamala Highland, Curtis Rankin and Phil Adams have to hide?

Gates didn't fit. Rankin? Could be shielding the real killer. He'd risen through the ranks shielding killers who owed him their allegiance. Adams? Whatever he was hiding would be well hidden. He'd been burying bodies under concrete his company trucks poured since he'd started in construction four decades ago. Kamala Highland was still the weak link in the chain, but I had to be sure Adams was satisfied I was through plying my trade.

"771-7711," Mari said as she stuck her head in. "Want me to call?"

"Got it. Thanks." I lifted the handset and dialed. A bored young woman's voice answered on the second ring.

"Mishkin, Jones and Greer. How may I direct your call?"

His personal secretary said Mr. Mishkin was in a meeting. Did I want to leave a number? I told her I was sure he had it.

And I had what I needed. The man was in his office.

I cut across Club Drive to Century Park East in all of seven minutes, and hurtled up an express elevator to the forty-fourth floor of the Century City South Tower, the priciest office building in California, matched only by its twin to the north. It never takes any time to get where you don't really want to go.

The tall, glistening mirror images rise high above the wealthiest part of a town where image is all-important, where men and women at the top of the food chain drive to work in obscenely expensive cars, dress in the latest fashions, and work hard to keep climbing higher, for the most part without worrying too much about the welfare of the people they're stepping on.

I stepped out into Marty Mishkin's penthouse office suite and was told by the attractive brunette behind a glass and chrome desk to take a seat. The brass plate on her desk said Lauren Taylor. I could see Santa Monica out one window, the downtown skyline out another, and my position on the plush leather couch was directly in line with Lauren Taylor's transparent desk and perfectly proportioned body. It was no contest as to which was the better view. The hour and ten minutes I sat waiting didn't seem half that long. It was especially pleasant when she answered the phone with a lovely, automatic smile. She even tossed a couple my way when she caught me staring.

At six twenty-two, according to the muted ticking of the burled-walnut grandfather clock sitting between two large Chagall's on an interior wall, the intercom on her desk buzzed twice, she got up and entered the inner sanctum. After a moment, she returned and crossed the polished hardwood floor to smile down at me.

"You win," she said.

"Good game," I said as I stood.

She smiled again and nodded me to the open door.

I heard a click as I stepped through it, and it closed automatically behind me as a man turned from a drafting table where he stood in front of a view that would stretch all the way to Catalina Island on a clear day. Today it looked out on a smog-red sunset, which had its own kind of ominous beauty.

Martin Mishkin was in shirtsleeves and wore a pair of thin, rimless glasses that almost vanished as they blended in with his thin features and lean frame. He smiled easily, but it was a formal smile that laid down a threshold not to be crossed.

"You're a patient man," he said.

"One of my many virtues," I said.

His smile stayed in place.

"Which one brought you here?"

"Self-reliance."

"I guess I'll have to rely on you for a little amplification," he said.

"Just trust your memory," I said. "You only have to think back to yesterday afternoon."

"I was in a deposition yesterday afternoon."

"I was in the back seat of Duke Catalano's car with a gun leveled on my bruised ribs."

"If we're going to communicate, Mister—" he peered down through his glasses at my business card, which was resting on the drafting table, "Drayton, is it? You're going to have to be more specific." He paused as he checked his watch, "And I have a dinner engagement at seven, so I'm afraid you'll have to be rather succinct."

I pulled the envelope with the twenty thousand dollars in it from my coat pocket and tossed it to him. He caught it with a startled look.

"Succinct enough?" I asked.

He looked at the envelope, then back at me.

"You know the specifics," I said. "And you don't have to amplify anything. Just tell Mister Adams I got the message loud and clear. And I appreciate his generosity, but there's no need for it. My client fired me today and I'm off to greener pastures."

I stepped back to the door.

"Open sesame," I said and tried the handle. It turned, and I turned back to Mishkin.

"Works every time," I said, and left him alone to ponder whether or not his client still had a binding contract.

Chapter Forty-Five

I took PCH home. Two gently undulating lanes unspooled in each direction as the coast curved gradually westward along the edge of the Pacific. It took longer than the freeway, but I wasn't in any rush. I had no client, and figured my show of good faith to Phil Adams meant I didn't have to worry about Duke Catalano tossing me off the pier to sleep with the fishes.

By the time I got through Malibu, veered away from the colony and started up the grade past Pepperdine University, the traffic thinned. After Trancas, it was clear sailing. The radio pulled more and more static, and I finally lost Vin Scully on a two-and-two count to Yasiel Puig with two out and two on just past Point Dume. I couldn't pull in any jazz, no country, no classical, so I snapped off the radio, rolled down the windows, and listened to the damp air rushing in around me while I tried to unsnarl my thoughts about the murder I'd been told twice in twenty-four hours not to do any more thinking about.

The city of Los Angeles said the case was closed. My client said the case was closed. My gut said different. I tried to convince myself that whatever I thought didn't square with the story being snapped up and spun out by the media could wait. That, in fact, the longer it waited the better. The people I seemed to have threatened would be less alert and I could operate more easily. There was no shame in that, no reason to let it eat away at me. I had to accept the obvious. There was no hurry, no worry, no urgency to any aspect of the case, if it was to be a case at all outside the privacy of my own mind. I certainly wasn't in danger, and neither was anyone else. Everyone else, in fact, had already put it behind them. Gus Chernak believed his son's slayer had paid for his crime; Jeremy Thomas's fans believed they knew the final chapter of their hero's life; and the public believed they were safe because Willie Gates had been shot to death. Five times.

It didn't matter what anybody else thought. They weren't walking around in my skin, feeling what I was feeling in my gut. I didn't know much, but I knew for a fact that it wouldn't have been the first time Curtis Rankin had ordered a public execution. And I knew if I was going to prove he was dirty this time without winding up in a shooting gallery myself, it might be better if I took a long weekend.

By the time I got off the 101 on San Ysidro, crossed back over it, turned onto Posilipo, and pulled into my garage, I had myself convinced that I'd get a much clearer picture of everything if I didn't let myself think at all about homicide.

I was in the moonlit ocean I'd been skirting for an hour by nine-fifteen, taking slow, steady strokes, working the kinks out after the long drive. I was out of the shower by ten, and sound asleep by ten-after. At ten-twenty, I was wide awake, staring at the ceiling. And the wide-eyed face of Willie Gates.

Chapter Forty-six

Daylight broke over San Marcos pass as I reached the summit and descended down 154 into a grass-covered, oak-dotted valley of sweeping flatland and gently rolling hills that lay fresh and clean and golden.

I wore my old Tony Lamas and a yoked chambray. My new favorite country singer, Darius Rucker, kept me company on the radio while I thought back to summers as a kid on my father's ranch, to the long days spent tending big animals under big skies that made me feel like I'd never be big enough to deal with any other part of the world they dwarfed. Two feet taller and nearly half a century later, I still felt small when I stared the grandeur of nature in the face.

Pidge Connors' spread was nestled against the foothills of the San Rafael range, where it backed onto the Los Padres National Forest. This was rolling hill country, more like the terrain outside San Antonio than the flat barren landscape of Del Rio where Pidge was born and raised. Maybe that's why he loved it so much. He'd owned it since 1960, paid for it with the money he earned alongside my father, making drugstore cowboys look like real ones in the spate of westerns that were in vogue from the thirties through the sixties. The original ranch was five thousand acres, but it was down to five hundred now, and the three hundred head of polled Herefords he ran were more for decoration than profit. His pride and joy was the fifty head of Texas longhorns he bred and raised. Whenever Pidge was missing, he could usually be found sitting on a rise looking down at the mottled herd of stringy long-legged throwbacks. Like Pidge, the longhorns were vestigial from another time, symbolic of values that once defined the quality of the mark an individual makes in the struggle to survive. Man and beast, they were a vanishing breed.

I'd grown up thinking of Pidge as an uncle, and knew him for a while as a father-in-law. Now I thought of him as a friend, and a man couldn't ask for a better one. He had raised his daughter on the land I was approaching, and it became a sanctuary she retreated to in her illness. I had moved to Santa Barbara to be closer to her then, and to the little girl who had grown so much bigger and, after her mother's death, increasingly distant from me.

Pidge and Liz's daughter, Julie, and I had grown up together, discovered our sexuality together, and sworn to be lovers forever. Then we graduated high school and realized there was a whole universe around us.

She had to be the prettiest freshman at USC when I went to work on location in Africa with my father. And when I came back, there were guys in every house on fraternity row lining up to show her what she'd been missing. One of them really didn't deserve the lesson I thought I was teaching him when I worked him up into throwing the first punch and then worked him over methodically with what I'd mastered in over a decade of martial arts training.

I learned two things that night. I had a capacity for violence I had to learn to control. And I had lost the respect of the only person in my life I really cared about more than myself.

A dozen years later, Pidge and Liz let me know that Julie's husband had left her and her little girl for someone else. My first impulse was to find the guy and beat him within an inch of his life, but I had, fortunately, learned to check those impulses and began a campaign for a chance at redemption.

This time I got the girl. And the gift from God that was her daughter. We were married less than a year when Julie's ex was killed, and I adopted Sheridan. I was a father, and determined to be the best father any child ever had. Then I learned that being a parent is the toughest job any person ever tackles, and before they take it on, they should be certain they know who they really are and what the consequences of their other life choices will bring.

As I rattled across the cattle guard and came to the gate, I could see a strawberry ponytail bobbing behind a rider on a sure-footed dun in the corral at the far side of the pens. I got out to open the gate and stood there, motionless, waiting for a wave, a freckled smile. It didn't happen. And it hurt.

I climbed back into the car and drove on up the dirt road, past an assortment of rusted machinery and ranch vehicles scattered behind the barn, to the back of a rambling, single-story, whitewashed house with a red-tile roof. The screen door opened before I turned off the engine. A buxom, wide-hipped woman in jeans, tennis shoes, and fuchsia T-shirt came through it with a dishtowel in hand and a broad smile on her face.

"'Bout time you showed up," she said. "Startin' t' figure you forgot the way."

I tugged on my straw Resistol and held my hands out.

"Take your best shots, Liz," I said, slipping into the relaxed diction I'd grown up around. "Get it all out now, 'cause I have come to repent."

"Thank you, Jesus," she grinned as we met and hugged.

Her short blonde hair had turned gray almost overnight when her daughter was diagnosed with lymphoma. Her fair skin had spent too many years in the sun, but Liz Connors was still a man's woman, a pleasure to hold and behold.

The screen door banged shut again, and Liz kept an arm locked around my waist as she turned back to the house where her husband stepped out onto the porch in sun-bleached plaid work shirt, faded jeans and narrow-toed boots. His old straw bull-rider sat back on his head, baring a patch of baby-white skin just below the brim. His sideburns were razored high, what hair he had was cropped short and as silver as the heavy brows over the time-hooded blue eyes. The rest of his face was a walnut-stained roadmap of good times and bad spent mainly out of doors. It was a strong face that never flinched and always looked you square in the eye.

He tucked his thumbs in behind his belt on either side of a big silver buckle and carved a dry smile around the toothpick in the corner of his mouth as he looked at Liz and me.

"Two o' you's fixin' t' run off," he drawled, "I got the gas money."

"Leave you with nothin' but holes in your pockets?" Liz said as she hugged me tighter. "We couldn't do that, could we, handsome?"

"That old fox's probably got a bank account in Switzerland neither one of us knows about," I said.

"He don't know where Switzerland is," Liz said.

"Know where them ol' coffee cans 're buried out back, though," Pidge said.

"Maybe we ought to think this over," I said to Liz.

"I know how t' find out where they are," she said. "Won't take but a minute."

"Waitin' for you only ever took a minute, I'd be thirty years younger," Pidge said as he stepped off the porch.

It was a given that anything in West Texas had horns, fangs or stickers, and anything born and bred there developed thick skin and a barbed tongue. Pidge Connors was true to his heritage.

"I'll just go saddle up some sorry ol' swayback this city fella might could stay aboard."

"Sounds like I better go make sure he doesn't throw my tack on some widow-maker," I said to Liz.

"He does, you make sure it's him climbs on it," she said.

I planted a kiss on the top of her head and caught up to Pidge as we headed for the barn. He seemed smaller to me than I thought of him as being. He'd never been a tall man, but gravity was taking its toll as he moved into his eighties. He still carried himself with pride, though. It showed in the jaw line that was as neat as a crease, and in the waistline that hadn't expanded the way it does on so many old wranglers. And, if you spent any time around him at all, you realized that it showed most in his character. It mattered to Pidge Connors that he liked the man in the mirror.

"How you doin'?" I said.

"How much time you got?"

"Can't be that bad."

"You a bettin' man?"

"Not with you. Last time I had a full house, you laid down a straight flush."

"Gotta keep your eye on the dealer," he said.

"Learn something every day," I said.

Our relationship had always been an easy one. He'd been a buffer between me and my father on more than one occasion while I was growing up. There were only a couple of men Jack Drayton ever totally trusted, and Pidge Connors was one of them. If I can trust Pidge, then, in the end, I was the other one. I'd like to believe that. Not just because Pidge Connors had never told me a lie, but because my father was, for better or worse, a man I knew to be authentic, and he would always be my benchmark.

As we drew near the corral, I stopped. Pidge looked at me, understanding my need to be alone for a moment.

"I'll saddle up Kobe," he said.

I nodded, and swallowed hard as I stepped to the corral fence. I saw the rider wheel the dun around, spur up to where I stood, and rein in. Her face was still a girl's face, but there was a woman in there trying to come out. It was a woman who looked very much like another woman I had loved and lost.

Chapter Forty-Seven

"So, how much longer, you figure?"

She looked at me sideways, questioning the question. My eyes were fixed on the shimmering water of a small lake a quarter mile down the canyon from where we'd reined in.

"For what?" she said.

"A good talk," I said.

Her eyes found the lake, too.

"Why?"

"I don't like it when you're mad at me."

"I'm not mad."

"Hurt, then."

"I'm fine."

"I don't think so," I said. "And I know I'm not."

I shifted my eyes to her. She met them.

"Why not?"

"I think I hurt you. And however I did it, I need you to know I didn't mean to."

She looked back at the lake. I swung down out of the saddle and dropped the reins to let Kobe graze. He was a white-footed sorrel, quick and long-legged like his Laker namesake, and big for a quarter horse. He had to be big to pack a load like me, but sitting high above Sheridan on her little dun mare wasn't conducive to the intimacy of the moment or minimizing the vulnerability she was already feeling.

"You know what detectives need most?" I took off my sunglasses and looked up at her.

"I guess private detectives need a lot of privacy."

There was more than a dollop of bitterness in the remark. And a fair amount of irony for a twelve-year old. I chose to ignore it, tucked my glasses into my shirt pocket.

"Clues," I said.

She sighed into the warm breeze that worried the ponytail beneath her wide-brimmed straw hat.

"If I were a really good detective, I'd probably realize that you just gave me one."

She was silent. Waiting. Or wanting me to shut up.

"That was a very heavy sigh. Which was probably a hint that you don't want to be having this conversation. That you think it's stupid and pointless."

More silence.

"There's another one," I said. "No response. A clue that you think if you don't talk there can't be any conversation, maybe just a lecture you think you can handle, and then I'll get off it and just go away."

The only sound was a big blue jay with a black topknot scolding us from the thick-limbed valley oak beside us. Kobe answered with a snort. Sheridan remained silent.

"And not looking at me, that's to make the point real clear. Right?"

Her eyes slid back to me.

"I do this for a living, you know," I said, trying to net at least a flicker of a smile. But there was only defiance.

"What do you want me to say?" she said.

"Whatever you want to."

"Maybe I don't want to say anything."

"Are you afraid you'll hurt me? 'Cause part of being a detective is being tough, you know."

I put up my dukes playfully. She started to rein away from me. I reached out and took the little dun's headstall in my hand.

"Hey," I said. "The biggest part of the work I do is finding the truth, okay? And the truth is you could do that, Sher. You could hurt me more than anyone else in the world."

Tears were forming as she glared at me.

"There's a clue in that for you," I said.

"I want to go home," she said.

"If you could hurt me more than anyone, that should tell you I care about you more than anyone."

The tears brimmed in her eyes. I kept hold of the mare's cheekpiece with one hand, put the other on Sheridan's shoulder.

"Talk to me, Sher," I said. "Please."

The dam broke and she leaned down to me, wrapped her arms around my neck.

Her hat tumbled to the ground as I lifted her from the saddle and held her tightly. Swallowing wasn't as easy as a moment before.

"I'm sorry, honey," I said. "I'm sorry."

"I'm not mad at you," she sobbed. "I'm mad at Mom."

She cried harder. I held her closer. I realized I really wasn't much of a detective when it came to a child's emotions. I hadn't seen that coming and I'd had months to consider it. I carried her away from the grazing horses, stood her in the shade of the old tree and dropped to a knee in front of her.

"Sheridan. Listen to me, pal. Your mom didn't want to leave you," I said. "She didn't get to choose."

"I know," she sobbed. "But—"

"But what?"

"But I didn't get to, either. And I didn't get to say goodbye. I didn't get to tell her I was sorry."

"Sorry for what?"

"For being mad at her."

"She didn't think you were mad at her."

"Yes she did. I told her I was when you went away."

She hugged me tighter. I felt foreign objects in my eyes and throat. They were hot and wet and I'd sworn I'd never feel them again.

"When I went away, that wasn't your mom's fault, pal. I told you that, remember?"

Her head bobbed on my shoulder.

"But you were just protecting her," she said. "Like you always try to protect everybody."

"I left for the reason I told you then," I said. "I couldn't live the life your mom wanted. There were other things I had to do."

"She could have stayed with you."

"No. She couldn't. And she shouldn't have. We were just two different people going in two different directions."

"It was her fault."

"No. It wasn't. It wasn't anybody's fault."

"I had everything before that," she cried.

I held her closer, but I couldn't stop the sobs that wracked her slender frame. I couldn't stop the salt of my own tears from sliding into the corner of my mouth.

"We can't go back, pal," I heard myself say. "It's one of the hardest lessons we have to learn. We can't go back. But we can learn from what happens. And we can try not to get hurt the same way again."

She squeezed me harder.

"Let's look at what we still have, okay?" I said. "Most of all we've got each other, right?"

She nodded and lifted her head to look at me.

"Could you come live here?" she said.

"No."

"Why not?"

"This is your grandparents' place."

"They'd let you."

"The point is, it's their life. One they built for themselves. I have a different one."

"Being a detective?"

"Yeah."

"You could do something else."

"Yeah. But right now, it's what I do. And I'm reasonably good at it."

"You're a good calf roper."

"Not good enough. And that's something I do for a release. For play. You know? We all have to find work we can do that we find some kind of fulfillment in, but we have to play, too."

"I could come live with you," she said.

"As much as I'd like that," I said, "I don't have that kind of life, pal."

"You know what I think sometimes?"

"What's that?"

"I think it's because you're not my real father."

I've been hit with gun butts, saps, wrenches, pipes, two-by-fours, crowbars, and more fists and feet than I can count, but I don't remember being hit any harder.

"That's why you don't want me with you," she said, fighting back her tears.

"Look at me," I said. "Look as deep into my eyes as you can see."

She looked.

"What's your name?"

"Sheridan."

"Sheridan what?"

"Sheridan Elizabeth."

"Go on."

"Sheridan Elizabeth Drayton."

"How do you suppose you got that last part?"

"You gave it to me."

"Damn straight. And the state of California made it legal. It's like a brand, okay? It won't come off in the wash."

To my surprise, I got a small smile. I reflected it, feeling some relief.

"You and I are the only two people who wear that brand, you know?" I said. "Now some day, you'll take a running iron to it and add on some other name, but not unless I think the sonofabuck who asks you to marry him is going to love you in his way as much as I do in mine."

Her smile graded into a small self-conscious grin.

"That'll be a while from now, though," I said. "So, till you're all grown up and off to college somewhere, we're the Draytons. You and me. Father and daughter."

She hugged me again, then wondered into my neck, "What if I don't want to go to college?"

"Then you won't."

"You don't care?"

"I care a lot. I think you should go. But that's a decision you'll make for yourself when the time comes."

She lifted her head again, wiped her eyes and nose with the back of her hand and smiled at me.

"You cried, too," she said.

I was crying again as I looked up from the lake to a red-winged hawk circling overhead, struggled to pull myself back to the present.

As always, the recall was crystal clear. It was a moment I'd played over and over in my mind for the past year, a moment I never wanted to forget. I would always be glad we'd had it. I would always ache for more. But there wouldn't be any more. No more misunderstandings, no more rides, or talks, or smiles or hugs. There wouldn't be any wedding, any college, there wouldn't be even one more day of school. All of that had been taken away in an instant when the bus was hit head-on coming through the pass.

The shock had been overwhelming. Not just for me, or Liz, or Pidge, but for seven other families that shared common values and goals, and were shaken to their core by the sudden reminder that hopes and plans and dreams for the future were but bubbles to be broken without warning.

I worked in a world of broken bubbles, worked at picking up the pieces of shattered dreams, looked for ways to revive dying hopes, but I was as broken and shattered and dead inside as anyone. And a rush of guilt compounded the shock, guilt for all the days we hadn't shared, all the reasons I'd had for not being with her the way she wanted. For not being with her that morning, driving her to school myself.

I'd been comparing my loss with Gus Chernak's since the moment I first played the message he'd left on my office machine. I had understood his mission, and probably seen a chance to vent some of my own frustrations by involving myself in it. And I knew that part of me needed to talk to him as much as he needed to talk to me. But when I stood with him in his office about to share my own grief with him, he had silenced me, and it was just as well. For me to imply that I knew how he felt when he was still a festering sore would have been a selfish thing, and could have been kerosene on the bonfire.

Sheridan's death and Ken's were both strokes of the absurd, but they were different in nature. The condition of separation from our children was different for Gus and me, too. The guilt he felt was measurably greater than my own. It still stared him in the face, ugly and unforgiving, a guilt for which there could be no moratorium now that his son was dead. That unalterable condition of his life made his elation at the death of Willie Gates entirely understandable. Because he didn't know what I knew about Willie Gates, or Curtis Rankin. And I couldn't tell him without putting him in harm's way.

For Gus Chernak, the hunt was over. If the true killer was going to be caught, I would have to be the hunter.

The sun was down when I got back to the ranch house, the crickets were out courting, and the familiar smell of livestock was heavy on the warm evening air.

"Michael?" Liz called from the screen door. "Telephone."

Chapter Forty-eight

Formaldehyde stung my nose and assaulted my lungs. The ME's assistant pulled down the cloth. Leah's face was bruised, scraped, and raw. A jagged gash ran from the right corner of her hairline to the left corner of her lips.

I nodded a positive identification, and I could feel the pressure building inside me. It wasn't just anger, it was rage. My whole body was bloated with a burning need to find a release for it, a target I could lay into, and I knew that target should be me, my own arrogance and stupidity.

"She's in there because of me, Eddie," I said.

"What the hell are you talking about?" Falcon said. "She lost control of her car. It only takes a second."

"I taught her how to put a Porsche into a power slide at ninety when she was half her age. She handled hairpins at Laguna Seca. She didn't drive off the road coming home from work."

"Work ended with a few drinks. It was the last day of shooting, somewhere between three and four o'clock in the morning, she's snaking across Mulholland from Laurel to Coldwater. It could happen."

"Somebody ran her off," I said. "Because of me."

We sat across from each other in a coffee shop. I don't know exactly where it was. I didn't care. It was late. I don't know how late. It didn't matter.

"That doesn't track," Falcon said in an unemotional tone intended to keep my emotions in check.

I stared into my cup, focusing on the black coffee, putting another liquid body in my mind, a pond whipped by the wind.

"Picture a small lake in your mind, Michael. A pond rippled by the wind. Now, take away the wind. Smooth the water."

It was a drill I learned on the mat in Ed Parker's *dojo* when he saw that a twelve-year-old with feet too big for his body had trouble controlling his emotions.

"The ancient masters called it 'mizu no kokoro,' the need to make the mind calm, like the surface of undisturbed water."

I focused harder, deeper, making the water calmer, flatter.

"Smooth water reflects images clearly. If you keep your mind calm, your opponent's moves will be clear."

"You hear what I'm saying?" Falcon asked patiently.

I heard him, but I was working on the pond.

"When you're calm, you're in control, Michael, not your opponent. All your energy is stored in one place. You're ready to block any attack, strike with precision in any direction."

When the last ripples were gone, when it was still, I looked up.

"When Wes Carter died, I knew a mistake in judgment killed him," I said. "My mistake."

"Don't keep beating on yourself for that, man."

"Wes knew that could happen. Leah didn't. Her last conscious moments were a nightmare because I made another mistake. I let her walk where we walk."

Falcon shook his head.

"Jesus, Drayton."

"I knew better," I said. "But I did it anyway."

Falcon waited while a waitress moved past, then he leaned closer.

"Look, I get where you're coming from. But it doesn't go anywhere."

"She knew something."

"What?"

"I don't know. I don't think she knew. But somebody else was afraid she did."

"What she told you about the star and the producer? That wouldn't get my boss to reopen the investigation. The cops came up with a viable perp, he's dead, case closed."

"You know he didn't kill those two kids. That's why you had me watch Rankin's star-turn on TV."

"It doesn't matter what I think. Or what you think. It's what the cops think. If somebody else did it, they're clear and they know it. There was no reason to kill her."

"As long as Rankin's story holds."

"That's it, isn't it?" he said. "Listen to me, Drayton. I know you. You want to think Rankin's dirty somehow so you can bring him down. You want revenge for something that happened a long time ago. Let go of that, man. And, friend to friend? Let go of what you're thinking now."

"You sound like Duke Catalano."

"What?"

"Muscle for Phil Adams."

"I know who he is. What are you talking about?"

I told him. About the beating and the payoff. About Marty Mishkin not denying anything when I gave the money back. I told him about being tailed by a PI Kamala Highland hired, and hassled by cops hooked up with Rankin, and being warned by the man himself to stay out from underfoot. I told him about Leah's house being staked out by a couple of *kamikaze* bikers who fed me to Catalano. I told him. And he stared into his own coffee cup.

"Jesus," he said.

He looked up, read my eyes.

"I can't go to Roselli, you know. Not without hard evidence."

"I know."

Chapter Forty-nine

Hard evidence. I had no idea what that would be, or where to find it.

I drove directly to a two-story, tile-roofed building on little Santa Monica, parked on the side street, and used my key to let myself in the back entrance. I stripped down at the locker I kept there, put on my *gi,* stepped into the dojo, and flipped on a switch that lit up the back of a large, high-ceilinged room with a polished hardwood floor and a wall of mirrors. The only furniture in the room, two chairs, a desk, and a low filing cabinet, sat behind a *shoji* screen just inside the front door. The bank of windows to either side of the door, and the door itself were painted black. The art in martial arts is all about focus, and Jimmy Torrenueva didn't want any distractions for his students.

I saw myself in the mirror. A bomb about to explode. I saw all the emotions I was feeling about what I let happen to Leah colliding with what I never stopped feeling about racist cops like Curtis Rankin and what they can do to a man like Willie Gates. That triggered emotions I'd wrestled with on and off from the first day I had to get on a bus and be shoehorned into a school that didn't want me, the first time my best friend told me I couldn't come to his birthday party because his parents didn't want me in their home.

A balcony protruded over the length of the back wall and a heavy canvas bag hung from it by a chain in one corner. Beside the staircase in the other corner, a leather punching ball was fastened to the balcony and the floor by strong rubber ropes. I went straight for the heavy bag. Normally, I'd warm up with stretches and some core exercises, but I hadn't come for a normal workout.

I earned my black belt in *Kenpo* by learning hundreds of techniques and over 400 variations on those punches, strikes, holds and throws, and I attacked the big bag without thinking about what I'd unload. Each *kiai* exploded from my gut as I delivered blow after blow and sweat began to run down my face and body, soaking into my lightweight black pants and padded jacket.

It was six or seven minutes before I was aware that I wasn't alone. Jimmy was standing in half-light at the base of the stairs that led to the balcony outside his upstairs apartment. He was barefoot, wearing a T-shirt and pajama bottoms, and a twisted smile.

I stopped, and leaned against the bag, sucking in stale air as sweat streamed down my back muscles and thighs.

"Keep that up, you're gonna owe me a new bag," Jimmy said.

"I thought you'd be in San Diego," I said.

"Jeannie's mom had a relapse. She wanted to stay with her."

"Sorry."

"Hey, man, no problem. Like I said, any time."

"Thanks."

His dark eyes were still searching mine for the reason fueling my fury.

"I heard the shouts, saw the light, had to be you," he said as he stepped closer, wiped some sleep from his eyes, and rubbed his bald head with both hands. The average, undiscerning American would call him black, but he was a colorful mix of ethnicities more diverse than my own, born to a Nigerian father and a Cuban mother, raised by a Filipino step-father who gave him his name, survival instincts, and raw courage.

"What's wrong, bro?"

"I'm okay."

"Not what I was watching. You were out of control, man. All fight, no focus. What's the point?"

"I just needed to vent."

"Bad habit. You know that," he said. "You want to climb in the cage with some yahoo, okay, maybe, I mean, your sheer power is lethal, but you get that sloppy against anybody any good, you could get yourself hurt."

He was still studying me. And he was right. When your only weapon is your own body, there is no margin for error. *Kenpo*, or fist-way, isn't a slugfest, it's about the concentration of strength at the proper time and proper place, the unity of mind and will.

Jimmy had watched me strike mindlessly at the bag. As a master who had trained under Ed Parker and, later, Bruce Lee, and a *Sensei* to his own series of black-belt students, he was concerned to see a fellow disciple displaying so little discipline.

"Want to work a while?" he asked.

"I should let you get back to sleep," I said.

"How much sleep you think I'll get knowing you're that far off your game?"

We went back a long way, trained together for years, and I'd been honored to be best man at his wedding fifteen years ago.

"Last time I saw you lose it was when you lost your partner," he said. "This that bad?"

"Worse."

He knew what that meant, but didn't comment, just nodded, then stepped toward me and stretched, working the kinks out of his lean, muscular body.

"Let's spar," he said.

It was a sincere gesture of friendship, his way of helping me exert control over my emotions and actions without asking me again what it was that had derailed me.

"You want to put on your *gi?*"

"I'm good," he said, stretching again.

"What do you want me to work on first?"

"No, no," he said as he stepped closer. "Like you were just working. Free-style."

Free-style sparring in *karate* is a lot like two boxers sparring in a ring, except the attacks are pulled just short of contact. Jimmy knew that if we weren't working on one move at a time I would have to find my control to keep from injuring him. I knew what he was doing for me. And I knew I had to find that control, not just for the moment, but for what I was determined to do about avenging Leah's death.

We faced each other, and bowed. He stands six-one, giving me three inches in height and the reach that goes with it, and he weighs maybe one-eighty, giving up a good twenty-five pounds, but he's a better fighter. It wasn't his training or his style that made the difference, it was what he learned in the back alleys of a little town in Puerto Rico and then the streets of East Los Angeles, the fact that fear cannot be a component of combat.

We assumed relaxed, ready positions and began to move, sliding our feet on the polished floor. He seemed to be wanting me to attack first, and I watched for an opening as I created the proper distance before I threw a right lunge punch to his face.

Like a phantom, he shifted to the left, avoiding the blow and counterattacking with a back-fist strike to the ribs. He was fast and he was smooth.

"Too anxious," he said. "Come on, Cowboy. Get a grip."

He let me attack again, and I went for his mid-section. He shifted outside and countered with a ridge-hand strike to the temple. Then he feinted an attack to my face, leaving his mid-section momentarily exposed and I went for it again, but that left an opening to my head and he attacked with a roundhouse kick an inch short of my temple.

"Good thing you can take it as good as you give," he said. "Way too many openings."

I attacked again, he blocked and countered, but I was ready and blocked his kick, countered with a combination of fists and elbows that put a smile on his face.

"Okay," he said.

I was finally focused, and we were finally locked in. We worked at our potentially lethal ballet for a good twenty minutes, pausing only briefly to be sure we were both not too winded or tired to continue safely. We shifted from offense to defense, and were sometimes on both simultaneously as we opposed, rode, and stole force from each other, delivered force to the other with hands, feet, knees, elbows and skulls in moves designed to dislocate, fracture, rip, tear, rupture, and maim.

When I felt my legs go, I raised my hands to signal I'd had enough. Jimmy smiled his twisted smile.

"Whatever it is," he said. "Keep it where you just put it."

CHAPTER FIFTY

It was mid-morning when I left the W, set out on foot down Hilgard, crossed Wilshire, and turned into a long driveway on Glendon that opened onto a little three-acre oasis of serenity where grass flourished, flowers bloomed, water trickled over stone, and shade trees stood like sentinels over hundreds of interment sites.

I had no idea what Leah's wishes would have been or where she'd have wanted to be laid to rest, but this peaceful private reserve felt right to me. It was a place where she could lie with Marilyn Monroe, Donna Reed, Natalie Wood and scores of others who had shared her dedication to an industry that, at its best, entertains and enlightens the world.

A family service counselor offered Sunday afternoon. I took it, and she graciously took care of all the rest.

The envelope from the Secretary of State's office with the domestic stock statements for Kamala Highland's company was on my desk when I came into the office. In typical bureaucratic fashion, only one statement was in the envelope, the one for Highland Productions. But it filled in a big blank.

The president and secretary of Highland Productions was Kamala Highland. The vice president and treasurer was Martin Mishkin. Mishkin was also named as the agent.

"Agent?" Mari said. "What's that mean?"

"The person who receives services of process in a law suit."

"A lawyer?"

"Usually."

"He's the one you went to see on Friday."

"Yeah."

"Because of this company?"

I was sitting at my desk. Mari stood looking over my shoulder.

"I think I'd better go over this myself."

"Why?"

"It's better if you don't know anything about it."

"You're still working on what happened, aren't you? Because you don't think that homeless man killed them."

"Drop it, Mari."

"You're right."

"What?"

"I went to the Veterans Hospital," she said. "I told them I was writing my dissertation on forensic pathology and asked if I could review the records on the man who killed Jeremy Thomas."

"You did what?"

"They wouldn't let me copy anything, but I read through the whole case file. His story made you cry," she said. "He needed help he never got. But you are so right, he didn't do what the police said he did. He wasn't a violent man."

"Mari, stop."

"Why?"

"Because another woman I liked a lot knew too much about what I was doing. I just booked her funeral."

I could see the chill course through her body.

"I thought she was in an accident."

"Listen to me. If you want to quit working for me today, as much as I wouldn't want that, I could accept it," I said. "If you ask any more questions about this, I'll have to fire you."

Her natural instinct was to question that, too, but she caught herself.

"Coffee?" she asked.

"Great," I said.

She turned, and walked out the door. I looked at the document and the one new piece of the puzzle: Martin Mishkin.

Mishkin represented Phil Adams. He had to be fronting for Adams in Kamala Highland's corporation. But why? Why would she cut anybody into something so golden that she'd built for herself?

I thought about the big house and the monthly nut that had to come with it. I thought about the fight between her and Thomas that Leah overheard. Was she falling out of favor? Was she spending it faster than she was making it? I still had to know more about Kamala Highland.

There were more papers beneath the envelope from the State. I looked at them.

"Mari?"

She came back with a steaming mug, set it on the desk.

"What's this?"

"I don't know," she said.

"It's more information on Highland Productions."

Mari leaned in to take a closer look.

"It looks like some kind of search from an online service," she said.

"HighNote Productions is here, too," I said, comparing the report to the document from the State. "But the State only sent us the DSS for Highland Productions."

"Yeah," she said, and began guiding me through the printout. "That one looks like somebody ran Jeremy Thomas and got HighNote Productions. Then they ran HighNote Productions and got the list of officers. Kamala Highland and Martin Mishkin show up there, see? The second one looks like they ran Kamala Highland and got Highland Productions and HighNote Productions."

My eyes left the paper for her poker face. She directed them back to the report.

"It looks like the controlling interest in Highland Productions was given to Martin Mishkin. And that Highland Productions is a full partner in HighNote Productions. So I guess that means Martin Mishkin was Jeremy Thomas's partner."

"Mishkin had the controlling interest in Highland Productions?"

"That's what the search says."

I looked at the printout. "How did you get all this?"

"I don't know."

I studied her face. It was still a blank. "Okay. How would anybody go about getting something like this from an on-line service?"

"I don't know."

"Take a wild guess."

"Well, I guess you'd have to have a friend who knew what he or she was doing. I suppose if they searched by the name of a company they could get a registration number. If they got the registration number, they could get everything they wanted right up to date."

"You mean, if you knew some computer whiz, they could just download all this?"

"I guess," she said. "But I really don't know anything about it."

CHAPTER FIFTY-ONE

"So what does that tell you?"

Falcon was silent, studying the creased copy of the report.

"Adams has his hooks in her good, that's what," I said. "Another laundry for his rackets."

"Maybe."

We were sitting in his car on a side street by Echo Park. He set the report on the dash.

"I got a couple things for you," he said.

"Yeah?"

"I checked the Valley unit that covered the crash. No skid marks except just before where she went over the side. They said she could've tried to miss a deer, or a coyote."

"Or a herd of wildebeests."

"I drove out to the tow shop in Van Nuys. Car was totaled."

I watched the steady stream of traffic on Wilshire Boulevard, my mind on Mulholland Drive.

"Silver Saab, right?" he asked.

"Yeah."

"See it lately?"

"Drove it."

"Notice any dings? Scratches?"

Falcon doesn't ask idle questions. I looked back.

"No. Why?"

"No black paint on the left front fender?"

"Sonsabitches!" I exploded.

"Hey," Falcon cautioned. "It was just a touch, easy to miss."

I responded reflexively again with my father's favorite West Texas epithet.

"Sonsabitches."

"Can it." Falcon snapped.

I met his gaze head-on. I was a teenager again, back on the mat with my *Sensei*. He lowered his voice and spoke again calmly.

"There's more."

I waited. So did he. Until he was certain I'd gotten the message.

"Kamala Highland," he said. "I called a guy I know with the State Troopers in Jackson, had him run a make."

"And?"

"No such animal born in Mississippi."

I looked back at the traffic.

"I found a legal name change in New York, though. Superior Court, 1982. Young woman born in Belzone, Mississippi, 1963, Jo Ellen Bates," he said. "Checked back with my friend. She was enrolled at Ole Miss in the fall of 1980, left after one semester. No degree."

"New York?" I said.

"Yeah."

"Eighty-two?"

"Right."

I rolled it around.

"What do you have?"

"I'm not sure," I said.

"Throw something else in the hopper," he said. "Insurance investigators come straight to our office when they know there's going to be a big claim. High-profile cases like this, celebrity deals."

"They called?"

"Yesterday."

"How big?"

"Fifty million. What they call a key-man policy. Covers a company for the loss of somebody who's basically a one-man band."

"What company? Universal?"

"HighNote Productions."

"Fifty million dollars goes to her corporation?"

He lifted the report from the dash.

"According to this—"

"To Martin Mishkin."

"To Phil Adams."

"Sonsabitches," I said, but calmly. He slipped the report into his breast pocket.

"I've got to have it all before I can take it anywhere," he said.

"I don't."

CHAPTER FIFTY-TWO

Mari was at a meeting with her Faculty advisor, and I was alone in my office. The sun had long since left my side of the building and was sliding off the buildings on the east side of the boulevard as I scanned the rooflines and checked the windows with a view of mine. I raked my eyes along the shadows of both sides of the street, then closed the blinds and opened the bottom drawer of the corner file cabinet. I took out two spare fifteen-round clips and six boxes of .40 caliber cartridges for my H&K automatic. I set the loaded clips and ammo in the duffle bag sitting on the chair beside the cabinet.

I wasn't going up against one heavyweight, I'd be taking on two. They each had legions at their command. All I had going for me was the element of surprise, if I could be patient enough to behave as though I bought the Willie Gates ending to the case I'd been working and Leah's coinciding "accidental death."

They had to be watching me. I knew I had to keep my impulses in my hip pocket and play possum, I had to be perfectly still at my center, had to be certain I wasn't creating any blind spots with the emotions straining to be unleashed. If I could do that, I might have a chance. I might also have to be someone else.

I reached back in the drawer and pulled out a zippered case, opened it and took out a snub-nosed Smith & Wesson .38. I put the case back, put the little belly gun in a belt clip and put it in the duffle. I took a speed loader and five boxes of twenty 125-grain .38 special plus P's out of the drawer, put them in the bag and pulled another zippered case from the drawer. I took out my dependable old Sig Sauer, jammed it in its shoulder holster and set it in the bag, grabbed two spare clips for it, a couple pair of handcuffs, and six boxes of 9 mm cartridges, set them beside the Sig, and zipped the bag. I closed and locked the cabinet, picked up the duffle, and left the office.

Thirty minutes later, Eugene Miller was bouncing on my knee in the kitchen area of the small apartment while his mother prepared mashed peas, pear sauce, and pureed chicken.

"You didn't tell me his grandmother was a famous movie producer," I said.

Karen Miller stopped in mid-motion to fix her green eyes on me. They were her son's eyes, her mother's eyes.

"What?"

"Kamala Highland."

"How did you—"

She caught herself, stopped, and set the plate she was preparing on a white plastic tray resting on the counter beside a blue-and-white plastic highchair.

"Is that why you came back?" she said.

"Partly."

She plucked her son from my lap, slid him into the highchair, buckled him in place.

"You remember the woman who was with me at Ken's funeral? The one who told the story about the big scene in the movie?"

She lifted a bib from the back of the chair seat and tied it over Eugene's bright red Winnie the Pooh T-shirt.

"She died," I said.

She glanced at me as she lifted the tray from the counter and slid it into the arms of the highchair, locked it in place.

"Car ran off the road on Mulholland Drive last Friday night," I said.

Her face softened. "I saw that on the news," she said. "That was your friend?"

"Close friend. Almost like you and Ken."

She studied me. Eugene flailed at the plate. She sat down in a chair beside him, spooned food into his mouth, and looked back at me.

"I'm sorry," she said.

"Thank you."

She fed the baby again, slipping the spoon in, pulling it up and out gently to scrape all the food off and keep it in his mouth. She was barefoot in a pale yellow, sleeveless dress. Her hair was pinned up and hung in wisps down the back of her long, slender neck. She was pretty. She was a good mother.

"I don't understand," she said. "Like, why'd you come here tonight?"

"I just found out today about Kamala Highland being Jo Ellen Bates. She is your mother, isn't she?"

"Yes. But what does that have to do with—" she hesitated, found the right phrasing. "With what happened to your friend?"

"Kamala Highland was Jeremy Thomas's partner. I think whoever killed him and Ken killed Leah, too."

Karen's eyes fixed on me.

"The police caught the man who killed Ken and Jeremy. They shot him," she said.

"They shot somebody," I said. "I don't think it was the person who murdered this little guy's father."

She got another spoonful into Eugene as she tried to compute what I was saying. A siren wailed somewhere in the distance.

"You think, like, I had something to do with what happened to Ken and Jeremy?"

"Any reason you didn't mention who your mother was?"

"I didn't think it mattered."

"Did you know she was producing the picture Jeremy put Ken in?"

"Yes."

"Did Jeremy know she was your mother?"

"Not at first."

"But he found out."

"Yes," she said, handling her stress and Eugene's with a command born of innocence. The siren had come closer, grown louder, and set off a chain of barking dogs.

"Ken and Jeremy got pretty close, and Ken, he, like, just opened up one night. I mean, it was, like, kind of freaky that we'd all be hooked up together after all that time, but he didn't know Jeremy would go off like he did."

"What do you mean, 'go off?'"

"He just got, like, really mad when he heard how she gave me away, how she never wanted to see me after that."

I felt an identity with Jeremy Thomas that I hadn't till that moment. I wondered if his anger had made him vulnerable, or blinded him to the possibility of what was yet to come.

"You're sure she's your birth-mother?"

"I told you, my parents didn't want it kept from me. I knew she'd changed her name. I knew where she was and what she did. But I never wanted to see her if she didn't want to see me."

"Even when you were in the foster homes?"

"No. Never. Not until Eugene was born. Then I just felt, like, this urge. I guess part of it was wanting her to know she had a grandson. Part of it was, like, actually wanting to see her face to face just once in my life."

"And did you?"

"This agent who comes to the shop got me a pass to get on the lot for a casting call. Then I went to her office."

"With the baby?"

"Yes."

"She let you in?"

"She didn't want to. But I wasn't leaving, and she didn't want a scene, you know?"

"What happened?"

"She thought I came to ask for money. But I wouldn't have taken any if she begged me. I just wanted to, like, see my own mother, wanted her to see my baby, her grandson. Is that crazy?"

"I don't think so."

CHAPTER FIFTY-THREE

The siren was gone. The dogs had stopped barking. Karen Miller sat in silent reflection for a moment. Then she fed her son another spoonful of peas as she spoke quietly.

"I guess maybe part of me wanted more than that, I don't know. Not money, just some, like, recognition, some connection, some way to acknowledge what we are to each other. I mean, like, half of me is her, you know? The other half was supposed to be some big Academy-Award winner who died a long time ago. There's no way I ever get to say hello to him. That's all I needed from her. Just, like, say hello, you know? All I wanted was, like, just to be in the same room together for a few minutes, see my eyes in her face, my lips on her mouth, and her to see that in me, too. I mean, it's like a miracle, isn't it? I look at Eugene and I see—"

She broke off, checking her emotion. "I'm sorry," she said.

"Don't be," I said, flashing on my own mother and how much of her I see in me.

"Oh, you're a mess," she said as she snagged a dishtowel from the counter to wipe the baby's face. Then she wiped at her own eyes. "Anyway, she didn't get it. She was sure I was, like, playing some kind of angle. But I wasn't. I just, I don't know, I wanted to, like, see her just once. And be seen. In case, maybe, she'd ever wondered how I turned out."

And I wondered what my mother would have thought about how I turned out, if she were still alive. Probably not much, given the work she did, all that she accomplished in such a short time.

The young mother across from me wiped the baby's face again, kissed the top of his head. I watched her in silence, her courage on display, her love for her own child.

"It wasn't anything like what Ken said he felt when he saw his father. I didn't have any of that anger, I guess. The people who adopted me were good people. They took good care of me. They loved me. When they were killed, I lived with some other good people. And I had Ken."

She stood up, unlocked the tray, put it in the sink.

"Jeremy was something else, though," she said. "He was a great guy, but he wasn't, like, big into forgive and forget. The day Ken told him who my mother was? That night, he told her he wanted a million-dollar trust set up for Eugene. She told him I hadn't asked for anything and she didn't feel like giving me anything. I was an accident, she said, a mistake she made thirty years ago. She'd taken care of hers without any help from anyone, she said. I could take care of my own, too."

She unbuckled Eugene, lifted him from the chair.

"'A mistake?'" I asked, remembering Leah's words, "She said that?'"

"That's what Jeremy told us. Then he said, like, yeah, it was a mistake she used to get her start and he figured every move she'd made since was just as cold and calculated, including the partnership with him. He said that was over, and as far as he was concerned she could go to hell."

"When was that?" I asked.

"Twenty-eighth of May," she said. "The day before my birthday."

Chapter Fifty-four

"Coverage on a battle sequence shot in Ireland you said?"

"Right. Middle of May, I think. How late did Thomas work?"

I was sitting in my office, Howard Alworth was in his going through production reports. The steady sound of evening traffic rose from the boulevard below and came in through the open windows.

"I'm gonna put you on the box," he said.

I heard the click. His voice grew thinner.

"What you need this for?"

"Just connecting dots. Something Leah told me happened that night."

"None of my business, I know," Howard said. "But if the cops are okay with things, why aren't you?"

"I used to be a cop."

I found I was staring at a photograph on the wall. It was the picture of my father with John Wayne.

"Okay," Howard said. "Here we go. Friday, May eighteenth. Pick up shots and coverage inside the castle. Thomas wrapped at eight o'clock."

Looking at the photograph, I realized that somebody walking into John Wayne's dressing room to glimpse my father for a moment in half light could come away with the same impression Leah had after seeing Kamala Highland with what could have been Jeremy Thomas's double.

"Thomas's double work that night?"

"Collingswood? Yeah, he would have. Here it is. Wrapped at eleven."

I felt the blood turn cold in my veins.

"You got an address for him?"

"Should have. Why?"

"You said he got the job because he's good with period weapons."

"Yeah, battle-ax, broadsword, mace, lances. He's good with all of it," Howard said. And then it hit him, too. He picked up the receiver.

"You looking at him as a killer?"

"Is he local?"

"2222 Summit Terrace," Howard said.

I jotted the address down on a pad.

"That's just off Mulholland," I said.

"Yeah. Valley side. Just a little west of Laurel."

"Not far from where Leah went over the edge," I said.

"No. 'Bout a mile, maybe," Howard said. "Jesus, Mikey. What are you doing?"

I was looking at the photograph, feeling I had finally locked in a piece of the puzzle.

CHAPTER FIFTY-FIVE

"Reggie Collingswood?"

He looked at me like a man looks when he's startled.

"How the fuck did you get in here?"

"I knocked, nobody answered," I said. "Heard the music and came around through the side gate." I didn't tell him I'd have taken the gate off its hinges if it had been locked, or that I was wanting to take his head off then and there.

The music was loud, big thumping bass, lots of screeching metal. There weren't any houses in sight from the rear deck, just a carpet of colored lights spilling out across the valley floor, but the sound had to be carrying down the bowl-shaped canyon to some unhappy neighbors somewhere.

"Who the fuck are you?"

"Michael Drayton." I showed him my ID. "Like to ask you a few questions."

He was bigger than I'd expected, with features chiseled out of granite and a body to match. The package wrapped in a black Speedo was impressive, or he'd stuffed it with sweat socks. He squinted at the ID, then back up at me as though he still couldn't believe I was there.

"Copper?"

"Private."

"Well, mate, this is a private party," he smiled too big, "if you know what I mean."

Two other men were watching us, both hooked on the same steroids as Reggie. They weren't smiling.

The rest of the party consisted of six shapely young women in thong bikinis. Two looked up from the table they'd been hunched over with the two men, two stopped splashing in the shallow end of the cantilevered pool, and two stopped dancing on the far side of it.

"It won't take long," I said.

"Not at all," Collingswood said. "'Cause it ain't happenin'."

He had a distinct West End dialect, laid on heavier for effect as his smile dimmed.

"You found your way in, you can find your way out."

He turned back to the pool. After all the years of training, the emotion fueling me this time made it hard to find the calm I needed.

"How well did you know Jeremy Thomas?"

He stopped, turned back. The smile was gone.

"You deaf, mate? This conversation's over."

"Conversation implies some sort of exchange," I said. "Ideas, opinions, thoughts, you know, a discussion."

"Cute," he said as he stepped back to me. "Okay. Here's what I think. I think you came to the wrong place at the wrong time with a wrong idea in your head."

He was looking up into my eyes. I knew the look. It was fearless.

"This is my home, all right? Mine. I pay a shitload of money every month for the privacy it affords me," he said. "So, that's what I think. An' here's how I feel about you droppin' in like this."

He stepped closer. "If you don't fuckin' bugger off, I'll break your fuckin' balls. Is that enough fuckin' conversation for you?"

"It's a start," I said.

And he smiled big again, glanced back at the pool and unloaded a sneaky left hook. I was so charged, I saw his move in slow motion and I met it with an explosion of force like I'd never known, stepping inside the punch, chopping forearm and bicep with the blades of my hands, driving my right elbow into his rib cage and bringing the back of my fist up hard against his head. He dropped like an anchor.

His two friends left the girls and started toward me. I pulled my jacket open, flashing my holstered automatic.

"Private talk," I said.

They froze in place. I reached down, took a handful of locks and the back of Reggie's trunks, carried him to the outdoor bar and dropped him on the mattress of a redwood lounge chair. As he struggled to clear his head, I dumped an ice bucket into a towel, twisted it into a pack and handed it to him.

"Put it where it hurts most," I said. "I'll tell you what I think."

The two men and the six girls hadn't moved, all were staring at their host as he put the ice pack against the side of his head and groaned.

"For openers," I said, "I think at least two of those nymphs are under age. That and the table top over there could lead to some legal bills that make your rent look like chump change. And you still might do time."

"What do you want?"

"See how easy that was?"

"I only did one picture with Jeremy Thomas," he said. "I met him in February, worked with him maybe three and a half months. Till June."

"And Kamala Highland? How long have you known her?"

"I met her three, four years ago. Worked one picture for her two years ago, then this last one. Why?"

"The night you did the pick-up shots for the battle scene in the castle. You went with her to Jeremy Thomas's bungalow, didn't you?"

"I don't know what you're talkin' about."

"I'm talking about Friday the eighteenth of May, about you and Kamala Highland, about Leah Sanders walking in on you. You know Leah Sanders. Her car was run off the road less than a mile from here."

His left eye was closing, but I had his rapt attention.

"Who'd you say you work for?" he asked.

"I didn't."

"And I don't have to say anythin' else to you."

"You want me off your back, you do."

He thought about that. I thought about Leah describing the tryst she walked in on and what it cost her. I wasn't going anywhere. He saw that.

"I don't want any trouble," he said.

"Talk to me about Kamala Highland."

"You want me to say I shagged her? I shagged her. That ain't against the law."

"Scored coke for her?"

"That would be against the law," he said. "I'm here legally. I'm not gonna let you fuck that up."

I glanced at the nymphets and the mirror on the table.

"Doesn't look like you need any help from me," I said.

The girls were huddled together behind the two men now. A million colored lights twinkled behind them. The music screamed on. Suddenly the whole tableau was freakish.

I looked back at the Brit. It was him Leah had seen that night, not Jeremy Thomas. He was an expert with broad-bladed weapons like the one that killed Thomas and Gus Chernak's son. He was an expert with cars, and Leah had been run off the road just down the block. But I couldn't make any of that add up to a charge of any kind. Whatever he knew, he knew that, too.

"So, are we finished, mate?" he said.

"Not if I can prove you killed Leah Sanders."

Chapter Fifty-six

I was on the track at Drake stadium before six. The light was thin, the air was as fresh as it was going to be. Olympic champions and world-record holders call the northwest corner of the UCLA campus home. I'd competed there, but was never a threat to break any records, and a long way past coming close to modest personal bests. I was working hard, though. Harder than I had since before my aerial ballet with a Rottweiler that ushered in the New Year, running in circles, looking for the straightest path to what I had to have.

I had to squeeze Kamala Highland, and I had to prove the police had executed an innocent man. After four laps, I decided to start with the executioner. His name was Timothy Lavin. He was a twenty-four-year old with two years duty in a West L.A. cruiser. His picture was in one of the L.A. Times articles I'd caught up with in the office after I left Collingswood.

I recognized him at once. He was the big red-headed recruitment-poster patrolman riding shotgun when I got stopped for the illegal turn my first day on the case. The article said he and his partner had responded to a disturbance in Bel Air and found Willie Gates wandering the grounds of an estate. The owners of the estate were out of the country. It didn't say who dialed 911 for assistance. It did say the partner's name was Ted

Wilkes. I remembered him, too, and the disagreement the two of them seemed to have when they let me go.

I thought back to my own days in a black-and-white, days filled with hours of mundane routine interrupted by seconds of sheer terror. I thought about how your partner was the only person you could be sure would back you up when you came to a life-or-death situation. And you would come to those situations. Patrol officers are in constant contact with citizens they need to protect and citizens they need to lock up. One morning they're in a five-star hotel taking a theft complaint from a woman who's lost jewelry worth more than they'll earn in ten years, that afternoon they're staring down a PCP-head high enough to take ten gunshots and still have the strength to literally rip out their throats.

Before an officer is put on the street, they're screened and tested carefully, but it's a wrenching change going from John or Jane Doe to John or Jane Law. When I first put on a uniform, I'd already met the hurtful half-smile of prejudice as a boy and faced naked hostility in the eyes of ignorant men as an adult, even after most of the country thought it had put the problem of race in the rearview mirror. It was something my father had prepared me for, and, sadly, still isn't totally unexpected. Confronting hatred and prejudice directed at you for no reason other than the uniform you're wearing, though, creates a kind of stress totally foreign to your nervous system. White, black, brown, red, yellow, male or female, there is no warm-up for that experience, no gradual exposure, nothing that parallels the sudden and complete change in how you are perceived and pre-judged by others. In dealing with it, most officers learn to control their baser instincts, but others get pulled down to the level of the lowest common denominator like quicksand claims strangers to the swamp.

Aware of the problem, LAPD started appointing veteran officers as counselors and confessors to rookies who worried about their job performance, their sanity and their lives. Not a bad idea, but a flawed one. Because of the flawed individuals who had come before and found their own way of dealing with the stress, found their own way of dealing with prejudice and hatred. It was dollars to donuts that the few I had known a decade before had used the well-intended policy to bolster their own ranks. Curtis Rankin was now their godfather. And they would do his bidding. But, maybe, with varying degrees of commitment. It was worth finding out.

I'd need Eddie Falcon to get somebody in West Bureau to pull 201's on Lavin and Wilkes and give me profiles. I'd need a favor from a genius kid who worked at a Radio Shack in Santa Monica, too. He was into all the latest James Bond gadgets in a big way and said he could set me up with a wire I wouldn't even know I was wearing.

When I left the W and headed for his shop a little after eight, I took enough turns and made enough stops that I knew I hadn't been followed. He checked me out with the equipment, I paid him cash, and drove to a gun club south of Santa Monica Boulevard. I fired a box of cartridges with the .38, the .40 and the 9. Then I drove to Jimmy Torrenueva's. He had a class going, but I staked out a corner at the back, loosened up and spent a half hour working on the heavy bag with precision strikes, and then focused on maximum power at impact against the canvas punching board on the back wall.

I was ready.

CHAPTER FIFTY-SEVEN

It was ninety-four degrees in Van Nuys when I pulled into the parking lot of War-Memorial Park a little before three in the afternoon. Patrolman Wilkes was hitting ground balls to five chattering twelve-year-olds in baggy blue-and-white uniforms on one of the all-dirt infields.

"Good job, gang! Good job! Come on in!" Wilkes shouted, and turned to a man in a red cap. "All yours, Coach!"

"Thanks, Ted," the man called back, and a team clad in red-and-white trotted out to take infield as Ted Wilkes addressed the boys in blue.

"Okay, guys, let's spread out along the sideline and stay warm, we're home team, so they bat first. Let's go!"

The boys hustled out on the edge of the grass behind first base. Wilkes stopped one of them. The gene pool man and boy shared was obvious.

"Matt?"

"Yeah?"

Wilkes put his hand on the boy's shoulder.

"When the ball goes over the middle like that next-to-last one I gave you, you gotta break fast. First step and a half, that's where you make the play, okay? See it into the glove, pivot and fire."

"Okay," the boy nodded. "Thanks, Dad."

He ran off to join his teammates and I drifted up to where Wilkes stood watching.

"Pretty good club," I said.

"Yeah, they hustle," he said with a smile that evaporated as he placed me.

"Got a minute?"

"I've got nothing to say to you."

"I've got a lot to say to the DA's office. But I caught something between you and your partner when I drove off the other day that made me think I should talk to you first."

I had his attention. Or the DA did. He shouted to another coach in a blue cap.

"Hey, Deck!" The man turned. "They're yours," Wilkes said. "Be back in a bit."

The man nodded, and Wilkes walked me away from the field, stopped by the parking lot and squared his broad shoulders to me.

"Talk about what?"

"Sometimes a guy gets pressure from too many places all at once, it's easy to make some wrong choices," I said. "Alimony, child support, legal fees, separate living expenses. All you need on top of that's trouble with a partner, a commander coming down on you for not sticking with the program."

"Get out of my face," he said, taking off his glasses.

"Stay cool, officer Wilkes. The score's a little different from the first time we met," I said. "A friend of mine's been killed to cover up what you and I both know is going down. So, if you want to waltz with me, we'd better call an ambulance first."

He wasn't afraid, but he wasn't stupid, either. While he thought about his next move, I stared down at him.

"Two minutes. That's all I want. You feel the same way then, I'm gone and you're back in the coach's box."

"I don't have to give you two seconds."

"That's true. But then you'll be giving the DA's boys a lot longer. Next it'll be Internal Affairs. This isn't going away."

He searched my eyes. He wasn't going to find anything more than I'd given him. He nodded me toward a shaded area away from the field.

"You're a father," I said as we walked. "Can you look at number four over there and imagine him being chopped down by somebody the way Gus Chernak's son was? That's my client, Gus Chernak, an ex-marine like you. Can you put yourself in his shoes? Can you imagine waking up to his nightmare?"

We reached the shade, but it wasn't any cooler. The ping of the aluminum bat on the diamond carried to us crisply through the dry air.

"And you're a cop," I said. "Framing the homeless and the helpless, is that part of the job description now? Execute them on the spot, guilty or not? Not care that whoever's really guilty of those murders is still walking around free because Curtis Rankin wanted the door closed fast? So fast he's willing to corrupt guys like you to bury the truth along with a human tragedy like Willie Gates?"

My lynch pin had put his dark glasses back on. His features were expressionless as he stared off at the boys on the diamond.

"When Rankin is Mayor of Los Angeles, or Governor of California, or sitting in congress, or the oval office, how are you going to feel about the job you did? The kind of cop you are? How will you feel when you hear yourself preaching to your son about how to be a better man?"

A voice came from the diamond, "Play ball!" Clapping and whistling came from the stands.

"That's it," I said. "Your call."

P-II Ted Wilkes didn't look at me. He looked at a twelve-year-old boy getting a quick jump on a ground ball hit into the hole behind second base, gloving it cleanly and turning to make the long throw to first.

CHAPTER FIFTY-EIGHT

Heaven is a little bar on Sunset Boulevard in Echo Park sandwiched between a bail bondsman and a dry cleaners. It's close to the Police Academy and Dodger Stadium, and its walls are lined with framed pictures of retired ballplayers and cops, old gloves, autographed balls, broken bats, and glass cases filled with police badges and caps donated since it became the LAPD's unofficial off-duty officers' club back in the 1970s. I sat on a stool at the far end of the long brass-railed bar looking at a sculpture of a revolver and a shoe resting in one of the cases. It was dedicated to a detective who shot himself in the foot. I hoped I wasn't about to inspire a bookend.

I hadn't seen anyone I knew and I didn't want to. It was ten after five, the cop I was waiting for hadn't shown yet, and I was booked for a command performance across town in Holmby Hills at seven. Another five minutes and I'd have to split with part of my plan still hanging in the wind.

Ted Wilkes had said Timothy Lavin dropped into *Heaven* for Happy Hour every Saturday between four and six when they were off duty. And he came through the door at five-fourteen with one arm around a shapely young Latina in a low-cut red dress that clung to her like Saran Wrap and his other arm around a carbon copy in a purple dress cut from the same pattern. The sight of him and all he represented triggered that familiar pressure inside. It was different this time, though. I could hear the chants of protesters in city streets, and the sense of calm I needed came quickly as I drew a strange comfort from the knowledge that what was about to happen was a long overdue brand of justice.

He was greeted warmly, touching knuckles with several men as he made his way to a table with the twin hotties. He signaled a busty bottle-blonde waitress in a white mini-toga and sandals, and she stepped to the table.

I got up from the stool, drink in hand. As the waitress turned for the bar, I stepped toward the table.

"Hey, hero," I said.

Lavin cut a glance at me. I opened my arms wide.

"Illegal signal, illegal turn," I said, having a little trouble with the double l's.

Annoyance and disgust mingled with Lavin's freckles.

"Something you want?" he said.

It was the first time I'd seen his eyes. They were gray-green like the sea off the coast of Donegal and Sligo.

"Saw your picture in the paper," I slurred, weaving my way closer. "Officer Timothy Lavin. Has to be the same guy, I said. No two guys in the department that big. Hell, no two cops in California. Man's a giant, I said."

I stood over him grinning stupidly.

"So?" he asked.

"So, you did it, huh?" I shot him with my finger and thumb. "Five rounds in the ten-ring?"

I was turning off the twins and turning heads my way.

"Meritorious Service Medal," I said with a degree of difficulty, "for that, right?"

"You're drunk, man," Lavin said. "Why don't you take it on out of here?"

"Hey," I leaned closer, spilling some of my drink, "just between us. Are they gonna let you keep that medal now?"

"What's that supposed to mean?"

"Shhhhhh," I said from behind the index finger I held to my lips. "Top secret," I whispered conspiratorially. "IAD's all over it. The set up, cover up. Whole shootin' match."

I snapped off another shot, and laughed into the bottom of my glass. Lavin stood up. I looked up.

"Let's get you on the road," he said.

"Wait a minute," I said, leering at the twins. "*Dos señoritas, dos hombres.* That adds up pretty good. Like you and Rankin."

He didn't wait for me to finish. My glass hit the floor, scattering ice as I let him crank my arm behind my back.

"Hey, whatsa problem?" I said without resisting as he marched me for the door.

A couple on the sidewalk and two plainclothes guys behind them gave way as Lavin used me like the cowcatcher on a locomotive to plow his way past the drycleaners and into an alleyway running alongside it. He shoved me hard against a brick wall on the far side. I took the shock with a shoulder, but stayed limp as I turned back to him, my head hanging like a rag doll's.

"Look at me, asshole," he said.

I lifted my head slowly. He braced me against the wall with his left hand, made a fist at his side with his right.

"What the hell was that about Internal Affairs?"

"Tried to tell you, pal," I smiled. "When you pulled me over, 'member?"

"Tell me now, you fuckin' nig–"

He was totally unprepared for what hit him. I didn't break his left arm, but there had to be nerve damage. I didn't rupture his Adam's apple, but it might be permanently out of alignment. I didn't put him through the brick wall but I used it to raise a knot on the back of his skull that could last a lifetime. I was pretty sure I did break a kneecap before he hit the pavement.

His left hand twitched at his side, he clawed at his throat with his right, gasping for air.

"Suck it up, big guy," I said as I sat on my haunches in front of him. He groaned in pain.

"I know," I said. "You hear me? I know."

He coughed up blood.

"You and your partner. You picked up the suspect on Sepulveda, and dumped him in Bel Air. You gave him that machete, got him worked up and used him for personal target practice. Then you let Rankin pin a medal on your chest."

I thumped his sternum hard with the back of my fist.

"Tell your buddy Wilkes the two of you are going down. Tell Rankin he's going with you."

I left him lying there like a fish on a landing fighting for air. I didn't feel at all bad about it. I felt good. I'd have felt better if it were Rankin, himself, but that ball was now in play. When his boy was able to talk, Rankin would get my message and he'd come for me.

CHAPTER FIFTY-NINE

"So how does a Southern Belle wind up in tinsel town?"

"Blame Cinderella."

"How's that?"

"When you're working in a dime store in Belzone, Mississippi, her fantasy looks pretty good."

"Prince Charming?"

Kamala Highland smiled. "Handsome, rich, famous? Who cares about the foot fetish?"

I'd grabbed a quick shower, splashed on some Polo and put on my gray hobnail suit for the audience I was being granted with the self-proclaimed First Lady of Film, ostensibly to prepare my eulogy for a memorial service which I said I hoped she'd grace with her presence and a few remarks of her own about Leah.

We had the remains of vodka gimlets in hand and were strolling a rose garden I'd inquired about. I'd inquired because it was a good two acres from the nearest turret and was laid out around a large fountain that splashed water down into a Koi pond. Out of earshot, I calculated, from the eruption I anticipated.

"You came to L.A. to bag a movie star?"

"Then I found the confidence to believe I had something to offer besides a full figure."

She offered a self-effacing smile, but true to form, she was pushing her best features in a low-cut, blue silk cocktail dress that defied you to look anywhere but at the full breasts bared to the nipples.

"Intelligence?" I asked, playing into the hand she'd dealt me.

"An ability to set a goal and attain it."

I set my empty glass down on the rim of the fountain. "So, your first goal was to skip the education and the work ladder, come here and hook up with a celebrity."

"First thought," she corrected. "I waited till I got the education."

"Yeah?" I said in anticipation of her first lie.

"University of Mississippi. I loved it there. Sometimes I think I should have stayed for my Master's."

There it was. Not damning evidence, but an indication of character and, if your name were George O'Leary, enough to get you fired as a head football coach at Notre Dame.

"Theater Arts?"

She looked at me with a vaguely suspicious smile.

"I thought we were going to talk about Leah."

"I'm fascinated," I said. "So, at Ole Miss? You were a cheerleader, too?"

"How did you know that?"

"I'm a detective, remember?"

She smiled. "I guess I mentioned that to Leah."

"Actually, someone else told me."

"Really? Who was that?"

She looked up beneath blue eye shadow, seeming pleased.

"Flora Richards."

"You know Flora?" she asked, feigning nonchalance.

"Long time," I said. "Had lunch with her just the other day."

"How is she?"

"Still waiting for you to return her call."

Sarcasm stained what remained of her smile. The tall fountain stood between us and the mansion where other guests were arriving for a private screening.

"My name just happened to come up?"

"So did James Cochran's."

Her eyes flashed a warning.

"I had a meal with your daughter, too," I said. "Karen Miller. She has your eyes, I think. So does your grandson."

"You fucking sonofabitch."

"Neither one has your mouth."

Her right hand struck like a cobra. It found my left waiting in front of my face and clamped around her wrist. Her eyes turned venomous.

"Get out of here," she said.

"Or you'll call the cops? Call Curtis Rankin, maybe?"

I forced her hand down and released it. She glared.

"You had a shadow on me as soon as Rankin told you who I was and what I might be doing. Why?"

"You're a small-time private investigator," she said. "I don't have to tell you anything."

"You're right," I said. "I'm a one-man band, and this is private. We can keep it that way, or I can take everything I know to the DA's office. Then they'll ask the questions, and your answers are a public record."

"Are you threatening me?"

"You threatened Jeremy Thomas. Leah heard you. The DA hears that, he might hear motive."

"Motive for what? Murder? That's insane."

She was good. So good she might even have herself convinced she was innocent.

"I had you followed because I thought if you investigated Chad Kennedy's background, there was a chance you'd come across things in mine that I'm not proud of."

"Not because you thought Leah might tell me about the argument you had with Thomas?"

That was the truth, of course. But it didn't figure truth was her long suit.

"Leah didn't know everything," she said. "She didn't know what really happened."

"Thomas told it to your daughter the same way Leah told it to me. He didn't make it up."

"He didn't know, either. I did threaten him, yes. I was desperate."

I'd spent the last decade talking with liars and cheats. She was right up there with the best of them. She knew I had a good idea of what had actually gone down, knew she had to make her story stick close to the facts, but twist it just enough to leave room for some doubt while she worked at convincing me she was a victim, not a perpetrator.

"For money," I said.

"Yes."

"To repay money you borrowed from Phil Adams."

"My last two pictures didn't do well, my TV company wasn't doing any better, I'd built this place. I couldn't lose it all."

"Because you'd lose your place in the pantheon?"

She looked at me as if I were an acolyte who didn't know the rituals.

"You think I'm shallow, don't you?" she said. "Selfish. That I'm getting what I deserve for the times I've mistreated people like Flora Richards or the child I never wanted. What about all the men who've been walking away from babies for centuries? A man who does the things I've done is CEO material, but I'm a slut?"

Her eyes were charged with hostility, but it wasn't so much directed at me as the gender I represented. Her voice deepened, her speech became more deliberate.

"You don't know me," she said. "You have to know that you and I share some things in our background, but you don't know the chubby little kid whose granny pulled her out of her own drunken daddy's bed, who grew up on welfare in that old woman's two-room shanty, grew up begging for the chance to prove the white part of her was as white as any other girl in town but found out the black part of her was all people ever saw. You must have gotten some of those same looks I did, same attitudes, but you don't know what it's like being the girl who got jumped too many times by redneck teenage boys, the girl who bent a rusty pipe over one of their heads and got sent to a youth detention facility to learn a lesson."

She was better than good. I'd expected a play for sympathy to what she figured had to be an empathetic ear, but that usually comes with phony tears. This was coming from a woman who knew how the best actors work. She was genuinely consumed with a loathing formed from ugly scars that had never healed and a kind of righteous zeal determined to keep that loathing from turning inward upon herself, and she was using it.

"That's some of what makes this 'Southern Belle' tick," she said. "Am I proud of coming so far with nothing but my own smarts, my own will? You're damn right I am. Do I wake up some nights in a cold sweat dreaming I'm back in that shanty? You bet your fucking ass I do."

The line was drawn. The residual anger in her eyes was a mute challenge to step across it with any further criticism.

CHAPTER SIXTY

"Tough is good," I said.

"Poor isn't," she said. "Poor and black is worse."

"And a woman to boot."

"I can see I've touched your heart."

"Is it anything I can identify with? Some. Is it the saddest story I've ever heard? Maybe, standing in the shadow of the palace you built for yourself."

"Highland's folly," she said, mocking herself as she looked at the imposing structure reflecting the last rays of sunlight off its myriad of windows.

"So, keeping up appearances being all-important, when a mogul can't pay her bills, she uses her TV library as collateral for a loan," I said. "When that loan can't be covered, she panics because if she loses the library, she loses everything. That's when you went to Adams."

"I just needed one more shot," she said, softening now, letting me see her *vulnerability*, her *innocence*. I almost wanted to applaud.

"You paid what? Five percent a week plus payment on principal? That's the going rate on gambling debts, isn't it?"

"You make me sound like an idiot."

"Just like every other addict."

"It wasn't drugs."

"Power. A lot more expensive habit."

She turned away.

"So Adams bailed you out," I said, softening to let her see that her charade was working, that I did understand the racism she'd faced, I did understand how she would be desperate, how her actions could be reasonable. "Then you couldn't pay him and he sent Duke Catalano around to talk to you. It didn't matter, you still couldn't cover the note, so you got another visit. From Martin Mishkin."

She turned back. The tears were finally there. She let me look into them, then dropped her head and nodded.

No Oscar for Meryl Streep this year. But I reacted as I knew all good actors do, going with what I'd just been given, as if seeing her in a new light.

"Then he takes control of all the assets and all the future income. You get a salary, he gets a beachhead in the entertainment industry and another way to launder money from the rackets and gambling he makes through the mob."

"It was a nightmare," she said.

"Adams set up your studio deal?" I asked, as if it were a new thought.

"Yes." She smirked. "One of the upstanding family men on the twelfth floor is addicted to his call girls."

"So, Adams doesn't even have to pay you, the studio does."

"He's never out of pocket a single dime," she said. "None of them play with their own money."

She sat on the ledge of the pond. I tried not to look down the front of her dress.

"Who hooked you up with Jeremy Thomas?"

She stared into the water. I was waiting for a John Williams score to rip my heart out.

"I knew the only way I could ever recover was a huge commercial hit," she said. "He was like a guarantee. His bungalow was next to mine on the lot. I was shameless."

"You were lovers?"

"Leah walked in on us one night," she said, and looked up at me. No mere embroidering this time. It was a lie calculated to coincide with what she assumed Leah might have told me.

"I imagine you know about that."

"Yeah."

But I suddenly wondered why Collingswood hadn't tipped her to our talk, and then I realized I could be wrong. Maybe she wasn't lying. Thomas wasn't working that night, but he could have been having sex. Collingswood might have said anything to get me off his back.

"We never talked about it, any of us," she said. "I think Jeremy and I both always had a soft spot in our hearts for her after that."

Was it her performance, or was I wrong? As I tried to gauge her credibility, she appeared to be gauging mine.

"I'd like to trust you, Michael," she said.

"With what?"

She hesitated, stared down at the golden fish swimming among the lily pads as she deliberated. I waited.

"I know who killed Jeremy," she said. "And why."

CHAPTER SIXTY-ONE

I rolled by the line of limos at the curb in front of *Spago* Beverly Hills and pulled into a public lot up the block. I took a pair of cuffs from the glove box, put them in a pocket, and started for the restaurant. There was a fundraiser for prostate cancer in progress being hosted by Phil Adams, and since I'd tagged all the other bases, I thought he and I should be formally introduced before his hired help tried to fit me with the Sicilian necktie Duke Catalano had mentioned.

Music was playing on the open patio and voices filtered onto the street to blend with the sound of evening traffic. I entered to a crowded bar and a young man in a double-breasted olive-green suit, purple shirt and burnished-orange tie standing at a lectern.

"Good evening, sir," he lifted his voice over the din. "May I help you?"

The extensive space behind him was teeming with tan men in expensive casual clothing and tan women in baroque babewear.

"Security for Mr. Adams," I said, giving him a look at my ID. "One of the other guys just called in sick, a brother. I don't remember his name, but he looks like that British heavyweight champ retired a few years back. You know where I can find him?"

"Yes, sir. He's with Mr. Adams. The room at the back across the patio. I can show you."

"I know where it is," I said. "Thanks."

I moved along the bar, being checked out by half the people pressed around it who weren't as interested in talking to the other half as they were in spotting someone they wanted to spot them. When I didn't compute as a career-booster, their eyes flicked elsewhere while their conversations continued without dropping a syllable. I had to smile. I was still batting a thousand.

I turned to the right at the end of the bar into an open pathway between the cloth-covered tables and mahogany chairs in the street-side patio and those in the big, open dining room. At the far end of the room, big glass doors and windows ran behind a bank of booths separating the diners from the kitchen. The preparation of food was in plain view, just like the old *Spago* Hollywood and *Al's Diner* in Eagle Rock.

Weaving my way through the crisscrossing table-hoppers and the bustling purple-shirted waitstaff, I caught whiffs of heavenly aromas from the passing trays. Then I caught a glimpse of a black heavyweight in a flower-patterned silk shirt and a lightweight suit. He was just to the left of a pair of doors off the semi-open hallway leading to the kitchen pantry and the restrooms at the back of the building. He did look like Lennox Lewis, with his bulging arms folded across his chest as he leaned against the wall, his eyes on a waitress with a bustline that draped her orange tie at an arresting angle.

I stepped behind a piece of wall, waited for traffic to clear the corridor, then doubled over slightly, left hand flattened over my stomach, right fist clenched at my mouth, and backed around the dividing wall toward where the big bodyguard was standing.

"Restrooms?" I coughed weakly.

Worried that I might lose whatever I'd had too much of all over his highly polished shoes, he nodded toward the rear of the building.

"Yeah," he said. "Down the hall and to the ri—"

My fist drove straight up into his light switch. The blackout was simultaneous with the crack of jawbone. I caught him as he bounced off the wall, grabbing one of his arms and ducking under it to take his weight on my neck and shoulders as I wrapped my other arm around his waist to grab his belt and propel him toward the men's room. Two guys pulled the door open and exited as I lugged my load past them.

"Great party, man." I grinned.

They glanced at me and my black pal like we were dirt and the door closed behind us. There was no one at the two urinals or in the first two stalls. I dragged two-hundred-plus pounds of dead weight across the tiles to the handicapped stall at the far end of the room, pushed the door open, and unloaded him next to the toilet. I pulled the cuffs out of my pocket, slapped one on a thick wrist and the other onto the pipe behind the toilet. Then I removed a 9 mm Beretta from his shoulder holster, put it in my jacket pocket, locked the stall door from the inside, and slid out under it. I checked the mirror in passing, dusted myself off, smoothed my hair, and stepped back into the hallway outside.

A busboy hustled past, headed for the pantry. He was the only person in the corridor as I stepped to the unguarded doors, opened one, and entered a small room with one large circular table. Another busboy was clearing the last dishes from the table, five women were still seated in conversation, seven men were standing, wine glasses in hand. The one nearest the door was Duke Catalano.

I eased up behind him, planted a friendly hand on his shoulder and pressed the barrel of the Beretta hard enough into a kidney that he knew precisely what it was.

"Duke," I said. "I need to see you and Mr. Adams alone."

Catalano's eyes fixed on me. I pressed the gun harder.

"Excuse me, folks," he smiled as he interrupted the conversations. "Excuse me. Something just came up. I wonder if you'd mind stepping into the other room."

Glances were exchanged, eyes fell on me.

"I'm very sorry," I said. "There's been a major donation with certain contingencies that I have to discuss with Mr. Adams. It won't take long. The bar in the room at the front of this corridor is open."

The men and women nodded pleasantries and *adieus* as they exited. Phil Adams stood calmly, his eyes never leaving me. When he saw the gun, it didn't seem to surprise him any more than the interruption had. I patted Catalano down and lifted a .32 automatic from a belt clip, slipped it into my coat pocket.

"Sit down, gentlemen," I said. "Hands on the table."

Chapter Sixty-Two

"You just made the biggest mistake of your life." Catalano sat, shoving his wine glass off to one side.

Adams sat without comment, resting his hands to either side of the glass he placed directly in front of him. I pulled out the chair across from him, keeping Catalano between us and both of their backs visible in one of the two large mirrors on the wall to the right of the door.

"My name's Drayton, Mister Adams," I said, resting my gun hand in my lap. "I won't take much of your time."

"How the fuck did you get in here?" Catalano growled.

"You're a business man," I said to Adams, ignoring the question. "I've got a proposal for you. A fifty-million-dollar deal."

Catalano started to respond, Adams silenced him with a gesture, his eyes fixed on mine. He remained relaxed.

"Would you like some wine, Mister Drayton?" he said.

"No, thanks," I said.

"Do you mind if I refill my glass?"

"Not at all. But so you know, this gun I took off Duke's watchdog is a nine. They make a terrible mess."

Catalano's eyes narrowed. Adams' flickered with amusement as he reached easily for a bottle of red sitting to his left, picked it up and poured into his glass. One of the doors to the corridor opened, and the young man in the green suit looked in at the three of us.

"Is there a problem, Mister Adams?" he asked.

Adams shook his head, smiled easily. "We just need a few minutes of privacy," he said.

"Of course, sir," the young man said. "I'll make certain you're not disturbed."

Adams smiled a dismissal, and the young man stepped out, closing the door behind him.

"You have my undivided attention," Adams said as he focused enigmatic hazel eyes on me. He was wearing another Kiton, a deep gray with a crisp white shirt and a black silk tie with small white dots. "That number again?"

"Fifty million," I said. "The death benefit on the life insurance policy payable to the corporation Jeremy Thomas formed with Kamala Highland."

Adams stared straight into my eyes, acknowledging nothing, sipping wine as he waited for the next card. I played it face up.

"I know you own her, so you own that policy."

Catalano's eyes narrowed. Adams put his glass down, sat perfectly still.

"There's one little hitch, though," I said. "The law says you can't benefit from a person's death if you caused that death."

"Excuse me," Adams said politely. "Are you implying that I had something to do with what happened to Jeremy Thomas?"

"I'm not into implications," I said. "What you get from me is what I know and I can prove."

"You're going to accuse me of murder?"

"No."

I looked straight at Duke Catalano.

"Me?" he said, an icy smile turning the question into a challenge.

I returned the smile. Long enough to make his falter. Then I spoke to Adams.

"You may or may not know that Duke here laid twenty K on me to give up an investigation I was conducting for the father of the other victim in that murder," I said. "You may or may not know that I returned that money to your attorney. I didn't want it. I didn't earn it. And I didn't like the threat that came with it."

Adams' eyes registered a faint glimmer of interest.

"Go on," he said, lifting his glass to drink again.

I had Catalano's interest, too. He was looking at me like a starving aborigine eyes a wombat roasting on a spit.

"I just left Kamala Highland," I said. "She says you had Thomas killed, and my client's son just got in the way."

The shadow of a smile slid across Adams' lips.

"You have an oddly cheerful disposition, Mister Drayton," he said.

"It's a nasty business," I said. "Levity is a little like the proverbial spoon full of sugar."

"Interesting," he said. The smile faded. He sipped his wine, looked across the glass. "Miss Highland's alleged accusation. Tell me more."

"Let's put 'alleged' to rest," I said. "First, I only knew to come here tonight because she told me this shindig is the reason you declined her invitation to a private screening at her home. Second, what do I gain from making it up? Turning you against her? I don't think you're with her. The records I dug up show a lien on that castle of hers and all her assets. The lien is held by a corporation in the Cayman Islands. The corporation in the Caymans is owned by a Swiss corporation owned by a corporation in the Dutch Antilles. I didn't get any further than that, but I didn't have to. I saw Marty Mishkin's fingerprints all over it. And it's his name on the corporation with Kamala Highland that started making sense out of all of this for me."

Catalano reached for his wine glass.

"Later," I said sharply.

He glared, but flattened his hand on the table.

"Have you considered the reasons Miss Highland may have told you what she did?" Adams said.

"Sure," I said. "If it's true, she may see me as a slim chance of getting out from under your thumb. If it's a lie, she may think I'm dumb enough to buy it and get myself killed trying to go after you. That way, she might not be rid of you, but she gets rid of me."

"Why should that be a concern to her?"

"Because she killed Jeremy Thomas."

His lips parted in a faintly mocking smile. "You know that and you can prove it?" he said.

"I know it and I will prove it," I said.

Chapter Sixty-three

"What makes you so sure of everything, you fuck?" Catalano said. "From where I sit, you look like road kill about to happen."

"You're an impressive guy, Duke," I said. "Until you open your mouth."

He kept his eyes on me, but he spoke to Adams. "Tell this clown to fuck off and let me have him."

"Relax," Adams said. "We haven't heard his proposal."

"It's simple," I said. "You cash in the policy, I get Rankin."

"Who?"

"Don't give me 'who?' I'm dealing off the top. You do the same and we both get what we want. Get clever, I make your life miserable."

"Tell him," Catalano implored again.

"He's got a lawyer for advice, Duke," I said. "Your job is keeping guys like me from getting to him in the first place."

"Fuck you," Catalano said.

I dismissed him with a smile guaranteed to pump up his blood pressure and turned back to Adams.

"I don't know you, Mister Adams. But I know Curtis Rankin. He's corrupt to the core. He's slick enough to hide that corruption from people he works for and charismatic enough to gain the trust of people who can't see through him. That makes him public enemy number one in my book."

"I gather you have a history with Captain Rankin," Adams said. "Are you looking for some kind of revenge?"

"I'm looking to expose him for the racist, self-aggrandizing disgrace he is to a department that has the toughest job in this city."

"So how do I give him to you?"

"When I drop him, let him sink. You'll find another stooge, the world is full of them."

"You fascinate me, Mister Drayton." Adams lifted his glass from the table. "You say you don't make implications, yet you've just implied I'm every bit as corrupt as you say Curtis Rankin is."

"You are," I said as Adams sipped his wine. "Trading favors with power players, buying beat cops and city councils, building networks to Sacramento and D.C., that's how you got to be top dog. You're so connected, a guy like me could never bring you down. But I can pull the curtain back, give people a look at the machinery you control."

"And how do you do that?"

I took a microcassette recorder from my inside pocket and put it on the table between Adams and me.

"If you don't give me Rankin, the original of this is addressed to the DA and will be delivered."

I flicked on the playback. It was cued up to Kamala Highland's voice saying, *"It was Phil Adams. He didn't want Jeremy to pull out of our deal. He wanted that company to wash his money, to have a major stake in the film business without buying a studio. He had Jeremy killed, and then he had Curtis Rankin frame that poor man so there wouldn't be any investigation and he could collect the fifty million dollars."*

I turned off the recorder.

"That's just an unfounded accusation," Adams said, holding his glass in hand.

"That's the next six months on network and cable," I said. "Talking heads talking about you. That's a *TIME* magazine cover, a *Sixty Minutes* special, a worldwide audience on *YouTube*. You're already rich, but that can make you famous."

Adams didn't look rattled, didn't look at the recorder. Catalano did both.

"How do we know you're not wired right now?" Catalano asked.

"You're definitely not overqualified for your calling, Duke," I said, and looked back to Adams. "Our discussion wouldn't interest anybody else. I won't say anything I don't want on record and you won't say anything that gets you indicted." I nodded to the recorder. "That tape is for you or the DA. It buys me Rankin, or it buys me nothing."

"It could buy you a funeral," Catalano said.

"Tell me about Rankin," Adams said.

"I know he framed a homeless person for the murders," I said, "and had him shot to death so he could close the case."

"You can prove that?" Catalano said.

"Even to you, Duke," I said. "I imagine you're exempt from jury duty, though, aren't you?"

Both of his hands balled into fists. But they kept contact with the table. Adams set his glass squarely in front of him again.

"So what do you need from me?"

"I need to know Rankin gets no support from you."

"What makes you so sure I'd help him?" he asked, his fingers slowly twisting the stem of his glass, its base rotating in a perfect circle.

"Because he helped you."

"How?"

"Shutting down the case before your part in it was disclosed."

"I believe this entire conversation is predicated upon the supposition that I had no part in what happened to Jeremy Thomas," Adams said.

"Of course," I said.

He stopped spinning his glass, studied me long and hard. Catalano sat quietly like an attack dog waiting to be unleashed.

"She's a cunt," Adams said as his eyes found the recorder, and he picked it up. "I help her out, she tries to stiff me. She's into me so deep, I have to help her again. I lean on somebody to get her a rich deal, I mean a deal like nobody gets, and she fucks that up, too. Sucking it up her nose, blowing it on that ludicrous fucking monstrosity she built to play queen of the world. Christ, what a cunt."

He set the recorder down hard.

"Then she goes completely fucking nuts, kills the goose that lays the golden egg, and comes crawling back again when Rankin tells her who you are and what you're doing."

"That's when you sent Duke to make nice?"

"That was Marty. He ran a make, said you'd jump at twenty K cold."

"You knew what Rankin was doing?"

"I just told him to shut it down. I don't tell people how they should do their job."

"You don't care."

"Only that it gets done."

"It did."

"And here we are," he said with his eyes locked on mine.

"Where is that, exactly?" I said.

"You don't make waves for me, I don't throw Rankin a life raft."

"There's one other thing."

"You pushy fuck," Catalano growled. I kept my eyes riveted on Adams.

"Something I think I know, but I have to be sure about," I said.

"What's that?" Adams said.

"I never figured you for the murders. There was nothing about it that said hit. The two vics knew the killer, the perp was all about rage. But the car that got run off the canyon, that came after I figure you'd stepped in to take over damage control. After you told Rankin to zip it up."

"Right," he said.

"The lady was a friend of mine. A close friend."

"I don't know anything about that," Adams said.

I looked at Catalano.

"You knew," I said. "And you knew she might know something about Kamala Highland that could blow everything out of the water. Something she might tell me."

"I didn't figure you to show up again," Catalano said.

"You didn't run her off the road?"

"Fuck, no."

"You didn't have it done?"

"You heard me."

"You hear me," I said. "If I find out it was you, all bets are off. If it means death row for me, I don't care, I'll take you out. *Capisce*?"

"It was the cunt," Adams said. "Stupid. The whole damn thing was stupid."

"She drove the car?" I said.

"The stuntman," Catalano said. "That Looney Tunes went with her and killed those two kids. Both tanked up on cocaine, fucking up everything."

"Collingswood?"

"Who?"

"The Brit," I said. "Doubled Jeremy Thomas on the picture."

"Nah, not him," Catalano said. "The one who sounds like a fucking chipmunk."

Chapter Sixty-four

    I sat in the parking lot, feeling shaken. It wasn't Collingswood Leah had seen with Kamala Highland, it was Frankie Tate. How did I look past him? I'd noted his initial defensiveness when I went to see him, his attitude about Ken Chernak, the axe to grind with Jeremy Thomas. I'd been so focused on the unholy trio that I'd scratched him off my short list. But it all fit. Frankie had always wanted what Jeremy Thomas had gotten, and he was always jealous of anybody he couldn't beat at something. Jealous of me, jealous as hell of my father. Jealousy is a garden-variety motive for murder. Or maybe he did it for hire, a different kind of contract, one that guaranteed his name above title.

    I thought about how long I'd known him. He'd broken into stunts working for my father, chafing under his demands the same way I had, feeling the sting of his blunt criticism, the frustration of never hearing a word of praise for even your best work, and the emasculating effect of bowing to the force of his will in any disagreement the way everyone ultimately did. Frankie and I had worked a lot together, depending on each other to find safe solutions for demanding gags, to rig explosives, fall horses and crash cars. He was working with my father the day he died. A former paratrooper, he'd grown up on a cattle ranch in Oklahoma, and he'd hit it off as well as anyone ever had with Jack Drayton the first time they met, Frankie in seeming awe of a legendary figure, my father aware of Frankie's willingness to tackle any challenge without fear.

He'd made a conscious choice to live on the edge a long time ago. And he'd made a good living. His ranch in Lancaster was a hundred and forty acres of land that was worth ten times what he paid for it. He'd turned it into a pretty good business venture, too, running a training school for would-be stuntmen and women with five thousand dollars to spend on various five-week courses. It was an isolated compound on the edge of the Mojave desert, run like a boot camp, set up to cover everything from handling cars, trucks, and bikes on a figure-eight track, to setting up jumps and falls from jagged rocks and ten-story scaffoldings; from working in an underwater tank to rigging fire and explosives. Gags, as professionals call the stunts they perform, keep getting bigger and better in order to keep up with a never-ending demand for testosterone flicks designed for the male teenage mentality and the males who never get beyond the teenage mentality.

My energy was flagging. I remembered I hadn't eaten since the hotdog I grabbed after I braced Ted Wilkes out in Van Nuys a little past noon. I'd promised Wilkes I wouldn't blow his identity and Falcon was sure his boss, Jim Roselli, would cut a deal to keep him from doing any time, but when all the cards were face up on the table, IAD would be another story. Section 805 of the LAPD manual defines four categories of police misconduct, and Wilkes had been coerced into violating all of them. Internal Affairs would want his ass in a sling. Personally, I thought they should plaster his chest with MSMs. If anybody earned a medal for meritorious service, how could it not be a cop willing to risk his future and even his life to see that the right thing gets done?

I heard my stomach growl. Seafood sounded good and *Hymie's Fish Market* was open till ten. I could just make it. I pulled out of the lot, drove past the limos, and turned left onto Wilshire. Then a black-and-white showed up in the rearview mirror, putting my heart in my mouth and making me forget about my stomach.

I turned right on Doheny and headed south on the narrow street lined with parked cars toward Pico. The cruiser turned with me and maintained about a four-car-length distance. I braked to a stop as a light changed to yellow. The cruiser changed lanes behind me and pulled alongside. I looked over. It was a dog and cat team, the man driving, the woman sitting by the window next to mine, blonde hair pulled back in a ponytail. She felt my eyes on her, glanced my way. I smiled. She returned it.

The man at the wheel saw our exchange, looked past the woman and nodded. He was Latino, had a strong face and a neatly trimmed mustache. I knew the makeup of the force was different now, that it was more inclusive, more diversified. The new Chief had made it a priority to root out any sign of racism, but Rankin was still there, and he still had cubs like Lavin in his den. I knew they all wore the same uniform and they could come in all genders. Knowing I'd summoned them, whoever they were, made me anxious about the whole department.

I acknowledged the driver and turned back toward the signal. I didn't like the place I was in, didn't like not trusting the most courageous people in the city, but I'd put myself squarely there. If I was a threat to Curtis Rankin, I was a threat to those who were loyal to him. And I was more than a threat, I was his worst nightmare, a guy who knew he was as racist as any KKK Grand Dragon to ever hide his face under a hood. If I could link him to the assassination of Willie Gates, all Curtis Rankin's dreams would go up in smoke.

He would know by now what I'd done to his poster boy. He would also know I hadn't brought in the evidence I said I had, and he would have to come at me before I did. I wished he'd come himself, but I knew he wouldn't. It would be people like the couple in the cruiser beside me.

CHAPTER SIXTY-FIVE

I glanced back at the woman. She was talking casually with her partner as the light changed, and I eased into the pedal. Halfway down the next block, a car pulled away from the curb in front of me and I slowed as the cruiser continued on, followed by two other cars. I signaled and changed lanes again, fell in behind the cars and kept an eye on the cruiser.

I checked my watch. Ten of ten. The kitchen was still open at Hymie's and I was still in the mood for the freshest fish in town, so I hung a right on Pico and watched the cruiser continue south. Hymie's was only a couple of short blocks west, and I could see the red awning running the length of the restaurant. Bold white letters proclaimed the place to be *Beverly Hills Surf & Soulfood Bar & Grill.* I'd forgotten they'd changed the name. The awning was pretty, but it was the only cosmetic change to the old nondescript building with peeling stucco and flaking paint. I hoped it was still just as flakey inside and the market was still there smelling like a fish market should. I turned left just past the entrance, then left into the alleyway between two old stucco-and-tile single-story apartments and the rundown commercial buildings on the boulevard.

I pulled into the lot behind the restaurant, gave the car to the valet, and started for the rear entrance, passing a dumpster filled with bricks and concrete from demolition of some kind beside the cement steps. I entered through the screen door beneath a small red awning and walked down the dingy narrow hallway toward the front of the building. Carlos Diaz was stacking menus at a counter beside the fish market that still smelled of fresh fish and made me hungrier and happier.

"*Señor Miguel*," he said.

"Still open?" I asked.

"For you, always," he said. "Until ten o'clock."

The tall, reed-thin host winked, and led me toward the bar in the back room.

"So, how do you like the facelift?"

"I hope it's only skin deep," I said.

"Two sides to the menu now. Southern style chicken, pork, and Texas barbecue on the right, fish on the left."

"I'll stick to the left. How's the swordfish?"

"You want the halibut."

"I'll have the halibut."

"Good choice," he said, and gestured to the empty tables scattered among a few couples lingering over after-dinner drinks. "Take your pick."

"Right here's fine," I nodded to the empty bar, and stepped to it.

"Stoli and tonic, Augie," I said.

"Good night for it," the chunky Chicano behind the bar smiled as he went to work.

One of the couples exited past me as I sat down facing the TV set over the bar.

The Dodgers had a rally going in the bottom of the ninth. I sipped my drink and thought about the day ahead of me. It could be a long one.

Gonzalez doubled in Kendrick and Turner and the crowd went wild as the Dodgers hung one on the Diamondbacks four to three. It made me remember warm summer nights at the Academy in Elysian Park. Doing pushups after a two-mile run, royal blue sweats soaked through, and hearing the roar from the canyon at Chavez Ravine. It made you feel proud to be a part of the city, proud to know some day you'd be wearing its badge. *"I recognize the badge of my office as a symbol of public faith and I accept it as a public trust to be held so long as I am true to the ethics of police service."* The words were burned into my brain. I wondered if Curtis Rankin still remembered them, if they were ever more than just words to him. I knew they hadn't been for a long time.

The halibut was primo as advertised, the second Stoli-tonic made me less cranky.

I was out the door by ten-forty. The parking lot was dark, the only light from the naked bulb directly over the door. The attendant was nowhere to be seen. I saw my car parked in the first stall off the alley and started toward it when I heard a snick that sent a chill through my blood. I dove behind the dumpster by the door as a burst from an automatic weapon stitched 9 mm slugs into the brick wall and chewed into the dumpster.

I pulled my Sig from under my left arm, the H&K from under the right, and stayed tight to the concrete-and-brick-fortified dumpster as the machine gun spent a full clip ripping into the steel bin and the closest car, sending glass flying around me like sleet.

Whoever it was, they weren't SWAT trained. No accurate two-shot bursts on full auto, just somebody freezing a finger and blasting away blindly behind the kick of the high-powered automatic.

I could see the flashes from a car in the alley. I could also see that I was in light and the shooter was in shadow. I fired a round from the Sig at the bulb over Hymie's door and dove quickly for the back of the closest car in the sudden darkness that swallowed me. The sound from the machine gun baffled by hardscape and metal cars was deafening. When the gun stopped burping, I squeezed off four rounds with the Sig, blowing glass in on the shooter and the driver. I heard a scream and broke for the cover of the next car in the lot, firing the .40 as I ran.

Another weapon roared, a twelve-gauge multi-round semi-automatic street-sweeper. It came from between two parked cars in the adjacent lot. I rolled behind the car as front and rear windows exploded. I came out on the other side, squeezed off a half-dozen shots with the Sig toward where I had seen the shotgun blasts. I heard another shout and the twelve-gauge fell silent as the machine gun opened up again.

I hit the ground and belly-crawled fast on my elbows behind the parked cars as bullets shredded metal and ricocheted off brick. I came up off the ass end of a Mercedes and opened up on the car with both guns. The shooter cried out in pain and the machine gun hit the pavement as the driver hit the gas. I emptied the Sig through the rear window and the car veered left, plowed into the wooden garage door of an apartment building and came to a dead stop.

Another car in the adjacent lot roared out of the darkness. I emptied the .40 into it. It didn't slow, but it didn't turn, either, and slammed into the first car.

The noise stopped, but I couldn't tell. All I could hear was my heart pounding. I re-clipped both guns and stayed low behind the Mercedes, tried to spit the taste of copper from my mouth. Nothing moved until I saw the screen door open at Hymie's. I leveled both guns on it and saw two figures silhouetted by the light at the far end of the corridor behind them, one tall and slender, the other short and stocky.

"Augie, Carlos—Get back!" I shouted, and both figures retreated quickly. I strained to hear what I could beyond the ringing in my ears, and retraced my steps to come out from behind the cars near where I had first taken shelter. Then I worked my way over to where the twelve-gauge street-sweeper had opened up. The air was heavy with smoke and the suffocating smell of potassium nitrate, charcoal, and sulfur. The shooter was dead on the ground, face down, three holes the size of baseballs in his back, the shotgun impotent on the pot-holed asphalt. I kicked it away from the dead man anyway and made my way cautiously toward the two cars.

The driver of the car from the adjacent lot had .40 caliber holes through his chest, his throat and his head. The two men inside the first car were riddled with nines.

I heard sirens coming, but I couldn't tell how close they were. I went to my car, opened the door to the strong smell of urine and found the valet bound and gagged in the back seat.

"It's okay," I said. "All over."

All over for Rankin, too.

CHAPTER SIXTY-SIX

The harsh light of a Xenon beam shined down from a hovering police chopper. Two local TV whirlybirds nearby, a voice on a bullhorn barked a command, a siren climbed somewhere in the distance. Yards of yellow crime-scene tape sealed off the alley and the parking lot, a coroner's team was on site, and the place was crawling with uniforms and plainclothes detectives.

Eddie Falcon had come as soon as I called. He'd brought in a team of his own investigators to eyeball the way things were being handled.

"Drayton?"

I saw his mouth move as he came back to where I was standing with Augie Ortiz, Carlos Diaz, the parking lot attendant, Bennie Corona, and two uniforms. He had three men in tow, a slender Oriental in a gray meat-and-potatoes suit, and two blue-suited, repp-tied men who might as well have been wearing nametags that said FBI.

I stepped away from the three witnesses and the two cops, glanced up at the thumping chopper.

"Sorry," I said. "Ears are still blown out."

"Let's go inside," Falcon shouted, pointing to the door where a uniform was posted.

Falcon led the way, opened the door, and entered the restaurant. I followed along with the three suits as the patrolman closed the door behind us. We walked down the long corridor to the empty dining room.

"Better?" Falcon projected.

"Thanks," I said.

"Benjamin Yee, Justice Department," the thin guy in the gray suit said. "Federal agents Cassidy and Shollin."

I took the hand Yee offered, returned nods from the two Feebs.

"I told them you'd been feeding me information they're going to want to hear," Falcon said as I strained to listen, studying his eyes for any clue as to how I was supposed to play things. "I've already told my boss," he said. "He made the calls."

I nodded.

"You think this attack was related to what you've been investigating?" Yee asked.

"I hope nobody buys a drive-by shooting," I said.

"Those were street gang weapons of choice," Cassidy said.

"Secure Property Room is bulging at the seams with confiscated weapons," I said. "These just weren't going to get the full deep-sea burial till after tonight."

"You think it was cops?" Shollin asked.

"I think they have badges that say they're cops," I said.

"Tied to Captain Rankin?"

"Tight."

"You're pretty cool for a guy who just killed four men," Cassidy said.

"How about that," I said.

"Are you aware of the civil rights investigation we've been conducting, Mr. Drayton?" Yee said.

"No." I looked to Falcon, got nothing.

"Suspicion that officers have been involved in beatings, unjustified shootings, false arrests, evidence planting," Yee said. "Similar to allegations I believe you made some time ago."

"You knew about it?" I asked Falcon.

"Our office has been involved," he said in characteristic, noncommittal fashion.

"There might have been an easier way to go about this," I said for his benefit.

"One of our members headed the Police Commission when you were on the force and initiated the charges against Captain Rankin that were dismissed," Yee said. "Over time, we've received similar excessive force complaints that weren't substantiated."

"Current Chief's changed the mind-set about policing minority communities," Cassidy said. "But he's been concerned there was still a pocket of prejudice. Justice asked for help from the Bureau. The Director put Shollin and me on it."

"Ferguson. Baltimore. New York. Protests from Boston to Denver. They told us a lot about racial bias going under the radar," Shollin said. "We're here to root out the rotten apples in this barrel, turn up evidence to bolster a criminal conspiracy prosecution."

"We want to let people across the country know there's zero tolerance for that kind of conduct," Cassidy said.

"Looks like you've expedited the process, Mr. Drayton," Yee said.

"Ten years since I started trying," I said. "Sort of gives a new definition to expedite, doesn't it?"

CHAPTER SIXTY-SEVEN

It was a quarter of five in the morning when Falcon turned his sedan onto a quiet street in Hancock Park where cruisers and unmarkeds covered both ends of the block. An IAD officer named Gerhart stepped to the car as we pulled to a stop.

"Got the warrant?" he asked.

Falcon showed it to him. He looked at it, then at me.

"He's with me," Falcon said. "Material witness."

Falcon's team of investigators and the FBI had ID'd all the shooters who came after me as off-duty officers, all tied to Curtis Rankin, and Officer Wilkes had given Falcon a preliminary statement about the shooting of Willie Gates. The DA, Jim Roselli, had gotten a judge to issue a warrant for Rankin's arrest on two counts of conspiracy to commit murder.

"Drayton, right?" Gerhart said.

I nodded.

"For a lot of us," he said. "Thanks."

I nodded again. He looked to Falcon.

"Let's do it," he said.

Falcon put the sedan in motion, and Gerhart climbed into an unmarked that led the parade of cruisers behind us down the block to a two-story Tudor set back off the street.

Falcon hadn't told me about the Justice Department's investigation because he couldn't. I hadn't told him about my meeting with Adams because I knew the arrangement I'd made wasn't one he could sit on. I didn't like the wall I'd put between us, but it had to stay there until I had the hard evidence his boss would need to indict Kamala Highland and Frankie Tate for murder.

He pulled into the circular drive, Gerhart pulled in behind him. Three cruisers stopped at the curb.

"Come on," Falcon said.

"You sure?" I said.

"Roselli already ripped me a new one for letting you freelance with what I gave you. But he's a results player, and this will be big for his profile. Besides, nobody can say you didn't earn the right."

He got out of the car. I got out on my side and walked with him to the front door. Gerhart and another plainclothes cop followed us, unbuttoning their suit jackets. Two uniforms from the lead cruiser fell in behind them, unsnapping the straps on their automatics.

As we stepped onto the porch, Falcon nodded toward the lighted doorbell, smiled with his eyes. I punched the button, and a mini version of Big Ben chimed inside the house. After a moment, the porch lights on either side of the door came on, then a small brass grill in the door opened. Falcon held his ID up to it.

"Captain Rankin?" Falcon said. "DA's office. Official business."

As the door opened, Rankin stepped into the doorway in slippers and navy pajamas with a military crease, not a hair out of place. If he'd been sleeping, it had to be standing up.

His eyes bore into Falcon's, then he saw me standing to one side, the other cops, the fleet of cruisers and unmarkeds. There was a quick flash of anger in his eyes, but no reaction that remotely revealed surprise or resembled fear.

Falcon pocketed his ID, pulled out the warrant and handed it to Rankin. He glanced at it.

"What the hell is this?" he said. "Roselli using good cops for political cannon fodder?"

"It's a warrant for your arrest, Captain. You have the right to remain silent," Falcon began to read the Miranda rights.

"Curtis?" a woman's voice called from inside. "What is it?"

Falcon continued as Rankin glared at me and his wife stepped to his side in robe and slippers. She looked at all of us, confused and suddenly fearful, then back to Rankin.

"Curtis?"

Falcon finished the Miranda. "You'll have to come downtown with us now, Captain," he said.

Rankin turned his disdain on Falcon, then stood taller and stepped out onto the porch.

"Cuff him," Falcon said to one of the uniforms.

As the cop locked the bracelets behind Rankin's back, his wife began to cry.

"Curtis?" she demanded. But Rankin spoke directly to me.

"You fucking waste of skin. You think you can do this to me?"

"Not me," I said. "The people you were supposed to be protecting, you morally bankrupt sonofabitch."

He didn't flinch as the two patrolmen marched him off toward the cruiser in his pajamas.

I started back to the car with Falcon while Gerhart and the other IAD officer dealt with Rankin's wife, who stood in the doorway shouting after me that her husband was a good man, worth ten times what anybody like me could ever be, whoever the hell I was, that he'd dedicated his life to serving the city, and important people knew that, important people who'd stand by him now and see that I got what I deserved.

What she didn't know and her husband was about to find out was that the VIP he'd be counting on most wouldn't be there for him. What I got at that moment had been a long time coming. The sight of Curtis Rankin in handcuffs being guided into the back seat of a black-and-white, and hauled off to be locked up behind bars.

CHAPTER SIXTY-EIGHT

I drove through the gate of Frankie Tate's ranch at eight in the morning. The heat already rising from the rim of the Mojave made the hazy foothills to the west and east shimmer in the distance.

I wasn't the first arrival. Several athletic looking young men and women in jeans, T-shirts, training shoes, and black-and-yellow ball caps were clustered around a hundred-foot scaffolding, white coffee mugs in hand. A young stud in a yellow jumpsuit and the same hat with the initials FT in yellow over the bill was demonstrating a body harness for the group.

I drove on down the dirt road toward a ring of newly planted trees and a low, white-stucco ranch house with a red-tiled roof. I rolled past a dozen dusty pickups, SUVs and sports cars, and pulled to a stop at the house beside a shiny black Porsche Cayenne Turbo. The personalized plate had only two letters, FT.

I sat for a moment, looking at the scope of Frankie's enterprise, listening to the constant shrill of cicadas coming from the trees. Another young man in jumpsuit and ball cap carried tack from a barn to a corral where horses milled, sending dust drifting up into the sunlight. A dark-haired young woman in the same uniform, holding one of the ubiquitous white coffee mugs in hand, supervised construction of a new flagstone patio being laid around a large swimming pool. It might have been Twila from Tulsa, but it didn't seem likely since she was firmly giving directions to the gang of Latino workmen.

I took long, slow, deep breaths to stem the tide of adrenaline I felt pumping through my body as I focused on the house sitting beyond the motionless pepper trees and a manicured stretch of green grass being mowed by a man in a wide-brimmed straw hat sitting astride a lawn tractor. As he turned to motor off in the opposite direction, I could read the logo on the back of his jumpsuit. The loop of a lariat formed a loose circle around a silhouette of a motorcycle rider in flight and the words First-Take Stunts.

When I knew I was ready, I got out of the car and became the instant object of attention for three black Labradors who came on the run with their inbred mixed signals of warning barks and wagging tails. I stopped to give each a scratch behind the ear and no cause to believe I was armed and dangerous.

They escorted me happily around the Cayenne beside me. I glanced at it and stopped short. The paint on the right rear fender was new. It was a perfect match, but wasn't completely buffed out. Something acidic rose in my throat. It wasn't the gas-station coffee I'd just downed to make up for the short night.

When I had a tight grip on myself, the adrenaline back in check, I started for the house. The smell of fresh-cut grass was sweet, the nickers from the corral pleasant and peaceful. I was feeling as deadly as the green Mojave rattlers that go unseen on stretches of lawn like I was crossing.

Chapter Sixty-nine

"Do you remember when you took that jump off the skyscraper for my father?" I asked.

"Don't forget a rush like that," Frankie said.

He was wearing one of the yellow jumpsuits and hats with his initials. I was wearing T-shirt and jeans, cross-trainers, and a light tan cotton jacket over a wire and my Sig Sauer.

We were standing in the kitchen drinking coffee from the same white coffee mugs I'd seen outside, mugs with the First-Take Stunts logo on one side and the foreign-looking words *OWA TA JER KIAM* on the other. It was a large, open room with dark, rough-sawn beams overhead and Saltillo tiles on the floor. Sunlight streamed through a large, undraped plate glass window behind a long, wooden table and six chairs.

"He told you to keep your eyes open all the way past camera even if the cable broke."

"For a fact," Frankie grinned.

"And you said the autopsy would find sand in your eyes."

"Prob'ly," he laughed.

"Anything ever scare you, Frankie?"

"Not that I recall," he said. "Gettin' the job's the hardest part."

"Not just work," I said. "Anything."

"Yeah," he grinned. "Dyin' old."

"I don't think there's much chance of that," I said.

He grinned again. I set my cup on the counter.

"What can I do for you, *hermano*? Thinkin' 'bout takin' a little refresher course?"

"You can tell me why you killed Leah Sanders," I said.

His smile slid toward the coffee mug, but he caught it.

"That's some serious shit you're smokin', man," he said. "Must be pure hydro. I never knew you were into that."

"You killed Jeremy Thomas, too. Did you kill Ken Chernak because you had to or just because you could?"

"That ain't fuckin' funny, *amigo*," he said.

"You see me laughing?"

I pulled my Sig from under my arm, jacked a nine into the chamber, leveled it at him.

"What is this?"

"Your day to be scared," I said. "No quarter-load blanks, Frankie. There's fifteen live rounds in this clip."

If he was afraid, he didn't show it. But his vocal chords tightened, pinching his voice higher.

"Shit, man, what are you doin'?"

"I want answers. I don't get 'em, you get the full clip one hunk of flesh at a time."

"This is crazy, man. This is fucked. I don't know what the hell you're talkin' about."

"Jealousy, maybe. Promises from a desperate woman? You tell me. You made the choices."

"What choices?"

"Kissing Leah off the canyon, was that your idea or did Kamala Highland say she'd make you a star?"

"Put that fuckin' thing down."

"You knew Leah saw the two of you, knew she might put it all together, or I would."

"You're not a cop. You can't pull this shit on me," he said, taking a step toward me. "I'll have your ass thrown in—"

I squeezed off a deafening round that singed his jumpsuit, slammed into the wall tiles behind him and drew a crimson crease on his right arm just below the deltoid. He grimaced, looked wide-eyed at the wound and back at me as the Labradors outside started barking.

"Answers, Frankie," I shouted over the reverb, raking my aim across his chest. "Like how paint from your Porsche wound up on Leah's car."

"What the fuck are you doin'?"

"Why kill Thomas? Because he dumped you? Because he had what you always wanted? You kill Chernak when he tried to stop you? Or were you so jazzed on coke you didn't know what you were doing?"

"Goddamnit, Mike—Back off!"

The Sig blasted his light voice away again, tore out more tile. He looked at the matching rip and ribbon of blood on his left arm.

"Tell me, Frankie. Everything."

"I am tellin' you, man. I didn't do any—"

I aimed the muzzle of the Sig between his legs.

"No! I just drove her up there so she could give him the fuckin' sword, okay?"

"What sword?"

"His fuckin' King Arthur sword. She put a fuckin' emerald size of a golf ball on the handle, had it engraved, wanted to kiss his ass with it."

"Instead, you killed him with it. Killed both of them."

"No. I—"

His denial was aborted when the door swung open and the three dogs charged in followed by a man and a woman in yellow jumpsuits. The couple froze when they saw the gun trained on their boss, and in the split second I reacted instinctively to them, Frankie dove through the glass window beside him while the dogs barked. I fired two quick rounds that missed as he rolled on the grass outside and came up running.

The Sig Sauer's report stunned the couple and frightened the dogs, who shied out of the kitchen into the adjoining living room to bark from a safer distance. The woman clamped her hands over her ears as the man grabbed her, pulled her away from me.

"Making an arrest!" I shouted. "Stay back!"

Frankie was sprinting for an overhang projecting from a large corrugated-steel shed. He was fast and forty yards ahead of me by the time I cleared the door and gave chase. He was headed for a half dozen dirt bikes parked in the shadow of the overhang. I stopped running as he slung a leg over a bright orange Honda 250. I gripped the Sig with both hands, v'd my arms as he tromped on the starter.

"Hold it, Frankie!"

But the engine caught and he popped the clutch. I fired and missed behind him, punching a hole in the shed. He gunned away, laid the Honda over as I fired again and missed high. He was full throttle and maneuvering like a jack-rabbit. I sprinted for the other bikes, jammed the Sig into its holster, and climbed on an apple-green Kawasaki. Voices were shouting, people were running from different directions.

Good stunt work takes the ability to be completely alone in a crowd. I knew that's where Frankie was and I had to be. I focused on him as the engine turned over and I leaped out of the shadows after the orange bike that settled into a straight line putting close to two hundred yards between us.

CHAPTER SEVENTY

We tore across wind-blistered terrain, dodging rocks and cactus. His rooster tail swerved, and I could see he was heading for an incline paralleling a wash to our left. I cut across at a forty-five degree angle, closing the distance between us rapidly. Then I saw the ramp he was gunning for.

I braked hard, sliding the bike to a stop. I yanked out the Sig, took aim, and squeezed the trigger as he launched airborne twenty feet above the wash two hundred feet away. The fuel tank he straddled exploded at the apogee of his jump.

I jammed the Sig back in its holster and accelerated toward the ball of black smoke and flying debris. I headed straight for the center of the ramp, cranked the gas wide open, and cleared the wash the way Frankie had planned to.

When I landed on the other side, I braked, and swung back toward the motionless figure lying in the narrow, boulder-strewn creek bed. I found a path down the slope and maneuvered close to where Frankie lay face down in the shallow, stagnant water at its center. Smoke rose from his charred clothes. He lifted his head. Half of his face looked like a burned marshmallow. A scorched hand reached out.

"Help me—"

I killed the Kawasaki and caught the faint sound of a siren.

"Not much I can do," I said.

Frankie shivered violently. His threshold for pain was at the breaking point, only that inborn belief that he could handle anything keeping him conscious.

"Put me down, man! I did it, okay? Did 'em both. Your bitch, too ...Put me down!"

"You're going to stand trial."

"Bastard! Just like your fuckin' old man!" he roared. "Hey, *Miguel*, you know how he died?" He grinned hideously. "That was me, baby—I rigged that charge just for him."

My hand went to the Sig.

"That's right, I killed the hard-ass prick."

I pulled the gun, levelled the muzzle.

"Yeah, do it, Mikey! Gimme the whole fuckin' clip!"

Images flashed through my mind: Leah Sanders lying under a sheet in a metal drawer, belted into a steel and glass cage, caroming into the abyss of a pitch-black canyon. Her terror. My father going into his last stunt knowing if the explosives around him weren't rigged exactly right, they were just as lethal as the Japanese shells and land mines he survived on Iwo Jima. A flawed but fair man, a hard man who made hard choices, who tried to teach his only son how to make the right choices, a son he knew would have to be ready to stand up to things no man should have to take from another.

"Bible says, 'turn the other cheek.' Harder 'n hell sometimes, but a man's got to remember we're all of us connected. Holdin' to the high road, that's the only sure way to bein' all you can be."

I lowered the gun, slid it back into the holster, and planted my hand on the bars.

"Go to hell, Drayton." Frankie glared, his vain good looks burned beyond recognition. "Go to fuckin' hell!"

The siren wound down into the compound, two more wailed somewhere on the highway. They'd be local County Sheriffs who'd be good at their job, and their job would be to lock me up and sort things out later. That was okay with me. I could use some sack time, and I knew Frankie Tate wouldn't be going anywhere but the nearest burn unit.

Chapter Seventy-one

"So, you couldn't tell me," Falcon said.

"Like you couldn't tell me about Yee," I said.

It was a little after eight the next night. I had slept all day, and we were sitting in *Mojo*, drinking *Negra Modelos*, the pulsating music muffling our conversation.

"I can tell you about the sword," he said. "You were right. It was under that new pool patio at Tate's place. And I can tell you his lady-producer friend's copping a plea to obstruction of justice in exchange for eye-witness testimony that gives him one last choice, lethal injection or the gas chamber."

"She's probably already made a book deal," I said.

"Hell of a thing," Falcon said, "her being the grandmother to your client's grandson."

"Sinners and saints," I said. "Never far apart."

Falcon nodded, sipped his beer.

"So, he know he's a grandfather yet?" he said.

"Gus? No. You only do because you had to."

"Be a good thing for him," Falcon said. "Big thing."

"I can't do that," I said.

"No," he said. "You can't."

We both reflected for a moment on the nature of the work we shared, the shared approach to that work.

"You believe what Tate said about killing your father?"

"No way to know," I said. "He was trying to buy a bullet. But I could believe it, yeah."

"Probably should," he said. "Put it to rest finally."

I nodded, took a pull from the bottle.

"So Adams gets his fifty mil and nobody's the wiser," Falcon said. "And how about Rankin, huh?"

"I didn't figure that," I said.

Rankin had gotten a high-powered attorney to spring him on bail, but it was clear he'd be standing trial. He left the courthouse, went straight home, put his Glock in his mouth and pulled the trigger.

"State pen's hell for a cop," Falcon said. "Looking over your shoulder day and night, wind up being a bun boy to the biggest guy who hates you most."

The best news of all was that Benjamin Yee, the assistant attorney general in the Civil Rights Division of the Justice Department, had concluded that a small segment of the LAPD discriminated on the basis of race and national origin in its law enforcement activities. Based on Yee's findings, the CRD had been authorized to file a police misconduct lawsuit, and every officer suspected of violating the public trust would be prosecuted.

"The feds forcing reforms in a city police department this size, that's big," Falcon said. "Maybe something's coming out of all this that gives some meaning to Wes Carter's death."

"Old perceptions die hard," I said.

"Not saying that wall of fear and mistrust's going to come down over night," Falcon said. "But people know a nation of laws has to enforce those laws. They know they need police. We just need some politicians now to stop making speeches and spell out what the police do, what grand juries do, so people understand how it all has to work."

"What we need most is to see each other, not uniforms and hoodies," I said. "All the tears that get shed by families burying young black men, the tears shed by families watching a flag-draped casket lowered into the ground while a bugler blows Taps, those tears don't have any color. That's what we have to see."

Falcon nodded.

"You're right about what just went down with the Department, though," I said. "Be nice to think rules and reality might be the same some day."

"Gonna have a code of ethics, it better have teeth," Falcon said. "Can't just be words in a manual."

We sat in silence for a moment, listening to the music. He drained his glass, leveled his eyes on me.

"How about you?" he said.

I shrugged.

"Give it time," he said.

I nodded. And flagged the waitress for another round.

CHAPTER SEVENTY-TWO

When I opened the door to my office the next morning, everything was neat and orderly, just like the young woman seated at her desk who wouldn't have it any other way no matter how hard I tried. Mari got up, stood on tiptoes, and kissed me on the cheek. She had on white sandals and slacks, a light-blue, tunic-length shirt with side slits and a mandarin collar. I had dewy, orange lipgloss on my cheek.

"What was that for?"

"If you don't know, you're not much of a detective," she said. "And according to all these people who want to meet with you, that's not the case."

She picked up a folder from the side of the desk and handed it to me. I opened it to names, numbers, and messages printed out in neat columns. Law firms, businesses, individuals. Some of the names jumped out.

"I may need an assistant," Mari beamed.

"We need to talk," I said.

I plopped into the wooden straight-back chair. She boosted herself up onto the edge of the desk, crossed her ankles and folded her arms.

"I won't be returning those calls," I said.

She frowned.

"My lease here is up next month. I'm not renewing."

"My uncle owns a building in Santa Monica. I'm sure he'd beat this price."

"It's not the price," I said. "It's me."

"You need a break?"

"I need a different life."

She straightened her back, squared her shoulders.

"It's your friend, isn't it," she said. "Leah."

"Partly."

"You feel responsible for her death."

"I am responsible for her death."

She nodded with an air of omniscience.

"Mm-hmm," she said.

"Mm-hmm what?" I said.

She unfolded her arms and put her hands on the edge of the desk.

"Next year I'll be Doctor Sabusawa, you know, and I'll charge a lot of money for what you get free today."

"It's nothing I really want to talk about," I said.

"I do," she said. "And you need to. You need to understand that none of us is responsible for every rotten thing other people do to us or to those we love. She could have told you to leave her alone, told you she didn't want any part of your world or your work."

"She didn't understand my world or my work."

"Bullshit."

She said the word quietly, but with force. It seemed so foreign to my perception of her that it shocked me in a way profanity never does.

"What?" I said.

She looked at me clinically.

"That is such self-indulgent, self-pitying bullshit."

"Excuse me, Miss About-To-Be-A-Doctor, you didn't know her. She never did anything to deserve what happened to her."

"What did she do to deserve knowing you? Loving you, maybe, being loved by you?"

"We weren't in love," I said. "This isn't about love."

"It's about life. The choices we make," she said, remaining calm, professional in tone and demeanor. "That's who we are. What we choose to do, who we choose to be with. She made her own choices, Michael, made her own life, the good and the bad, we all do."

"Michael?" I said, reacting to the sudden familiarity.

"The seriousness of your condition requires a degree of formality, I know," she said with faint imperiousness, "but we're friends, aren't we?"

"My 'condition?'"

"You're borderline clinically depressed, for God's sake," she said. "You have been since Sheridan died, but you're too tough, and too stubborn, and too resilient to deal with it the way you should. You'll just clam up and talk like a smartass and shut yourself off from the rest of the world, so you're damned lucky you know me, because I respect you too much, and I'm too genuinely fond of you to see you carry a load of shit like that around and fuck up any chance you have for a half-way normal relationship with any other woman who cares about you."

"You know, if you're going to do this for real, you might want to work on your bedside manner."

"This is for real," she said. "Don't be so damned egotistical. There's no way you could predict what happened to your friend, or your daughter, either. There's no way you can guarantee control of your own life, you can't expect to control anyone else's. My God, if we all thought everything that happens to people we know or love is a result of our being in their life, how could we ever be intimate with anyone?"

"I was responsible for Leah," I said again.

"You want to be responsible. You need to be responsible, because that's who you are. But don't belittle her intelligence or her integrity by holding onto that," she said. "Do you think that's what she'd want? Is that the kind of person she was? She'd want you to live in that kind of bondage forever, want to have you be a martyr to her memory? Want you to kill a part of yourself?"

There was concern in her face. It was touching. And she had touched me. She had punched buttons and cut straight to the chase. I did want to be responsible. I didn't know how not to be.

"Get over it, Michael," she said. "Grieve for however long it takes, but make that grief for her, not for yourself. And then get on with it."

I looked into her young face, her old eyes.

"Okay," I said. "I'll try, Doc."

CHAPTER SEVENTY-THREE

I walked from the office through busy streets to a quiet oasis, and sat alone with Leah Sanders beneath a giant elm tree. The bouquet of yellow chrysanthemums and white daisies I placed beside her small brass plaque was cheerful in the dappled light.

I looked around at the other graves, thought about some of the famous people who lay dead beneath the ground in the little enclave walled off from the bustle of the sprawling city that collected them. Like metal shavings to a magnet, they were drawn to its power, energized by the thought that so many others had proven you could earn a living in pursuit of individual passions here, find recognition, however fleeting, for individual talents, even a shot at a kind of immortality.

I thought about Jeremy Thomas and Eugene Prentis, Chad Kennedy and Ken Chernak, Kamala Highland and Jo Ellen Bates, three people who led six lives. People who weren't happy with who they were, who came to this city to re-create themselves, whose idealized personas all came to tragic ends.

I thought about how we all live two lives. How the creation story in all cultures tells us good and evil are woven into the fiber of every human being. Wise and concerned men way back when had thought it was a good idea to make us aware that we will all know pain, to make us conscious of desire and mortality, temptation and corruption. In Eden, Eve's hunger for knowledge and a life without restraints gave us all a warning to be careful what we wish for. And old Adam's reluctance to take responsibility for his actions mirrors a weakness we all need to guard against. The snake? He wasn't evil. He was a rebel. He questioned whatever rules stood in the way of human progress. For better, or worse, he was my hero.

I tried to focus my thoughts just on Leah. Her spirit, her soul. Had it moved on, taken flight? Is there a heaven? Paradise? Nirvana? She believed there was. And it was good to think of her being there in that place, a place without pain or prejudice, without envy or vengeance, or cemeteries.

By the time I got my car and headed west on Wilshire, the midday traffic had congealed into an unpleasant mass creating unpleasant moods on streets that weren't built to handle the eighteen million people who wanted to drive them.

When I got to the *Tavern* on San Vicente, Gus Chernak was waiting at a table in the large, glass-roofed atrium.

"Sorry I'm late," I said.

"Just got here myself," he said. "Damn traffic." He shook his head, knowing the thought needed no amplification.

The room was splashed with sunlight and alive with chatter, the clinking and clanking of silverware, china and glasses. Laughter rode over the sound waves on the aroma of good food.

"They put us here," he said, indicating the extra chairs. "I told 'em we were just a deuce, but they had us down for four."

"It's fine," I said.

A perky waitress in a white blouse, white tie, white apron, and dark jeans stepped to the table. "May I get you gentlemen something to drink?"

"Couple of drafts," Gus said.

"Light or dark?"

Gus looked to me. I shrugged.

"Dark," he said.

"I'll be right back to take your order," she said, smiling brightly as she moved off toward the bar.

"So," Gus said. "Good to see you."

"You, too," I said.

"How you doin'?" he said. "You know."

"Leah?"

He nodded.

"I accept that she's dead, and that I can't do anything about it. I get that I'm not dead, and I have to get on with it."

"You're lucky. Got somethin' to do worth doin'."

"You think?"

"Hell, yes. Long as there's psychos like that screwy bastard stunt-guy killed Kenny, and SOBs like that bent cop you brought down," he said. "Not everybody can do it, either. Not like you."

"I don't know," I said. "I might hang it up. Thought I had till you called."

"Quit?" he said. "Leave the tough stuff you know how to do for somebody else? I told you how I feel about quitters."

"It's a young man's game."

"You got plenty of miles left in you," he said.

"You haven't looked under the hood."

"Hell I haven't," he said. "You think I'd be sittin' here, I didn't like what I saw?"

"Thanks," I said. "That goes both ways."

The waitress returned with the beer in two frosted mugs, set them on the table.

"Are you gentlemen ready to order?"

"Give us a few minutes," I said.

"Sure. Any time," she said.

Gus was studying me as she moved off to another table.

"So, okay, let's say this was it. You close up shop and walk away," he said. "To what?"

"Not sure. Take some time to figure that out."

I took a pull on the draft. He watched me, read me.

"You're serious," he said.

"Jury's still out," I said, "but the pros and cons are definitely under consideration."

"Let me tell you somethin'." He paused to be sure he had my full attention. "Havin' a life worth livin' means findin' a reason for livin' it. That's all. A reason for livin' it. You got one," he said. "No. You got two."

I knew one of the reasons was Sheridan. And I finally got around to telling him about her. He was stunned. And he understood why I hadn't been willing to back off when he told me to. He had a lot of questions about her. It was good to share the answers with him.

"Geezus," he said. "I'm sorry, buddy."

"I just wanted you to know," I said.

"It's like we both served in the same outfit, in a way."

"Yeah."

Our talk brought us closer and touched a lot of bases. It took us through two more beers and a couple of burgers.

"So, whatta you think?" he said. "We put anything to rest?"

"Not enough."

"No," he sighed. "Thing about ghosts, I guess."

"What's that?"

"They don't die."

We fell silent. I drained the last of my beer. Gus stared into his.

"I guess nobody ever finds out what the hell it all means," he said. "But I don't even need that. All's I want is just a way to keep some kind of faith, you know? Some reason to keep on grindin'."

He lifted his glass, swallowed the last of his beer. Then I saw Karen Miller walking toward our table, and I stood to greet her. She was wearing a white pantsuit and a pink blouse, her dark hair hung over her shoulders. Gus frowned up at her as she stepped to us carrying his grandson.

"Hi," she said self-consciously. "Sorry I'm late. Traffic was really bad."

ACKNOWLEDGMENTS

There are many people to thank for launching this maiden voyage into uncharted waters. Chief among them are: my publisher, Randy Morkved, of Balcony 7 Media and Publishing, for his venturesome spirit and rock-solid integrity; Simon Green, for his good counsel; and Shelly Lowenkopf, who bracketed the development of these pages from first thoughts to last with his trained eye and veteran's savvy.

I owe my profound thanks to Ty Hutchison, whose vast experience in pursuit of justice while wearing an LAPD shield, and later packing a private license, ensured the accuracy of the practice and procedure of law enforcement portrayed in this story.

My deepest gratitude to Patrick Hasburgh, whose enthusiastic response to the earliest draft of this first book let me know the target I was aiming for was in the crosshairs, and whose criticism sharpened my focus.

Gifted writers Bruce Murkoff, Frank Strunk, Alice Randall, and Carla Malden, Michael Gleason, and Jeb Rosebrook all took the time at different stages to read, comment, and encourage; Mike Warren and George Crosby, treasured friends intimate with interracial relationships, made sure I was on track with that crucial element; Mary Sheldon, of Tecolote Book Shop, made me believe the effort was a worthy one. Thank you, my brothers and sisters in spirit. For caring. For advising. For inspiring.

As the core of this story is about parenting, I must also belatedly thank my parents, Mac and Sally McGovern, for hard lessons patiently and lovingly taught.

Finally, I want to thank the incorruptible Janice Wilder for being a daily reminder that true goodness does exist.

ABOUT THE AUTHOR

John Wilder is an award-winning writer, producer and director of nearly 400 hours of prime-time drama on network and cable television, spanning over forty years. Wilder's deep Hollywood roots shine in his long-awaited fiction debut, now coming to fruition through his new Michael Drayton series. Among other projects also in the works are several sweeping screen adaptations, including Timothy Egan's National Book Award-winning novel *Short Nights of the Shadow Catcher.*

Wilder is also Writer in Residence and Adjunct English Professor for prestigious Westmont College in Santa Barbara, California, where he currently resides. He is a graduate of UCLA.

SOME OF JOHN WILDER'S NUMEROUS CREDITS:

- Received the **Writers Guild Award** for **Best Long-form Drama**, the **Western Heritage Award**, and a **Golden Globe Nomination** for his adaptation/production of James A. Michener's *Centennial*, the epic, 26-hour NBC mini-series, and one of the biggest television events of its time. Wilder also Executive Produced the film for Universal Pictures.

- Received the **Western Writers of America Award** and second **Western Heritage Award** for Writing/Exec-Producing the 7-hour CBS miniseries, *Return To Lonesome Dove*.

- Received a **Golden Globe Nomination** for *The Bastard*, a 4-hour mini-series he adapted and Executive Produced, from John Jakes' bestselling novel, for Operation Prime time network.

- Created, Wrote and Executive Produced the critically acclaimed NBC series *The Yellow Rose* (starring Sam Elliott and Cybill Shepherd).

- Developed, Wrote, Executive Produced and Directed the top-rated ABC series *Spenser: For Hire* (starring Robert Urich and Avery Brooks), from the bestselling detective series by Robert B. Parker.

- Wrote, Produced and Directed the number-one rated ABC series *The Streets of San Francisco* (starring Karl Malden and Michael Douglas). Received a **Writers Guild Nomination** for **Best Teleplay**, and **Two Emmy Nominations** for **Best Dramatic Series**.

Thank you for taking the time to read this book. Please leave a review and share your reading experience with others by posting on any or all of the following suggested sites:

• Amazon's *Nobody Dies in Hollywood* page
• Barnes & Noble's *Nobody Dies in Hollywood* page
• Disqus on the Author Profile page on www.balcony7.com

The authors and the production team appreciate all feedback you may share. Please follow John Wilder on these social media sites:

Facebook

Google Plus

Disqus

Saucy Jaw

CPSIA information can be obtained at www.ICGtesting.com
Printed in the USA
BVOW02s1003030915

416441BV00001B/42/P

9 781939 454409